Tamiko Brown and the Mystery of the Lone Girl

TAMIKO BROWN AND THE MYSTERY OF THE LONE GIRL

CHRISTOPHER J. MORIN

CreateSpace, Inc.
Seattle

Tamiko Brown and the Mystery of the Lone Girl

ISBN: 978-0-9881249-0-5 (sc)
ISBN: 978-0-9881249-1-2 (ebk)

Printed in the United States of America
CreateSpace rev. date: 11/08/2012

For my wife Valerie, and my daughters Alexandra, Marie-Chantale, and Annabelle—I love you all.

True compassion isn't about what you feel—
it's about what you do.

CONTENTS

CONTENTS (CONTINUED)

CONTENTS (CONTINUED)

CONTENTS (CONTINUED)

INTRODUCTION

There she lay in the darkness, fast asleep on the front porch of some shabby little house in an old wicker basket, looking like a lost Japanese doll. Tied to her right arm was a little name tag with "Tamiko" written on it. Not a sound disturbed the silence of this foggy Australian night except for the first drops of a gentle rain. With tears in her eyes, the young Japanese widow looked at her newborn baby for the very last time. "Good-bye, Tamiko," she whispered before she turned and slowly walked away.

When the surprised old man discovered the baby the following day, he immediately called the authorities, and the child was soon whisked away to one of the few remaining orphanages in Australia—St. Alfred Orphanage, just north of Brisbane. There, Tamiko—half Japanese and half Australian—began her life in a very stern and structured environment. Still a baby not yet subjected to the hardships of reality, Tamiko was quite content. But when Tamiko grew older and her school years commenced, she was often teased and bullied by her peers.

Interestingly though, life as an orphan didn't cause Tamiko to become cold or hateful; instead, she became warm and compassionate and developed a passion for fighting injustice and helping those in desperate times. Like most people, Tamiko would get angry when she was pushed to her limit from too much teasing or fighting. However, there were times when Tamiko would lose control of her anger and fly into a terrible rage. Regardless of how furious she became, Tamiko never lost her gift of compassion.

Her one sadness came, though, every time a couple showed up at the orphanage to adopt a child. On those occasions, Tamiko would sadly gaze out the window of her room hoping that maybe she'd be the lucky one that was chosen. Yet, years went by, and she still remained without a family to call her own.

PART 1—
TAMIKO: ORPHANED, ADOPTED, REFORMED

Chapter 1—
The Orphanage

St. Alfred Orphanage in Queensland, Australia (2010): Seven-year-old Tamiko is hiding behind an old hot water tank in the mechanical room with her friend Laura. The room is dark, and the air is stale. Over the rapid breaths of the two young hiders, there are sounds of bubbling from the water tank and rapid, little footsteps from the seeker in the basement hallway of the two-story building. The door of the mechanical room opens just before Tamiko lets out an accidental giggle. "Gotcha!" exclaims the victorious discoverer. "Arrrg!" says Tamiko in a loud whisper. "I knew you'd find us, mate! Let's go upstairs now before the nuns see us!"

After recess, Tamiko attends school upstairs, followed by lunch in the eating house. Lunchtime is with Laura, and lunchtime is good ... until "The Smirk" shows up. Her real name is Ivy, and she's not exactly Tamiko's closest buddy—far from it. A year older than Tamiko, she has the face of a well-groomed pig with bulky brown eyes and the build of a young football player. They call her The Smirk because of her big, smug smile, though some call her Poison Ivy as she can have a rather poisonous effect on certain people, especially Tamiko. Because Tamiko is half Japanese and half Australian, she has distinct Japanese characteristics—darker skin, thinner-looking eyes and a somewhat larger nose—and thus stands out amongst the other children who are Australian, making her an easy target. With dark brown eyes and short jet-black hair, Tamiko is just under four feet tall and of slightly larger build than most girls her age. She also has a slight scar over the second knuckle on her right hand—the kind that says she had hit something hard and it had hit back.

Today, just as Tamiko reaches for her apple at the lunch table, Ivy appears. As usual, she is wearing her arrogant smile, but this time, something's different. It's as though she knows something—something bad about somebody—and just can't wait to blurt it out and ruin that somebody's day.

"How's the apple?" Ivy says as she gives Tamiko a penetrating stare.

"G-good," Tamiko replies.

"Enjoy it while it lasts … 'cause it ain't gonna taste good for long."

She is right. For Ivy had somehow dug up some ugly information concerning Tamiko's past. The Smirk tells Tamiko what she claims to know; Tamiko was essentially born an orphan—that she was abandoned just after birth like a worthless, little doll.

"That's … that isn't true," says Tamiko.

"Is too!"

"Is not!"

"Your mommy never wanted you. Your daddy didn't either. They didn't want some stupid Japanese doll. You're a reject. From the day you were born—"

"Shut up!"

Then, out loud for all to hear, The Smirk repeats what she had told Tamiko.

"I said shut up!"

"Reject! Reject! Tamiko's a reject!" Ivy hollers.

With that, Tamiko pushes Ivy onto the table, almost crushing Laura's lunch. Ivy pops back up and shoves Tamiko. Everyone else moves out of the way to watch the fight unfold.

"Truth hurts, don't it?" says Ivy.

"It's not the truth!" Tamiko yells back.

"Leave her alone!" shouts Laura.

Filled with anger, Tamiko charges at Ivy and plunges her into the table once again. This time, however, Laura's lunch is pummeled. Now, both girls are at each other on the table while wearing muffins, ham sandwiches, and pepperoni pizza. First, Tamiko's on top of Ivy, and then Ivy's over Tamiko. They punch each other. They slap each other. They grab each other, and they even spit at each other. The crowd roars with shouts and cheers. Some root for Tamiko and others for Ivy.

"Slant-eyed Japanese reject!" Ivy utters.

Tamiko had heard enough. Now, she flies into a rage and grasps Ivy's hair from behind with both her hands and pulls with all her might.

"IT'S NOT TRUE!"

Ivy screams. Tamiko yanks her hair again. Ivy elbows Tamiko and gets away. Then, Ivy swings at Tamiko and knocks her to the floor. Ivy jumps on Tamiko as Laura pushes her. Tamiko rolls Ivy over, and now Ivy's the one who is on the floor. Tamiko punches her enemy over and over again, screaming, "I hate you! I hate you!" Finally, the nuns arrive and break up the fight. Tamiko is dragged away, kicking and screaming.

For her punishment, Tamiko's hair will be shaved off, and she'll be forced to wear a sugar bag as a dress every day for the next week, even in school. As for Ivy, The Smirk, she'll only have to scrub and polish the floors.

And then, in almost a blink of an eye, it happens.

"Now stay seated, don't move and don't say a word!" orders a nun as she turns on the electric hair clippers.

Shaking and almost crying, Tamiko hears a crescendo of humming and buzzing as the clippers fly over to the front of her scalp like a giant bee about to sting her. The clippers hit her head and the buzzing turns into an awful garbling noise. The sound reminds Tamiko of the times when she and Laura picked flowers at the edge of the field in the summer and heard the landscaper's lawn trimmer as it cut through the thick grass. The nun mows a wide, ugly line right down the middle and to the back of Tamiko's head. Tamiko, with her eyes hanging low, avoids looking into the mirror. Just as the nun brings the clippers swiftly forward for the next pass, Tamiko gathers up all of her energy to keep herself from crying. Like a pressure cooker about to explode, Tamiko groans as her face trembles and reddens with anger. The clippers make another pass and then another. One tear, then two trickle down her cheeks while Tamiko still barely holds on. Tamiko flickers her eyes up and down once, giving her just enough time to see her almost hairless head in the mirror and still tries to keep it in. But it's too much; Tamiko sobs, more tears pour down her face and then, all at once, Tamiko screams and cries like a baby. *It's not fair! It's not fair! Ivy should be the one having her hair shaved, not me! It's so not fair!* she thinks.

In addition to her angry, feisty side, Tamiko had a strikingly different side that first appeared when she was in kindergarten ...

Tamiko is in kindergarten doing a puzzle. Just as Tamiko completes the puzzle, the teacher says it is nap time. With that, the children lie down on their blankets and sleep for a while. A bell rings. Class is over and one by one, all of the children slowly pick up their blankets and exit the room in a single file—all, that is, except for a blonde, curly-haired Australian girl named Laura and one other person, Tamiko. At this point in time, Tamiko had never really played with Laura before; in fact, she didn't know her at all. Yet, while everybody else, including the teacher, had seen Laura as just another orphan with nothing very special going on in her life, Tamiko sensed that something was wrong. Tamiko didn't know any specifics—she didn't know that Laura just had a bad dream about the loss of her baby sister—but she somehow sensed the grief. Now, as the teacher is about to say something, Tamiko walks over to Laura and hugs her. Finally, Tamiko whispers two simple words of compassion into Laura's ear, "It's okay."

But after Tamiko's days of kindergarten, it wasn't long before she began to see and experience the true hardships of life as an orphan. It all started with her first discovery of the orphanage's brutal ways of punishment and discipline ...

At the orphanage, just outside of the Beating Room in the basement, Laura, another friend, and Tamiko peer into the room through the narrow slit of the partially open door. They watch in awe as the punishment is carried out. Three boys are bent over a long wooden table, each held down by two older boys. Their bodies squirm. Their pants are down. Their buttocks are shaking. It reminds Tamiko of a row of confined ponies that she saw in an animal picture book with Laura during kindergarten.

"She's gonna put a beatin' on them," Laura whispers.

A nun raises a black leather belt behind them and strikes the bare bottom of the boy on the left. The boy screams. Then, the nun whips the other two and repeats the beating over and over again—at least another four times. Shrieks and howls fill the room. The air turns foul. At the end of it all, the boys are panting like dogs, and their buttocks are about as red as a fire truck.

Most often, life as an orphan is like being trapped in a giant cage, like a prisoner. There are eight kids to a room with bunk beds. The blankets aren't soft or fluffy, and the sheets stink. The bathrooms are disgusting. Birthdays aren't celebrated. The toys are broken. Life as an orphan is school, dusting, washing floors and windows, working in the kitchen, cleaning bathrooms, setting tables, working in the laundry room, shining shoes, and making beds. Most of all, though, life as an orphan is taking orders—orders most always given by the nuns. They're like drill sergeants telling everybody what to do and when to do it. "They're always behind you, watching you," Laura often says.

If a child disobeys, even the smallest of things, the offender either ends up like the three boys, beaten and humiliated, or is punished by one of many other means, such as "no meals for the next 24 hours" or "if you wet your bed, you will parade around the room with your wet sheets over your shoulders while everyone else laughs at you." Tamiko thinks, *This isn't right! Someday, I'm going to stop this from happening to anyone else!*

As for love, there's little of it—only love amongst friends—or none at all. To the nuns and staff, no child is an individual. Each child is just a number. There's no real "nurturing" or hugging or kissing or comforting or affection of any kind. Nor is there anybody to tuck you into bed, read you a bedtime story, and say a simple, "Goodnight." Like most orphans, Tamiko dreams of a family—a caring mom and dad that spend time with her and are always there for her no matter what. Children don't find that here. Here, they learn to keep a straight face and hide their emotions or else …

But it wasn't always like that. There were some good times, too …

Tamiko likes hide-and-seek, playing cards, picking apples, playing checkers, coloring, playing tag, and "Duck, Duck, Goose!" She also likes to skip and play hand-clapping games. But Tamiko's favorite things are exploring the wilderness behind the orphanage and climbing trees with Laura. They eat together, sleep together, and talk to each other as they share their hopes and fears; they're best friends.

True to Tamiko's nature, she comforts Laura and helps her in any way she can just as she often does for others. Unlike most everyone else, Tamiko puts other peoples' concerns ahead of her own and doesn't expect anything in return. For Tamiko senses the sorrows of others, listens to what they have to say and gives them a simple hug whenever they need one. Every so often, when nobody's around, Tamiko sneaks into the kitchen and steals food that she gives to the younger ones who are poorly fed and to the local bum through the fencing in the far corner of the yard behind the dumpster. That's just Tamiko.

And there were other happy memories and other times when Tamiko, along with her best friend, did certain things that they weren't supposed to be doing ...

Tamiko and Laura sneak out to the wilderness area at the back of the orphanage where they can be free. Where they can just be themselves without being bossed around or constantly watched by the nuns. They run into the forest like a pair of kangaroos, zip down the trail and climb the tallest tree. It's late spring. Birds are chirping and distant cars are buzzing. The air is clear and the sky blue. From high above, they see everything; they see houses and green parks nearby, tall gray buildings of downtown Brisbane further away and blue ocean beyond.

"Do you think we'll ever get out of this orphanage mate?" asks Laura as she gazes off into the distance. "Do you think we'll ever have a mom or dad?"

"I don't know," Tamiko replies. "Maybe we will soon ... before we die, I hope."

"Tamiko. What do you, like, want to be when you grow up ... if you get out of here?"

"I don't know," says Tamiko. "Wait! I *do* know. I want to be ... an angel. An angel that flies around and helps people and stuff. And I could also learn, like, karate or something and beat up all the bad guys!"

Little did Tamiko know that, one day, not too many years from now, her life would be drastically transformed. It would start with something tragic—something totally unexpected—and many tears would be shed. Then, not too long afterwards, something absolutely wonderful would come about. As a result of this astonishing transformation of Tamiko's life from tragedy to marvel, the lives of many other people, especially that of a mysterious lone girl and a stolen twin, would be forever changed.

Like usual, Tamiko's fun times with Laura in the wilderness didn't last very long. And soon afterwards, Tamiko's chief enemy was at it again with her teasing and bullying …

Through the trees in the park behind the orphanage, Tamiko is running after The Smirk who has just stolen her hairbrush. Tamiko huffs and puffs as she tries to catch up to the thief. She finally does; in fact, Ivy—clever as she is—lets Tamiko do so at just the right time and place.

"Give it back!" says Tamiko.

Ivy, smiling, still refuses, saying that she doesn't have it. The two push and shove each other. As Ivy had planned, the girls are only a few steps away from a group of nuns around the corner. Ivy calls Tamiko a "Reject" and, like the previous times, Tamiko loses all control and tries to rip off Ivy's hair while nearly strangling her. The nuns come running, stop the fight, and once again tell Tamiko that her head will be shaved and that she will be wearing a sugar bag for the rest of the week. Ivy wins again. But Ivy isn't the only source of Tamiko's anger, leading to violent rages; there's also Debra The Tarantula, Timmy The Meanie, and one of Ivy's friends amongst several others. Most often, they bully Tamiko simply because she's Japanese. *This isn't fair!* Tamiko thinks. *One of these days, when I get older, I'm going to put an end to all of this unfairness!*

As she's being dragged away by the nuns, Tamiko hears the revving of car engines in the distance and sees flashes of sunlight flickering through the green trees. Tamiko sees an airplane draw a thin, white line across the clear blue sky as it announces its presence with a crescendo of screaming jet engines. Tamiko thinks, *oh, how I wish I could be in that airplane right now … flying me away from this dreadful dungeon, from all of my troubles and off to a far away place.*

Then, before she knows it, Tamiko is sitting in the Cutting Room waiting for her hair to be sheared off once more.

"Stay seated and don't move an inch! You know the drill!" says the same nun that shaved her head the first time.

The nun grabs the electric hair clippers and goes straight to her work. Just like before, she starts at the front and plows down the middle and towards the back. Same awful buzzing noises. Same ugly first cut. Tamiko clenches the armrests as she shakes, pouts and refrains from crying. The nun makes a second pass and then a third while Tamiko continues to fight her emotions. Above all, she doesn't look into the mirror. The nun puts on a grin; it makes Tamiko think of Ivy's snotty little smirk as well as the face Debra The Tarantula makes when passing by Tamiko in the hallway or eating across from her in the eating house—a smile similar to Ivy's but one that says, "I'm really laughing at you, silently, and you don't know why." Tamiko struggles with her anger to keep herself from lashing out at her haircutter.

By now, Tamiko's hair is almost all shaved off and, like before, her face becomes red like ketchup and she's just about to blow up. But then, Tamiko acquires some mysterious rush of strength. It enters her bloodstream like a jolt of lightning and she now has the courage to look into the mirror. So she looks up at her reflection with a grin on her face, almost as if she is proud of her new look. Tamiko thinks, *I'm not going to let Ivy or anyone else take me down! And I'm certainly not going to give any nun the pleasure of watching me cry!*

But Tamiko's days with Ivy soon came to an end. For only a few weeks later, just after Tamiko turned eight, it happened ...

Tamiko is looking out of her bedroom window and sees a bright green car pull into the parking lot below. It's summer. The sky is sunny; the birds are singing, and the trees rustle in the gentle summer breeze. Yet, Tamiko is visibly sad as a young couple gets out of the car—a white man with an Asian woman. Tamiko had met with them briefly twice before because they expressed interest in adopting a child—possibly her or maybe somebody else since Tamiko wasn't the only one they had met with. They are very nice people, and Tamiko would love to live with them. Looking at them through the window now, Tamiko thinks, *Like all the other times, these people are going to pick someone else. They don't want some Japanese kid. They don't want me. I'll just stand here, hopeless, and watch as they drive away with today's winner.*

Tamiko stares and stares, waiting for the inevitable. Then, the wind stops blowing, and the birds stop singing. There's a long silence. The man goes back to his car as curious children run around him. It looks as though the couple has chosen someone else after all, as one of the girls outside appears to be walking beside the man. With that, Tamiko turns around, jumps onto her bed, buries her face in her pillow and cries. *I knew it*, Tamiko thinks, *No one wants me. Like Ivy keeps saying, I'm just a reject—a Japanese reject!*

Then, suddenly, the door opens.

"Tamiko," someone calls.

Tamiko looks up and ... there they are!

CHAPTER 2
ADOPTION

Tamiko gazed into the faces of the young couple. Like the other times, they were accompanied by a staff member. The Asian woman must have been in her late twenties. She had jet-black hair just like Tamiko but longer. She, too, had dark brown eyes and was of medium build and slightly taller than Tamiko. She could have very well been Japanese. As for the man, he was white, had short brown hair, and was about two inches taller than his partner; also, he looked slightly older than his mate. He had blue eyes, a well proportioned face, and large ears that stuck out more than most. Both were dressed in blue jeans and souvenir Australian T-shirts.

They stared at Tamiko with dazed looks on their faces. There was a moment's silence, and then …

"She's the one!" said the woman in Japanese.

"You're Japanese. Right?" said Tamiko in English.

"Oh yes! Yes, I'm Japanese," the woman replied. "Again, my name is Kana."

"That's really a lovely name," said Tamiko. "And I'm Japanese too, like I told you the last time, I think. I mean I'm half … I'm Japanese!"

"Shorter hair now, but … you're beautiful!" said Kana.

"What we've always wanted," said the man. "As you may remember, I'm Thomas Brown."

"You're the one that we want!" said the young couple.

"Really?" replied Tamiko.

"That sounds like a done deal," added the staff member.

"Yes!" cried Tamiko, jumping with joy.

And that was it! After years of waiting, enduring cruelties, and losing hope, Tamiko's life had suddenly changed. But from deep within her, Tamiko sensed that something just wasn't quite right with this couple. She couldn't put her finger on it, but it reminded her of a time when one of her lady school teachers made a promise to her—a promise that she would help Tamiko get through her difficult times with the nuns—only to learn afterwards that the teacher was really on *their* side, working with them all along. *Oh well ... don't let it bother you. Just let it go*, Tamiko told herself.

Tamiko packed her things and said her goodbyes, especially to Laura.

"You take care now, mate, you hear?" said Laura.

"I'm ... I'm going to miss you," Tamiko responded as she began to cry. "I love you."

"I love you, too."

"Good on you, mate!" said Tamiko, wiping her tears away.

"Best friends!" Laura said.

"Best friends forever!" said Tamiko as they knocked their fists together.

They hugged and said goodbye.

Tamiko's new parents walked her to their car and drove out of the parking lot. Tamiko waved goodbye to Laura and her other friends as the car rolled away.

"So this is ... this is a car," said Tamiko. "Wow! I've

never been in a *car* before!"

"Well, I guess there's a first time for everything," replied Thomas.

"So tell me ... tell me all about yourselves," said Tamiko as the new family of three drove away from the orphanage.

"I was going to ask you the same thing," replied Kana.

"Can you tell me first?" asked Tamiko playfully.

Tamiko "hit it off" very well with her new parents; they shared a few laughs and giggles and then the couple began their story.

"We were going to keep it a surprise ... but I'll just tell you," said Thomas. "We're going to Japan—that's where we live—in a city called Fujinomiya."

Thomas intentionally didn't talk about Mount Fuji or tell Tamiko that it was right next to the city; that was one surprise that he planned to keep.

"So then, what are you doing here in Australia?" asked Tamiko.

"We are on vacation," replied Kana. "We really wanted a child, so we come to the orphanage ... and find you."

"May I ask ... are you married?" asked Tamiko.

"Yes, indeed we are," said Thomas. "Actually, we got married five years ago in Japan."

"And where do you come from?" Tamiko asked Thomas. "You're not Japanese."

"I originally come from Canada," said Thomas. "From Ottawa—that's the capital of Canada. After I grew up, I went to university in Alberta—that's a province or region of Canada. That's where I met Kana."

But that was only the beginning. Thomas and Kana had lots more to tell.

Thomas completed an undergraduate degree in nanotechnology at the University of Alberta. Kana studied

English. The two fell in love, moved to Japan, and got married. They tried to have a child but things didn't work out as they had planned. While vacationing in Australia, they heard about the orphanage of St. Alfred and how badly the children were treated there. They had planned to adopt when they got back from vacation, but given what they had learned, they decided to consider adopting and "rescuing" one of the poor children from St. Alfred instead. A young Japanese girl is what they had always wished for and Tamiko, being Japanese, just happened to be there waiting for them.

"Do you work?" asked Tamiko.

"We both do. I own craft and furniture store, and Thomas … he is a crazy scientist," said Kana laughing.

"A scientist?" asked Tamiko. "What … what kind of scientist?"

"I'm called a nanotechnologist. I study—"

"A nano … technolo what?" asked Tamiko.

"A nanotechnologist. I study super tiny, microscopic particles and how to make them and use them—I try to put them together in various ways to make new materials and things."

Then, Kana described her work. She owned a country furniture and craft shop not far from their home. She liked to collect things, fix things up, and sell them. Like Thomas, she really loved her job.

"Now that you know a little about us, how about you?" asked Thomas.

Tamiko recounted the story of her life at the orphanage, including her friends, her enemies, the school, her daily work routine, the living conditions, and her punishments. Above all, she talked about how much she longed to be part of a real family.

"I'm SO glad you picked me," said Tamiko. "You saved

my life!"

"It sounds like we did," said Thomas. "After what *you've* been through!"

"Do you have any friends and family?" asked Tamiko.

Kana spoke of her best friend, Midori. They met in kindergarten—like Tamiko and Laura—and had been good friends ever since. They looked very much alike, though Midori appeared a bit younger than Kana and had shorter hair. Midori was a real thrill seeker, enjoying everything from zip lining to parasailing. She even planned to go skydiving one day. Midori was also a pilot. Often, at least once a week, she would fly high into the sky as she explored the Japanese Alps in her sea plane and took pictures.

Then, Thomas said that he had an older sister and two younger brothers he left behind in Canada along with his parents and grandfather. He visited them every year or so and saw his brother Dylan most often as he frequently came to Japan on business trips. As for Kana, she had her grandmother, her dad, and an older brother Makoto living in Tokyo but no sisters.

"So, do I have any ... cousins?" asked Tamiko.

"In fact, you do," said Thomas. "There's three on my side and ... two on Kana's. Yumi and Nobu. They're around your age. You'll probably meet them sometime soon."

Tamiko treasured the openness and acceptance of her new parents as they described their life in Japan. She looked forward to getting to know them more as they traveled throughout the country and towards Brisbane Forest Park.

"Okay, let's have some fun!" said Thomas.

Before waving goodbye to Australia, the new family of three explored the country for several days starting with Brisbane Forest Park. In the park, they walked down numerous paths and trails within a natural bushland filled with lizards, owls, giant barred frogs and various Australian native snakes and birds. After, they made their way north towards Beerwah to visit Australia Zoo—the zoo that was owned and made famous by wildlife expert Steve Irwin. There, they made friends with all sorts of fascinating zoo animals ... like kangaroos, cheetahs, dingoes, elephants, giraffes, koalas, tigers and zebras along with a wide range of reptiles and crocodiles. Tamiko's favorites were the elephants, snakes and crocodiles. Thomas and Kana especially enjoyed the Wildlife Warriors show and all three had a great time feeding the animals.

Soon enough, their Australian adventures came to an end; it was now time for Tamiko to be transported to her new home—and new world—awaiting her in Japan. So they drove to the airport in Brisbane and, after a three-hour wait, boarded a plane to Japan just before lunch. Airports were something new for Tamiko—she found her first experience both fascinating and exciting. Flying in a plane was also new for Tamiko. She felt thrilled as the plane roared its engines, shot down the runway and lifted up into the air like magic. From the view through a window, the ground below soon looked miniature; cars looked like little toy cars, buildings like little toy blocks and people like ants. It wasn't long before the aircraft crossed over the shoreline and flew high above the ocean. Through the window, Tamiko could see the coast of Australia—and all her troubles—getting further and further afar until the last sign of any land faded away past the scattered clouds. Suddenly, all went white for a short while ... and then bright blue as the plane soared above the puffy clouds like a giant eagle. In just over eight hours, they would touch down in Japan. Like a new diary waiting for words to fill it, Tamiko's new world was waiting for her to fill it with new adventures.

Finally, they landed in Tokyo, Japan, and the three spent the rest of the day walking around the city, shopping, and eating some sushi—raw fish on rice. Tamiko was blown away by the city's culture and size; just a few hours ago, when Tamiko got a glimpse of downtown Brisbane on her way to the airport, she thought it was the biggest city in the world. But now ...! Big buildings, cars and trains were everywhere. The air was filled with smells of beer and car exhaust. The streets were packed with busy people, mostly Japanese, and were moving around in every direction like there was no tomorrow. Food—especially fish and seafood and miso soup—sent its tantalizing aromas on the night air from all corners. Bright, flashing lights lit the night sky. Signs with funny looking Japanese writing—hiragana, katakana and kanji characters—cluttered the scenery. Tamiko had never seen anything like it. For her, it was like a whole new world! On a street corner, a large group of women wearing fancy, colorful costumes—kimonos—gathered together for what appeared to be some kind of religious ceremony. On the other side, several people were lying down in special chairs to have their heads massaged. Further down the street, a couple of musicians played a long vibraphone, while others played a guitar and sang Japanese songs.

"This is awesome!" said Tamiko.

They spent the night at a fancy hotel, and Tamiko had never slept so well! The next day, the small family climbed into Thomas's car at the airport, and they made their way over to the city of Tamiko's new home and where her new world was waiting for her on the edge of Fujinomiya located under the shadows of Mount Fuji, the highest and most famous mountain in Japan. The mountain was stunningly beautiful with its white, snow-covered peak and broad, wooded foothills below.

"Wow!" said Tamiko when she first saw the mountain up close. "That's gorgeous, mate!"

Soon, they approached Fujinomiya, only minutes away from their house. The sky above was partly cloudy, and the wind gently blew with the occasional "Whooooosh!" on this quiet early summer's day. Much unlike Tokyo, Fujinomiya was surrounded by farms and fields with a few small buildings and scattered houses. The main feature was the utter beauty of Mount Fuji.

"We're almost there!" said Thomas.

And the car slowed down and finally pulled into the driveway. There stood Tamiko's new home—a charming, little, two-story house located in a quiet English enclave on the outskirts of Fujinomiya. It had a stone walkway lined with cherry trees, two bow windows, turquoise gables, and a front door with a round top. There was a little front porch. There was also a couple of wind chimes hanging from the eaves—one on each side of the door.

"Wow!" exclaimed Tamiko.

Filled with excitement, Tamiko hopped out of the car, and Thomas and Kana gave her the guided tour.

"Welcome home, Tamiko!" said Kana and Thomas.

Compared to where Tamiko came from, the house was magnificent. The main floor housed a charming, little kitchen with maple cupboards, wallpaper printed with roosters, a large food pantry, and a dishwasher. Also on the main floor, there was a living room, a dining room, and a bathroom. The floors were finished with large slats of mahogany hardwood. In the back, Tamiko found a spacious yard featuring a trampoline and a large, rectangular deck with a barbecue. The tour ended with two bedrooms upstairs.

"And here's your bedroom," said Thomas as he slowly opened the door to reveal the room that he and Kana had prepared for their soon-to-be adoptive daughter.

Tamiko's room contained a platform bed, a small wooden desk, a white dresser, and an empty closet.

"Later, let's fill the closet with the dresses, jeans and Hello Kitty T-shirts you bought in Tokyo," said Kana.

The walls were covered with animal wallpaper in pinks and purples. Elephants (Tamiko's favorite animal), giraffes, tigers, zebras, and monkeys danced across the walls. On the wall hung various pink hearts and several pictures of Mount Fuji and Tokyo. In one corner, there was a bamboo plant; in another corner stood a Japanese floor screen. On the wall above Tamiko's bed were two large windows that provided a spectacular view of Mount Fuji.

"Incredible!" said Tamiko. "I love it!"

"We're glad you do," said Thomas.

"This is like ... the *best* day of my life!" exclaimed Tamiko as she shed tears of joy.

And so it went. The three were now one little happy family, all under the same roof. Not only did Tamiko have a family, but she also had a home. No more orphanage! So no more stinky bed! No more dirty bathroom! No more broken toys and no more taking orders before working all day long like a slave! Although Tamiko valued her new freedom, family was what she treasured most.

Over the next four seasons, the three were virtually inseparable. They ate together, played games together, read books together, went shopping together, went camping together, went fishing together at Lake Tanuki, and went hiking together in the Japanese Alps as well as biking, tennis, and kite flying. Tamiko even met Kana's brother Makoto and his wife Hiroko—Tamiko's new uncle and aunt—and their children Yumi and Nobu—Tamiko's new close-aged cousins. There were days when Thomas showed Tamiko his scientific toys, including magnets and microscopes. There were other days when Kana shared her book collection with Tamiko and taught her how to make cakes and pies. All throughout, they shared laughs and tears.

Although the three shared many good times, there were a few bumps along the way; every now and then, especially when she was asked to do certain chores around the house, Tamiko would get upset—even angry sometimes. One day, Tamiko played a game of Old Maid—a simple card game—with her parents and lost for the third time in a row. Thomas and Kana laughed and laughed at her chanting, "Old maid! You're the old maid!" Tamiko got so angry, she grabbed all of the cards and threw them across the room.

"I knew it! I knew it!" yelled Tamiko "I knew I'd lose again!"

However, Thomas and Kana had been informed of Tamiko's anger problems at the orphanage, and they began to read books on how to deal with it as parents.

Thomas took off as many hours from work as he could, and Kana found someone to replace her while she wasn't in her shop; they spent this extra time with Tamiko. When Thomas had to return to work, he would rush home to spend more time with his new daughter. While they were at work, they hired a woman named Sakura—an older Japanese woman who worked as a home tutor and had long wavy hair—to come to the house to educate Tamiko rather than enrolling Tamiko in regular school. Sakura taught Tamiko many things … especially the Japanese language and writing. Sometimes Midori, Kana's good friend, would stay with Tamiko when neither the parents, nor the tutor was around. Midori and Tamiko got along quite well. In fact, Midori was almost like a big sister to Tamiko.

The best time of all, though, was bedtime—when

Thomas and Kana tucked Tamiko into her little bed and read her a good bedtime story. Her favorites were *Charlotte's Web* and the *Junie B. Jones* books. After each story, Tamiko's mom and dad would tickle her, squeeze her and finally kiss her and say, "Good night."

Tamiko had never been so happy.

But one day, Thomas came home late from work and rushed upstairs to read Tamiko her bedtime story only to find her fast asleep. Nonetheless, Thomas said "Good night" and quietly shut the door.

"*I* read her the story since you were late," said Kana after Thomas went downstairs.

"Oh."

Gradually, Thomas was feeling more and more pressure from his job especially due to the fact that he had taken so much time off work over the last few months. Kana was pressured, too, although to a lesser extent. Despite all of this, Thomas and Kana were still able to spend a decent amount of time with their daughter. Midori was there for her, too.

But it just wasn't the same as before.

One night, when Tamiko was exactly nine and a half years old, Thomas didn't even come home. Instead, he worked all night, returned home late the next morning, and slept for the rest of the day. The following night, he came home late. The rest of the week was fine until early the following week when he came home late again and in a bad mood. His work was slipping because he was trying to achieve a certain "breakthrough" while his boss had told him to do something else instead. Furthermore, he had to finish making up for all of the hours that he had missed to spend with Tamiko.

"Don't ask me! Don't ask me why I'm late!" he said to Kana. "You know it's all because of that stupid boss of mine!"

As for Kana, she'd come home late, too, sometimes—more often than before, but Midori was always there to fill in for her.

Just before she turned 10, Tamiko became suddenly fascinated with the martial arts, so her parents enrolled her in karate and tae kwon do lessons. Tamiko did very well, ... she learned quickly and even showed her compassionate side as she comforted one of her buddies whose cat had just died. But there were a few rough spots. A boy named Allan McCoy was sort of a class bully, and he and his friends liked to tease Tamiko, telling her that "karate isn't for girls." On one occasion, Allan used a phrase with the word "reject" in it—Tamiko's most hated word—and Tamiko flew into a rage. She was suspended from class for several days, while Allan and his buddies got away with their comments. "Don't let him get to you. He ain't worth it," Tamiko's partner had told her.

At the karate school every now and then, there came a Grandmaster Shun who talked about the spiritual side of karate. He was a plump, elderly Japanese man with white hair, a beard and a little mustache. He reminded Tamiko of Mr. Miyagi, the Martial Arts Master from the Karate Kid movies she watched with Midori the other day. Clever, funny, a great teacher, a very good listener and, of course, an excellent fighter.

In times of trouble, especially when Tamiko was concerned about her parents' pull away from her and toward work and her problems with Allan the bully, Tamiko would talk to Grandmaster Shun. Tamiko received wise advice from him. Shun always had a certain magical way about him in that he could somehow see another person's feelings and know exactly what to say. Instead of answering directly like most people, he would say something completely unexpected, and it would, strangely enough, make perfect sense. "If you are patient in a moment of anger, you will escape a hundred days of sorrow," Shun often said to her.

To cheer up Tamiko, her parents bought her a dog—a golden cocker spaniel pup with a white spotted snout. Tamiko named it Butterscotch after its color. It put a few more smiles on her face, but it wasn't a good replacement for time spent with her mom and dad.

Her parents also bought her a little netbook computer and a camera. But doing so only encouraged Tamiko to spend more time on the computer than with her parents. What Tamiko needed right now was a friend she could talk to. There were a few kids around her age in the neighborhood, but somehow, she didn't really "click" with them.

"Where are you Laura?" she asked herself in bed one night.

Now, just after Tamiko turned 11, things had degraded to the point where Thomas was returning late almost every night—even on weekends. He was often in a bad mood and had little patience. Kana was still there for her more than Thomas, but she, too, was spending more and more time trying to fix up her shop, which was slowly beginning to fall apart.

Tamiko didn't know what to do; now she felt like just a timeslot to her parents. She tried to talk to her parents, especially during calls to work, but they were impatient with her.

"We'll discuss this later Tamiko," they'd say. "I have to go now! I have work to do!"

Shun helped and so did Midori and even Sakura. But, again, Tamiko needed a friend her own age to confide in and lean on.

One day, as a "last effort" to come through for their daughter, Thomas and Kana promised to take Tamiko to the Hamaoka Nuclear Exhibition Centre after work to watch an IMAX movie on dolphins and to visit various energy science attractions. With new hope and impatience, Tamiko sat by the front window watching the birds in the trees and the gray rain clouds roll by while she anticipated the arrival of her parents. It felt like the times when she gazed out her bedroom window at the orphanage, waiting for someone to come and adopt her and, when a couple showed up, hoping that she'd be the chosen one. It was now just a couple of minutes after 4:00 p.m.—the time they told Tamiko they'd pick her up—but they didn't show up. At 4:10, they still didn't. Then 4:20, 4:30 and still no sign of mom or dad. Like the raindrops rolling down the window, tears ran down from Tamiko's eyes with each passing minute. She looked at the clock and then through the window … and then at the clock again as she waited and waited and waited …. Finally, just after 5:00, they arrived but that was far too late.

"It was … it was traffic!" said Thomas as Tamiko stomped up the stairs like a young elephant, ignoring his words. "You have to understand. I had to make a turn onto … look, we'll go next week Tamiko. Tam—!"

Humiliated, Tamiko didn't even look back. Instead she went straight into her bedroom and slammed the door behind her.

One warm, cloudy Saturday in autumn, Tamiko stopped by the neighborhood park to take pictures of the beautiful maple, ginkgo, and beech trees with their vivid red, yellow, and purple autumn leaves. The air was misty from a light rain. Kids were playing at the playground with their parents who were happily pushing them in their swing seats and chasing them around the play structure. Some were even showing their children how to draw Japanese characters in the sand and how to make little sand castles.

Tamiko wished that, now, she could be one of those children.

Then, one daddy threw his daughter high in the air, caught the child, and wiggled his face on her tummy. The little girl giggled and …

Tamiko couldn't take it anymore. She sat down on the empty park bench, surrounded by damp, freshly fallen leaves, put her face down in her hands and burst into tears.

That's when Tamiko met Hina, and that's when everything changed.

Chapter 3~
Hina, Rin, and Jeremy

"Ya soko! Doushita no? Doushita no?" said a young female voice.

At first, Tamiko didn't respond to the "Doushita no?" (that is, "What's the matter?"); she was too involved in her emotions. After a short pause, the voice started again, slowly penetrating Tamiko's shell, and Tamiko slowly looked up.

Standing in front of her, Tamiko saw a Japanese girl around her age—11 years old—but slightly taller and thinner. She was dressed in pink. She wore a bit of makeup.

"Ugh ... never mind," Tamiko responded in Japanese with tears still rolling down her face while staring at the girl in pink.

The girl gave Tamiko a gentle hug.

"What happened?" asked the girl. "Did he just dump you? Did he—"

"No, it's not like that. It's ... kind of personal."

"Then if it's not 'him', then it must be ... let's see," said the girl. "Is it school? Homework?"

"No."

"Friends?"

"No."

"Parents?"

Tamiko hesitated, and her peer took that as a "yes."

"Tell me about it," said the girl. "My mom and dad don't know me—they say they can't trust me. They won't let me hang out after supper, but why should they care? They don't have time for me anyway. They—"

"I know what you mean," said Tamiko as her tears began to dry.

"Then, welcome to the club."

"Yeah, my parents *used* to spend time with me. Lots of time. And now, it's all 'I have to go to work' or something else … it's like I'm always in their way," said Tamiko.

"I understand. My name's Hina, by the way."

"Nice to meet you. I'm Tamiko. I like your clothes!"

And what clothes she wore! Hina looked like she had just jumped out of a fashion magazine. She reminded Tamiko of the girls she had seen in the Harajuko Shopping District in Tokyo. She was dressed in a flamboyant pink jacket with white stripes over a pink blouse and T-shirt. She also wore a black skirt with pink polka dots and a pair of zany looking pink and white shoes. She had all kinds of stuff in her long, black hair, including a tiara, a couple of colorful hair bands, and many little pink and purple hair clips. She also had several necklaces and bracelets as well as a Hello Kitty shoulder bag. She could have almost passed for a clown.

"I like them too," said Hina.

So Tamiko had just made a new friend. They stayed at the park and talked and talked under a light shower of autumn leaves. And in only a few minutes, Tamiko felt like she had known Hina all her life.

"Want to come to my place?" asked Hina.

"Sure!" said Tamiko. "I'd love to!"

The two hopped on their bikes, and Hina lead Tamiko over to her home several blocks away from Tamiko's house.

Hina lived on the second floor of a small apartment building with her parents and two brothers. For a family of five, this was quite a small place—a little kitchen and dining room with a tiny living room and only three bedrooms and a bathroom. There, Hina introduced Tamiko to her parents and then to a Japanese friend of hers who had been waiting at her house while Hina was talking to Tamiko at the park. Her name was Rin. Unlike Hina's wacky clothes, Rin was dressed much more plain—a long beige dress and a long-sleeved shirt with black and white horizontal stripes. Rin was slightly overweight and shorter than Hina. Her eyes were brown, and her hair was just a bit longer than Tamiko's. She had a round head and wore little makeup.

"Konnichiwa," said Tamiko, greeting Rin with the traditional Japanese "hello."

"Konnichiwa."

"Nice dress," said Tamiko.

"Thank you."

"So, do you both go to school together?" asked Tamiko.

"Yes, in fact we do," Rin answered. "Junior High, first year. And we're in the same class too. We have to wear uniforms now."

"And she's got the better grades. Let me tell you!" added Hina, pointing to Rin.

And so it went. The three played Koi-Koi (a popular card game in Japan) and had a good chat. Rin was more reserved than Hina. She was very smart—a computer whiz—and seemed to know everything, whereas Hina was a little dense or even stupid at times. After another game, Rin looked at the time and said that it was "time to go."

"Where are you going?" asked Tamiko.

"To Jeremy's birthday party," said Hina. "Want to come?"

"Umm ... sure. But I should call my parents first."

So Tamiko called and talked to her mom. Kana asked a few questions and finally let her go, telling her that she should be home by 8:00 p.m. Then, Tamiko asked who Jeremy was.

"He's my boyfriend," said Hina. "My Japanese BF."

"He's my boyfriend, too," said Rin, somewhat confused.

Hina and Rin grabbed their birthday presents and put them in their knapsacks, and the three made their way over to Jeremy's place.

They pedaled down the streets of Hina's neighborhood and then through a small forest, which provided them with a fantastic view of Mount Fuji surrounded by the beautiful autumn foliage. Once they exited the forest, they sped past several old houses, a spooky little home on a corner, more old houses, and finally arrived at Jeremy's neighborhood. It consisted of a cluster of old townhouses. It looked tougher—more like a "hood"—compared to where Hina lived. Aside from a few slight differences, the houses looked pretty much the same. Most were in need of some kind of repair.

Finally, the three girls arrived at Jeremy's place. His house was a brown brick bungalow with metal siding—like all the rest. The driveway was rather broken up, and they had a basketball hoop set up on the side of the driveway. A short, spiny little tree without leaves offered the only décor in front.

Hina rang the doorbell, and the girls heard voices penetrating the door; so, the three opened the door and walked in. Standing in the hallway were three boys, none of whom were Japanese.

"Happy Birthday, Jeremy!" shouted Rin along with Hina.

Tamiko turned to the girls.

"But … where's Jeremy?" she asked them, just loud enough that the boys could hear.

"*I'm* Jeremy," said one of the boys.

"But I thought you were … Hina said that you were … Japanese!"

With that, everybody burst out laughing while Tamiko stood there smiling. Then she, too, laughed along.

"Hina, you little trickster you!"

"I should have taken a picture of you," said Hina. "You looked *so* confused!"

"When you said that Jeremy was your Japanese BF, I was a little confused myself," added Rin.

"Well … Tamiko, this is Jeremy and his friends, Dave and Peter. Everyone, this is my new friend, Tamiko!"

Jeremy was as white as his friends—North American, actually—and he was one handsome guy. He had short brown hair, blue eyes, and bright white teeth. He was well built, and his head was tilted slightly upwards. Jeremy had on light blue jeans along with a purple hooded sweatshirt. He smiled when he looked at Tamiko, and Tamiko smiled back a little.

"Oh … well … Happy Birthday," said Tamiko. "So how old are you now?"

"Thirteen," said Jeremy. "How 'bout you?"

"I'm eleven. I guess I'm still a kid."

"You're a tween," said Jeremy.

The party began and everyone had a great time. Jeremy showed off his pet spider and his drums. After that, they ate spaghetti with meatballs and cake with green tea ice cream. Jeremy opened his presents—hot spices and a model motorcycle, and then they played Monopoly till the sun went down.

"Oh, I ... better go now," said Tamiko. "It's past eight and it's getting dark outside."

Tamiko exchanged phone numbers with her new friends, said her goodbyes, and left. When she got home, an angry Thomas and Kana were waiting for her.

"I told you I wanted you back by eight. It's now past eight thirty!" said Kana.

"But I was having so much fun, I forgot," explained Tamiko. "Sorry."

"Look how dark it is," said Thomas. "Don't let this happen again. Now, brush your teeth and go to your room!"

Even though she did not like upsetting her parents, Tamiko wasn't very upset herself. She had just made three new friends—Hina, Rin and Jeremy—and felt a new sense of happiness. It all happened so quickly; only hours ago, she was down in the dumps, but now she was back on her feet again. It was as though Hina and her friends were zapped onto earth in order to rescue her. In not even a day, they felt like good friends. In fact, they almost felt like family to her. It felt warm. It felt secure.

This was the beginning of a friendship that would last forever.

From day one, the three new companions quickly filled Thomas's and Kana's absence. They biked around town, explored the countryside, took silly pictures of one another, caught small animals and insects, played tetherball and basketball, played video games, and sometimes just "hung out" at the corner store, school, or shopping mall. They even wrote and performed songs together sometimes—Hina played keyboard, Rin played bass and Jeremy hit his drums; Tamiko and Hina were the lead singers.

For a young Australian girl who had lived in Japan for just over three years, Tamiko had experienced many things—big and small—that are part of the Japanese culture and etiquette. Her first lesson was at Narita airport in Japan, just after she arrived there from Australia. When Tamiko stepped on an escalator leading to the subway, she stood on the right while her parents stayed on the left. Almost immediately, several Japanese individuals came bolting from behind as though their pants were on fire. They squeezed by Tamiko and her parents who, together, were kind of blocking the way. At least two of the hurried fellows blurted out something as they passed by. "What was that all about?" asked Tamiko. "On the left, Tamiko!" said Kana. "In Japan, you always stay on the left to let others pass by." Her next experience was later that day, just before drinking her first miso soup at a restaurant in Tokyo. The soups and teas started shaking a little all by themselves. "What ... what's happening?" asked Tamiko. "Oh, don't worry Tamiko," said Thomas. "It's just a few tremors ... you could say a miniature earthquake. You'll get used to it. It's very common here in Japan." Other very Japanese things in Tokyo: posters of "Mr. Children"—a popular Japanese rock band—and parlors filled with people playing with "pachinko machines", an extremely addictive Japanese gambling game consisting of glass-covered cabinets with colorful flashing lights and containing little silver balls moving around all over the place. Quickly, Tamiko learned more about Japanese etiquette. For the Japanese liked to bow a lot to show respect to one another. The Japanese also liked to give certain things using both hands ... especially when offering gifts like expensive melons or other fruits. "Tsumaranai mono dess ga (This is a small thing, but please accept it)" or "Dozo (Here) ..." the giver would say earnestly with both eyes fixed on the recipient. "Ee tah dah kee mass (I humbly receive)," the other would respond.

Having met her friends only a few weeks ago, Tamiko already knew a lot about them. She knew that Jeremy first met Rin at school in the Detention Room where Rin, as a volunteer school assistant, first helped Jeremy with his math and science homework. She knew that Jeremy, on at least one occasion, privately ate birdseed for lunch. She also knew that he won a cupcake eating contest and joined the school chess club with Rin one day ... only to give it up two months later as it was "too nerdy" for him. Tamiko learned that Rin played hooky once and that she accidentally set off the fire alarm last year—the same year she was voted "Most Quiet Student". Like Jeremy "tried out" for chess, Rin tried out for girls' football but just didn't make the team. And Hina, she came in 2nd place at a fashion show in Tokyo, had a monkey as a pet (or claimed to) and began collecting basketball and hockey cards three years ago and has been trading them with Jeremy ever since.

One of their favorite places to go was a big oak tree in the forest beside Lake Tanuki. There, they would climb the tree and talk and play for hours while listening to the soft sounds of nature and admiring the magnificent view of Mount Fuji. Hina talked about her love of fashion, her waning grades in school, and how she dreamt of becoming a figure skater or maybe an actress or singer. Rin spoke of her love of books, how she skipped a grade, and how she wanted to be a doctor. As for Jeremy, he bragged about his popularity, shared his passion for sports and promised that, some day, he'd be an Olympic athlete.

Every now and then, the four went around town and played a harmless prank on someone, like going to the clock store and setting all the alarms to go off at the same time. Or they would dress up as store clerks, and when someone needed help, they would all surround the customer and speak at once.

Then one day, Hina asked Tamiko to meet her alone at the big tree. As soon as Tamiko laid eyes on her, she knew that something wasn't right. Hina's usual cheery face had been replaced with a sadder one.

"What's wrong?" asked Tamiko.

After a long pause, Hina spoke.

"My parents. They just got a divorce," she said, crying.

Tamiko hugged her and talked about it with her. It turned out that Hina's dad left the house, and they planned to split up the children—Hina and her younger brother with her mom and Hina's older brother with her dad. They discussed it some more and Tamiko eventually shared that she was an orphan and told Hina all about her life in the orphanage. She spoke about how wonderful it was when Thomas and Kana rescued her, about their lovely times together, and as Hina already knew, how things had gone downhill. Even though Hina felt better afterwards, she wasn't the same as before.

Hina changed and the others changed with her.

At the next "big tree" meeting, Hina dared the other three to jump into a deep spot of Lake Tanuki from a tall tree by the shore. First, they started low. And then, as they got more daring, they jumped from higher branches. Although she had changed quite a bit, Hina hadn't lost her crazy side, and she urged her friends to jump from even higher spots until Jeremy nearly slipped and fell to the ground.

"I think we're going a bit too far now Hina," said Tamiko.

But throughout the days, Hina got the gang to do crazier things. Their pranks were not so harmless anymore; they were rather mean or offensive. Her daring ways ran deeper, and her plans became more insane. They loitered behind schools and stores after dark, especially on weekends. The gang even began to vandalize a little. Often, Rin would hesitate before going through with Hina's plans. But, somehow, Hina was able to win her over and finally get her to do it. Tamiko was hesitant, too, but she didn't want to "drop out" and risk losing her friends. As for Jeremy, he seemed to be having as much fun as Hina even though he seemed a bit doubtful at times. Although the acts were harmful in some ways, the four stuck together; they shared a special bond that just couldn't be broken. They were like one small family together. They were almost like soul mates.

Hina's clothes, if not already wacky enough, became even wackier. For she began wearing a few Kermit the Frogs on the front of her jacket—similar to the ones found on rockstar Lady Gaga's crazy Kermit the Frog coat—along with lightning bolt earings and more necklaces. On some occasions, she even wore tall, peach-colored lace-up boots with black laces—also out of Lady Gaga's wardrobe. Hina and then the others started swearing more often. They also began to play violent video games together. They'd listen to all sorts of crazy music together. Then, Hina got a lip piercing and put pink highlights in her hair. Rin dropped out of the school chess club, failed a test for the first time in years, and her clothes changed from ordinary to more extraordinary—a bit like Hina had done when Hina first met Tamiko: black skirts with pink polka dots, wacky looking pink shoes, hair bands, purple hair clips, and necklaces. As for Tamiko, her nature changed from caring to conceited. Her clothes changed from the usual jeans and Hello Kitty T-shirts to pre-ripped jeans and shirts with rock band logos on them. And for the first time, her friends saw a bit of her angry side during an argument that Tamiko had with her mom over the phone. "I've never seen her like *this* before," said her friends. Surprisingly, her karate skills actually improved in the lessons because Tamiko was pumped up with more energy as her arrogant ways drove her to prove her greatness, and Allan didn't tease her so much. And Jeremy changed from a gentleman to some kind of a punk. "Unko dreams!" he'd say, the Japanese word "unko" meaning "poop" in English.

As for the parents of these gradually misled youths, they didn't really seem to know what was going on. Thomas and Kana were working later than ever, and they had problems of their own. They didn't care too much if Tamiko went out to "chill" with her friends or returned home after dark. Rin's parents were stricter; therefore, she didn't stay out as late. Jeremy made up excuses—that he had a football practice at school or that he had a detention, and his parents believed him. As for Hina who lived with only her mom and younger brother, whenever anyone asked her about her coming home late, Hina would say that her dad wasn't there and that her mom didn't care since she was too involved with "something." Whatever that something was, it seemed to bother Hina from time to time and she didn't want to talk about it, not even with Tamiko. Even stranger, Hina wouldn't let people into her house anymore. "My mom's sleeping," she'd say.

By now, the four were out and about, wrecking up the town, in full swing like mini tornados. They littered the streets, pulled nasty pranks, destroyed gardens, took apart playgrounds, knocked over flower pots, set off fire alarms, sprayed people's chairs with water, and smashed bottles. They even began slashing bicycle tires.

Then, Hina bought several cans of spray paint and the gang sped over to a closed 100 yen shop near a dark street alley in the poorer quarters and the four sprayed Japanese writing and art all over the building. As they were packing things up, they heard footsteps, and then the voice of an angry man. The kids dropped their things and …

"I know you around here!" yelled the man as he marched around with a baseball bat in his hand. "I gonna find you—and when I do—you gonna pay for all this! Got that?"

Shaking like a leaf in the wind, 11-year-old Tamiko scurried stealthily around the closed shop and then into the foul air of the dark, barren alley behind her friends where she tripped over a stone and fell. Tamiko let out a short scream. The man froze and then stomped towards Tamiko. Hearing the crescendo of footsteps, Tamiko quickly picked herself up only to realize that her friends had already run away. With her heart pounding like a Taiko drum, Tamiko thought quickly and made a beeline to a nearby dumpster and hid behind it just before the man caught sight of her.

"My new shop … it just been painted," said the man as he rampaged through the alley, waving his bat, "and what you do to it? You spray graffiti all over! That called vandalism! That a crime, and you gonna pay for it!"

Within seconds, the man arrived at the dumpster. He paused, listened and then sensed Tamiko's presence on the other side. Slowly, the angry store owner plodded about the dumpster. Just in time, Tamiko stepped silently out of the way and moved around the other side of the wastebin in pace with the man, making sure that the container stayed between them. It was like one of the times Tamiko gave some stolen food to the local bum at the orphanage—behind the dumpster in the far corner of the yard—and almost got caught right afterwards. The shop owner went around one way, then the other, but didn't find anything. Confused, he finally left.

When the coast was clear, Tamiko made her move to escape, but out of nowhere, two big dogs—German Shepherds—suddenly came onto the scene. They barked and growled and sniffed all over the place but they thankfully didn't go after Tamiko as they were more interested in the smells coming from the other side of the open dumpster. Nonetheless, Tamiko stayed in her hiding spot behind the trash bin as she trembled with every "Arf!" and "Woof!" from the unwelcome visitors.

Sitting with her head down low in her hands, Tamiko waited and waited for the dogs to go away. The canines had ceased to bark but continued to growl every so often and were still intrigued with the odors of the trash. Finally, they gave up and fled. But Tamiko, having waited for what seemed like hours, had gradually drifted off into a sort of trance. Then, suddenly …

"Tamiko!" Jeremy called out. "Tamiko!"

Still in her sleep, Tamiko wasn't quite sure whether this was reality or just part of some dream.

"Tamiko!" Jeremy cried even louder.

With that, Tamiko awoke from her trance and suddenly realized that this wasn't a dream after all. She crept out of her dark, little corner behind the dumpster and a bright flashlight lit her face.

Standing in front of her were her friends—Hina, Rin, and Jeremy. And beside them holding the flashlight was … the angry shop owner! Tamiko and her friends had just been caught!

Chapter 4
Change

There he was, a black silhouette standing under a trace of moonlight, waving his flashlight in one hand and holding a baseball bat in the other. He was a tall, stocky, and intimidating Japanese individual who appeared to be in his late 40s—though it was difficult to tell with the lack of light. He wore big glasses and a hat.

"Great!" said the man. "Now we have the whole darn gang here! And now … you gonna listen."

Tamiko shook with every word that shot out from the man's angry mouth.

There was a long pause, and then the man began.

"Do you … do *any* one of you … know what you just did?"

The four graffiti artists just stood there, trembling and speechless.

"You have nothing to say? You don't care about what you did to my building … what you did to me!?"

Again, the four partners in crime didn't say anything. They were still shaking but also sobbing now as their mouths twitched with guilt.

"Say something! Why do you do that? Why? Do you enjoy ruining other people's things? I see you before, you know. Making big mess. Breaking everything you see. I even saw you cut tires. Would *you* like that if someone did that to *your* bike?"

Then, he pointed to Tamiko.

"What your name again? Tam …?"

"T-Tamiko," she replied, her head hanging low.

"Tamiko, would you like that if I cut your tires … or if I spray paint on your house?"

"No," answered Tamiko after a short pause, still sobbing.

"I didn't think so. Then why you do it? Just for fun? Because you think it cool? Or maybe you just bored and got nothing better to do with your life. People like you, you got no purpose. No future. Your parents probably don't know where you are … and probably don't even care. You good for nothing. You come here and decide to spray all that—"

"But it was *her* idea," said Tamiko, pointing to Hina.

"Oh! So you *good* now. It don't matter if it not your idea. You can do it anyway."

Rin was about to say something like, "but I didn't do anything" but was too shy to say the words. Unlike the others, Rin felt wrongfully accused as she, more or less, only watched her comrades do the work.

"It's not like we broke anything," said Hina. "It's just paint … and everybody else does it."

"It just paint!?" said the man. "You don't have to break something to ruin it. You spray over my brand new store and destroy the looks! And you think that okay to do if everyone else do it, too. I ought to spank you little—"

"Okay okay," said Jeremy, playing it cool. "We're sorry, we made a mistake; we won't do it again. Now let - let's just chill—"

"Just chill!? I worked so hard to get money to pay to have it built! It just opened, not even a week ago! Who gonna to want to come to my store now? Huh? You even put paint on the windows! What am I going to do!? It cost money to remove paint! I don't have more money! You nothing but a gang of bratty little kids—worthless little rejects—that will go nowhere in life!"

As soon as Tamiko heard the word "rejects," her fists clenched, and she ground her teeth together. She was just about to yell out, but something within her stopped her from doing so.

"NOW GET. GET OUTTA HERE BEFORE I THROW YOU OUT MYSELF. GET AND DON'T EVER COME BACK!"

With that, the four raced to their bikes and sped down the dark alley and through the empty streets. With Hina leading the way, and with the help of their bicycle headlights, they pedaled down the forest trail that led them to the big tree. There, they stopped and jumped off their bikes under the moonlight that pierced through the trees.

"What a jerk!" said Hina. "It was just a little paint. He was all like, 'You totally destroyed my building'!"

"Yeah," said Jeremy. "Did you see him with that bat? It's like he was going to kill us or something! And over what? A bit of freakin' paint. What a doofus, man!"

"I know," said Rin, simply going along. "What a ... what a dope."

"His 'building' actually looks better now," said Jeremy, laughing. "We did him a favor, man. Unko dreams, baby!"

"And did you hear the way he talked?" said Hina. "It just paint ... who gonna to want to—"

"I know," said Rin. "That was funny."

"What about you, Tamiko? You're pretty quiet. Aren't *you* going to say anything?"

Tamiko just stood there like a statue with her head low, still sobbing while the cutting words of the angry store owner rang in her head, over and over again, like a stubborn alarm clock: "You nothing but a gang of bratty little kids—worthless little rejects—that will go nowhere in life! Worthless little rejects—that will go nowhere in life! That will go nowhere in life! Nowhere in—" All at once, she received flashes of her and Laura in the tall tree at the back of the orphanage. Then, she remembered what she said to Laura after Laura asked her what she wanted to be when she grew up. *Look at me! Look at us!* thought Tamiko. *Look at what we've become! This isn't me and what I really stand for! I'm going to show that man—I'm going to show the world—that we're no worthless little rejects! I'm going to change things and, together, we're going to make a difference ... once and for all!*

"Tamiko, what are you ...? Say something," said Jeremy.

But Tamiko's mouth didn't open, and her body didn't move an inch.

"Tamiko, what's *wrong* with you? Aren't you going to open your mouth and say—?"

"Today's the day," Tamiko finally said.

"Today's the ... what?" asked Jeremy. "What do you mean, today's—?"

"Today's the day," Tamiko repeated.

"What are you talking about? I don't get it. This isn't really you talking. It's like—" said Hina.

"Today's the day we do things differently ... that we change our ways," said Tamiko.

"What do you ... change our ways ... I don't get it," said Hina. "What's this 'changing our ways' thing? Explain, Tamiko!"

45

Tamiko took a deep breath and then spoke.

"I see … I can see now what we've become. At first, it was kind of fun. The jokes. The pranks. But things went … down from there. I'm not talking about our friendship—as far as I can see, we'll always be together—I'm talking about how we treat ourselves and how we treat other people. I ask myself, what—"

"But we didn't really *hurt* anyone," said Hina. "We were just having some fun. Come on, Tamiko. Lighten up! Snap out of it! Don't be so serious!"

"But like the man said, what if somebody cut *your* bicycle tires? Or what if somebody wrecked *your* garden? Or what if you stepped on broken glass with bare—"

"You know, she *does* have a point," said Rin.

"Kind of," said Jeremy. "But like Hina said, we were just having fun, man. But, Tamiko's kind of right, too."

Tamiko continued.

"I look at all of you—and myself in the mirror, and I ask myself, "What good have we ever done? Like the man said also, we're nothing but … you know … that will go nowhere in life if we keep going on like this."

"I've done a few nice things," said Jeremy. "Like, I don't know …"

"What good have we done? That includes you, too, Hina and Rin."

"She's right," said Rin. "We haven't really done … anything really good … come to think of it."

"But Tamiko," said Hina, "it's good to have fun. Take the prank where we put Jeremy's habanero chili powder in that guy's hamburger. It not like he was going to die or … okay … I'll admit that stuff is kind of hot."

"*Kind* of hot?" said Rin along with Jeremy. "That's, like, the hottest spice in the world! If we had put any more inside, he would have gone to the hospital!"

"Okay, so we did some not-so-nice things," Hina admitted. "But why now? Why, all of a sudden, did you go all 'goody' on us?"

"I ... I had a dream," said Tamiko. "I was half asleep in the alley back there and I dreamed about my past—from when I was at the orphanage to when I was adopted to when I met you, and the things we did after—"

"Wait, wait, wait," said Jeremy. "You ... you were an orphan?"

"Yeah," said Tamiko. "I only told Hina. It's a long story. Let's just say that my life wasn't very easy in that dungeon of a place."

Then, Tamiko had a confession to make.

"All along, I wondered why I went along with you ... doing all these mean things with you. That wasn't really me. Well, it was ... but. Now, I understand why I did them. I did them because you're ..." said Tamiko as she began to cry.

"Because what?"

"Because ... because you're my best friends—my only friends really—and I was afraid that if I didn't do them, I would lose you. That I'd be ... rejected!" she said bursting into tears. "Like I was when I was sent to the orphanage."

There was a long pause, and then Rin opened her mouth.

"Me too," Rin said as she, too, began to cry. "I just went along because I wanted to be someone cool ... like the rest of you. Not some kind of nerd ... like me."

Tamiko gave Rin a gentle hug just as Hina joined the parade of confessions.

"There's something I didn't tell you," she said. "Only Tamiko knows. Well, she doesn't know the whole story. I guess it's what made me do all these things. My—"

"What Hina?" asked Jeremy. "What's your big secret?"

"My parents ... a few months ago ... they got a divorce. But that's not all."

"What else?" asked Tamiko.

"After they told me about the divorce, my dad left the house with my older brother. And then, my mom ... she started drinking. At first, it was just a few glasses. And then she just drank more and more ... until she was, like, drunk every day. That's why I didn't want you to come into my house anymore."

"Oh Hina," said Tamiko as she put her arms around her.

"I'm so sorry," said Rin. "Is your mother still ...?"

"She's getting a little help now. She's doing better."

"That's good to hear," said Jeremy.

After more discussion about Hina and her mom's drinking problem, Jeremy looked to the ground as if he, too, had a secret.

"And you, Jeremy," said Hina. "Do you have something to say?"

"Umm ... no. Not really. I'm fine!"

But everyone else could see that he was hiding something.

"Well, I—"

"Come on, Jeremy. Be a man," said the girls.

"Okay, I'll admit it. I didn't make the basketball team. My dad's kind of ashamed of me, and my friends—especially Dave and Peter—think that I'm a ... wuss. So I found 'other' things to do like try out for football and ... you know," Jeremy said as he shed a tear or two.

The girls comforted Jeremy, and then Hina raised an important question.

"So where do we go from here?" she asked.

"I was just thinking about that," said Tamiko. "Well … I was thinking of going around town and helping people in various ways. Sort of like angels on special missions. And maybe I could use my karate."

"Like angels?" said Rin. "Sounds intriguing."

"I kind of like it," said Hina.

"I can't wait to see this!" said Jeremy.

"Now let's go out and prove that angry man wrong. Let's show him … let's show the world that we *can* go somewhere in life … and that we can really make a difference!" said Tamiko.

And so it was decided. The four would set out to change the future and change the world. Their first mission— remove the graffiti from the 100 yen shop.

Part 2—
The Mystery of the Lone Girl

CHAPTER 5
505!

Things had really changed. No more wrecking things. And no more pranks—except for, maybe, a harmless one every now and then. The four now dedicated their time to helping others in any way they could. They started the very next day by removing the graffiti from the poor man's store. In actuality, they sprayed over the wall graffiti using the exact same color as the original paint; as for the windows, they used paint thinner to remove their works. Just as they were finishing up, the man came to check on his shop. And what a surprise he had—no more graffiti! But he had a second surprise when he saw the four kids.

"*You* do this?" he said. "I don't know what to say!"

"We're sincerely sorry we ever did this to you sir," said the four.

"Apology accepted. I don't know how you do it but … it look like brand new again. Thank you! Thank you so much!"

Over the next few days, the four came up with a couple of ideas for their next missions—they were really determined to make some kind of difference in the world. As for their friendship, the four were closer to each other now, since there were no more secrets and they understood each other's feelings. Hina didn't feel so ashamed about the divorce and her mother's situation; she could now talk about it freely amongst her friends. Rin didn't feel so bad about herself. She no longer felt "pushed" into doing things simply to prove that she was "cool" … and her grades started to climb again. And Jeremy didn't feel like such a loser. He didn't give up on basketball, though; he was still determined to eventually make the team and hopeful in making the football team as well. As for Tamiko, she wasn't afraid of being rejected anymore and she was now able to share all her orphanage stories with her friends. It was like a giant weight had been lifted off of her shoulders, and she could now walk again. At the same time, and for reasons unknown to her, Tamiko's relationship with her parents improved somewhat; Thomas and Kana made an effort to spend more time with her and talked to her more, but they still had a ways to go. Furthermore, Kana's friend Midori took Tamiko on one of her exploring expeditions around Mount Fuji in her seaplane. Tamiko took lots of pictures and showed them to her friends.

Now, it was time for them to plan their next mission.

So the next sunny and windless day below Mount Fuji, Tamiko slipped out of her house, sped through the forest on her bicycle, and made her way toward the village corner store where she was to meet with her club members. When she finally arrived, there were her friends, Hina and Rin, straddling their bicycles.

"Konbanwa!" cried Tamiko as she braked her bike. "Where's Jeremy? Is he coming?"

"He said he's going to be a bit late but should be here soon," said Rin.

"I expect *all* the angels to be on time, even cute little boys like Jeremy," said Tamiko jokingly.

"And what about you?" asked Hina. "You're a little late

yourself."

"Well ... as I'm the leader now, I *do* have special privileges, you know," said Tamiko.

They got off their bikes and started to mosey around.

"And as for Jeremy, he's more than just cute," said Hina. "He's a cutie patootie and I'm his biggest crush now ... no offense!"

"You just *think* you're his biggest crush!" said Tamiko. "You may be the prettiest, but ..."

"Ooooh, someone's getting a little bit jealous," said Hina.

Then, Rin broke in. "What Jeremy wants ... what Jeremy needs ... is a girl with good grades. What he needs is me!"

"Well," said Tamiko half-jokingly, "I've got both good looks *and* good grades—just what it takes for Jeremy to be my BF. It's just that I'm too busy studying and doing other stuff these days ..."

Then, Tamiko talked about the "other stuff"; the others had heard it before. Tamiko, with her older friend Midori, had been searching the foothills of Mount Fuji by plane for a cluster of ancient shrines dating back to the Yayoi period, many centuries ago. Legend had it that they contained all sorts of treasures worth many yen. Tamiko wasn't in it for the money, though; she only wanted the simple glory of finding them.

"Are you serious?" said Rin.

"Yeah," said Tamiko. "They're out there somewhere!"

After a bit more discussion about the treasures, it was time to get down to business.

"So, first, any new missions?" asked Tamiko.

"Well, let's see. We have Maya, and the expired food thing, and that's about all," replied Rin.

"Still no donor for Maya?" inquired Tamiko.

"Not yet," replied Rin.

After that, the three discussed summer break; by then, their missions would hopefully be accomplished.

"I think my summer is going to be kind of boring without you two," said Tamiko. Hina and Rin were both going away to a summer camp in China. "Oh well, I'll find something to do. It's only for one month."

"Why don't your parents let you go to school like us?" asked Hina. "Why do you have to have a home tutor?"

"My parents told me that I'd learn more and get better marks with a home tutor," replied Tamiko. "They *always* have an explanation for everything."

"How's your mom doing by the way, Hina?" asked Rin. "Any better?"

"A bit," said Hina. "She's drinking less now, but she needs more help."

"Really?" said Tamiko. "Let's hope that she—"

Just then, Jeremy's voice blasted from the walkie-talkie.

"Moshi moshi!" he cried. "I was on my way, and I got an SOS from that spooky little house at the corner where—"

"Yeah, we know the one you mean," said Tamiko.

"I heard some screaming and stuff when I passed by the house. Get over here fast!"

"Roger that! We're on our way!" replied Tamiko.

With that, the threesome sped off on their bicycles.

Meanwhile, Tamiko's parents had just finished sharing a peaceful meal together in the dining room. As Thomas went upstairs to grab his briefcase, he spotted Tamiko's agenda on the stairs, where, apparently, she had dropped it. Looking over her plans for the day, he uttered, "What in the world?"

"What's wrong?" asked Kana.

"Tamiko's agenda ... I can't even read it!" said Thomas.

"It's in code or something."

"Really? Oh well, forget about it, Thomas. She'll be back soon," said Kana. "Let's have dessert! How about some anmitsu?"

When the bicycle gang finally arrived at the source of the distress signal, Jeremy was standing next to the little old two-story house looking like a news reporter. Alone on the corner, partially hidden by a cluster of mature Japanese maple trees in front, stood the house. The old dwelling was built of dark red brick with wooden trim. An old navy blue car sat in the driveway, and a tall brown fence enclosed the backyard. The grass in front had not been mowed for weeks. Two gray and slightly crooked wooden dormers poked through the treetops as though they were searching for sunlight. The side of the house was bordered by a long hedge. If the house could talk, it would be saying, "Please fix me up a bit … I'm starting to look kind of old!" The kids had seen the dreadful place before, but today it seemed different … it seemed more isolated and sort of spooky. Was it the dark clouds behind it? Was it the way the sun was dimly lighting the front of the house? Or something else? It was rather hard to tell.

"So, what exactly is going on here?" asked Tamiko.

"See anything?" said Rin.

"You said you heard screaming?" asked Hina.

"Yeah! Sounded like something pretty bad was going on in there," said Jeremy. "Let's go take a look!"

They got off their bikes and hid them behind a nearby hedge. Then, following Jeremy, they crept over to a partially opened window and peeked inside the house. They listened. They waited. The inside was dimly lit and smelled of mold and stale nuts or sushi. As they glanced around the small, narrow dining room and down the hallway, they noticed all kinds of things—boxes, bags, books, clothes, and toys, to name just a few—scattered everywhere. As of now, however, there were no signs of life.

"I don't hear anything," whispered Tamiko.

Suddenly, they heard the sound of footsteps. Louder and louder the noise grew, like a soldier proudly practicing his march, and then a man came into view. Quickly he opened what appeared to be the basement door and then stomped into the room in the far corner. Immediately afterward, he yelled something, but Tamiko and her friends couldn't make out the words. Then, the kids heard a little girl crying. The man shouted something and then turned and headed toward the window.

"Duck!" said Tamiko.

After a short while, the kids slowly got up, shaking. The window was now almost fully covered by heavy curtains! Nonetheless, there was a small gap in between them that was just wide enough to look through. The kids peered inside trying to get a glimpse of what was happening. They didn't see anyone now, but they heard rapid footsteps getting louder and louder. Two big, rough-looking men dressed in white uniforms stomped down the stairs from the second floor like a pair of sumo wrestlers and frantically searched the house. Then, in the corner of a mirror between the living room and the hallway, Tamiko saw the third man—the one the kids had first noticed—play with some kind of belt or strap in the kitchen like some kind of a lunatic. Then, suddenly, the man left the kitchen and joined the two others. It was kind of hard to make out their faces, as they were moving around quickly and the viewing range was rather limited. They ran from one end of the house to the other and then back again.

"What are they looking for?" asked Jeremy. "What are they trying to find?"

"Beats me!" said Hina.

Then, the girl in the house slowly peered around the corner of her bedroom door; only half of her face was showing. From what the kids could see, the girl was about five or six, had long black curly hair, and she looked pretty frightened.

As for the three men, they continued looking—behind boxes and behind furniture, inside cupboards and under tables. Then the men stopped momentarily. They appeared to be listening for the slightest noise as they silently peered around the room. It was as though they were playing a serious game of hide-and-seek.

"Maybe they're looking for a dog or cat," whispered Tamiko.

Then, the men froze completely, but after a second or two, they raced down the basement stairs. From below the kids could hear a battery of dull, stomping footsteps. Then, everything was dead silent. The stomping resumed for a minute and then once more all was silent. Suddenly, there came a loud, sharp squealing accompanied by angry voices from the men. What exactly happened? Did they just find a dog? Whatever the men found, they were dragging it upstairs as it made agonizing and increasingly bizarre noises. The girl bolted out of her room, crying and screaming. The man without a uniform quickly grabbed the girl and pushed her back into the room. "Nooooo!" cried the girl. Then, there were a few thumps and the man shut the door. From the room the girl was in, there came screams and a deep, banging sound.

"What on earth is going on?" said Tamiko.

The other men dragged their catch over to the far side of

the hallway, and one of them took out a syringe and injected something into its body. The kids tried to make out what it was, but they just couldn't see well enough. After only a few seconds, the howling and squealing stopped, and the two men in uniform put the body into a big bag and carried it out the front door. The kids slowly crept to the front of the house and peered around the corner just as the men reached a gray truck parked on the street. The back of the truck was equipped with several large cages, and the men opened one and pushed in the cloth bag. Then, they jumped inside the truck and raced away with tires screeching. All was silent for a moment, but then the kids could hear the crying of the little girl.

"What exactly was *that* all about?" asked Rin.

"That's what I'd like to know!" said Tamiko.

"What … what were those men doing?" said Hina, frightened.

"I'm not totally sure," said Jeremy, "but the way I see it is that those men came to get rid of the girl's dog. You know … drug it and then take it to the pound."

Hina froze. "Did they, like, *kill* it, you think?" she asked.

"I don't think so," said Jeremy. "The dog was so aggressive that they had to sedate it. I wouldn't worry about it. It'll be all right."

"Of course," said Tamiko. "It all makes sense. See the truck? It had cages in the back of it."

"That was a pound truck," said Jeremy. "They take pets away to animal shelters."

"Maybe that's why the girl was crying."

Everything seemed to make sense now. In fact, it was kind of obvious to them as they looked back on the situation.

"Poor girl!" said Hina.

"And poor dog!" added Tamiko.

"That place gives me the creeps!" said Jeremy.

"You seem to know a lot about dog removal and pound trucks, Jeremy," said Tamiko.

Jeremy recounted the time when his dog was taken away. He was almost ten when it happened. According to Jeremy, the dog had been peeing and pooping all over the house. This drove his parents nuts until they finally reached their limit and had the canine removed. The whole experience was very similar to the one the little girl had just been through— the bag, the needle, the truck, and the crying afterward.

With that, the group of four peddled away together, talking a bit more before they split up and made their separate ways home. As Tamiko approached her house, she thought back on what she and her friends had just witnessed. She couldn't quite put her finger on it, but she felt that there was something pretty strange about the whole situation. Something creepy. Something very ominous. They would have to go back and learn more.

Chapter 6

Furniture, Crafts, and Bulletproof Vests

"Urusai! Urusai!" yelled Tamiko.

The word *urusai* is Japanese for "shut up," and that's what Tamiko wanted the family dog, Butterscotch, to do early next morning as the golden sun was just beginning to light the Japanese countryside. The distant barking of another dog had caught his attention, and now he was barking and running around the house. The noise was a sharp, ear-piercing "Arf! Arf! Arf!" with the occasional "Woof!" This immediately woke up the whole family.

"Hey, hey, hey! Quiet!" yelled Thomas from his bed, hoping that this would be enough to silence the dog.

Butterscotch stopped for a short while but soon continued.

"I said quiet!" Thomas repeated as Kana joined in, screaming, "Butterscotch, no bark!"

With that, the air was peaceful once more, and Butterscotch didn't start in again. The family, however, was all awake. It was almost time to get up anyway; a new day had begun. As usual, Tamiko's mother was the first to get out of bed. She slowly walked to the kitchen and let out Butterscotch so he could do his morning *unko*—again, that's the Japanese word for "poop"—and then she began making breakfast. On this morning's menu was steamed rice, miso soup, and tamagoyaki.

As Thomas washed up and Tamiko sifted through her clothes, Kana called out, "Asagohan!" the morning word that signaled everyone to come to the table. With that, Tamiko and her father hurriedly finished readying themselves for breakfast and raced to the dining room. As for Butterscotch, he had already sniffed his way to his food bowl. After saying *ohayo* and sampling a few spoonfuls of rice, Thomas and Kana began to question Tamiko about her time spent with friends.

"So tell us more about this gang of yours, Tam," Thomas said. "What exactly do you do?"

"We—my friends and I—we go around helping people and stuff," Tamiko explained. "We like to think of ourselves as some kind of angels."

"But how, though? What do you actually do?" asked Kana. "Tell us about your latest thing."

"Well, all right," began Tamiko. "Here it is. Yesterday, as Jeremy was biking by, he heard screams—actually, from a little girl—coming from this house way past the corner store, and … well, we all went over to the house and checked it out. Through the window, we saw—"

"Now wait just a minute," Thomas interrupted. "You were actually *spying* on these people?"

"Well, kind of," said Tamiko. "We were just curious. We wanted to make sure that—"

"You know shouldn't be looking through other peoples' windows," said Kana. "That's an invasion of privacy."

"I know, but—"

"Anyway, go on," said Thomas. "What happened next?"

"We saw these men running around looking for something. At first, we weren't really sure what. Then, we realized it was some mad dog. They caught it and put it in a big bag and then …"

"And then what?" asked Kana.

"And it was moving around and making so much noise they had to put it to sleep. Then, they took it out of the house and put it into a cage in the back of a pound truck and took off. The little girl was crying after."

"That's kind of sad," said Kana.

"Happens all the time," said Thomas.

"Right," said Tamiko.

The conversation went on for a bit longer before ending with an air of "That's no big deal; the girl will get over it." Thomas and Kana left the breakfast table and got ready for work. As for Tamiko, she went into her bedroom to get her books and papers for the day's session with her home tutor. After Tamiko finally gathered her school things, she ran over to the front door and gave her parents a good-bye hug. For the first time in a while, Thomas and Kana kissed their daughter. "See you later Tamiko," they said just before leaving. "Don't forget to wash the dishes."

Then, Thomas drove Kana to the country furniture and craft store that she owned, which was in the countryside south of Mount Fuji on the way to Thomas's work. It was actually a small barn that had what appeared to be a doghouse or a second miniature barn placed halfway up into the sloping roof of the main structure. It was a very charming little building. In it, Kana sold all sorts of furniture—sofas, platform beds, shoji screens and lamps, chairs, stools, tables, bookcases, cabinets, tatami mats, and even footrests. She also sold various crafts like kokeshi dolls, toys, quilts, furoshiki, pillows, picture frames, Kyoto folding fans, kumiki puzzles, lanterns, bamboo baskets, and carry bags. Kana often liked to buy old, beat-up pieces of furniture and repaint them or fix them up somehow. She even sold a few antiques as well as some wild plants and flowers. Kana's work suited her well, as she was naturally creative and, though somewhat quiet and submissive, quite ambitious. When she was a girl, Kana collected all sorts of things: dolls, toys, coins, gems, and even bottle caps. She still had some of these old items in boxes up in the attic.

On a regular basis, Kana's childhood friend Midori explored the landscape by plane, searching for anything new that Kana could sell. These days, Midori, along with her flying buddy, Tamiko, had been searching for a set of ancient Shinto shrines that, supposedly, were filled with all sorts of treasures. If Midori were to ever find them, she would be tempted to take a few and try to get Kana to sell them at a very high price. A part of Midori told her that this would be theft and that she should just look—not touch or take. Another part of her, however, said that it would be fair, since she would have earned—even deserved—the treasures after all of the time and effort involved in finding them. *Besides, what's the harm in snatching a few gems*, Midori thought. At the end of the day, Midori would land her seaplane on a lake close to Kana's store and, as usual, come back with some beautiful flowers from the countryside as well as a couple of plants, such as phlox, balloon flowers, and hostas, for Kana to sell.

Just before Kana got out of the car to start another day at work, Thomas gave her a quick good-bye kiss and continued on his way. Thomas arrived at his office at the edge of Tokyo just on time and began his day like most of his co-workers normally did—by having a cup of coffee. He was a research scientist and process engineer at the new Tokyo branch of the Nanotechnology Research Institute (NRI). The lab there was like something one would see in a movie—there were computers, cables, electron guns, chemicals, and test tubes everywhere. There were also all kinds of other fancy devices like electron microscopes, spectrometers, calorimeters, and even little robots zipping around performing various tasks. He collaborated with four other scientists on his team. Two were Japanese, and the others came from different countries. There, he designed and developed various materials using extremely small particles. Thomas continued to work long hours some days—from 9:00 a.m. to 7:00 p.m. and sometimes later. He was the kind of person that always had to finish what he was working on before being able to really concentrate on anything else.

Whether at home or at the office, Thomas loved to analyze things. Whenever there was a question that was the slightest bit complicated, Thomas would break it down into several components, rate each of the components on a scale of one to ten, and, finally, calculate the answer. For example, the other day Thomas was having a hard time deciding which vanilla ice cream to buy. So he bought one of each brand and wrote down four components for his analysis: taste, consistency, calories, and price. Afterward, he gave a rating—on a scale of one to ten—for each component for each ice cream and performed the final calculations to determine which ice cream was the best pick. As it turned out, Haagen Dazs was the winner; Thomas immediately bought ten tubs of it!

Most recently, he was working on improving the strength of bulletproof vests. He was already able to create thin layers of an extremely durable material made up of carbon nanotubes—tiny particles that are hundreds of times stronger than steel. The only problem now was that it took him a great deal of time to produce just a small amount of it.

He also worked on recreating existing objects and inventing new ones. With his undergraduate degree in nanotechnology, Thomas had hopes of pursuing a master's degree and then a PhD with the possibility of NRI funding his tuition. His career goal was to work his way up to Senior Research Engineer. His dream was to discover a breakthrough in finding a way to speed up the carbon nanotube manufacturing process; if he managed to do so, he would become world renowned ... and maybe even win a Nobel Prize! Those were just dreams.

After finishing his coffee, he made his way toward the lab to continue his testing of several different bulletproof vests. As of now, he was able to increase their strength by 20 percent—nothing incredible. His goal was to reach 50 percent before the end of summer. Once in the lab and having said good morning to his fellow scientists in three different languages, he turned on his computers and did some computer programming. Then, he aimed a fancy-looking laser gun toward a sample bulletproof vest and pressed several buttons, which caused a burst of funny noises followed by a blue light shooting from the laser gun. At the end of the day, and after some calculations and analysis of the vest, Thomas discovered that he had increased the strength from 20 percent to ... only 20.5 percent. *Oh well. Maybe I'll do better tomorrow*, he thought.

As for Tamiko, she practiced karate and tae kwon do after her tutoring session with her teacher Sakura and then got together with her friends at the park to discuss their next mission.

"So, what next?" asked Hina.

"How about we go check out that house again," said Tamiko. "There's something about what happened the other day that just doesn't seem right."

"Like what?" asked Jeremy.

"I don't really remember," said Tamiko. "But there was something … something about the girl … and man and how he was acting."

"How was he acting?" asked Hina.

"Like I said, I don't remember. It was just all kind of weird, that's all."

"I have to admit the guy was a little strange," said Rin.

After more talk about the man and the girl in the spooky old house, the subject changed to romance.

"FYI … Jeremy kissed me! And we're going out," said Hina proudly when Jeremy left momentarily.

"Kissed you where?" asked Tamiko.

"Where do you think?"

"It was just a little love peck," said Rin.

"Was not," said Hina. "Jeremy's my boyfriend now. We're kareshi-kanojo!"

"Yeah, right!" said Tamiko. "I have a feeling he's more in love with your fancy clothes than he is with you."

"Look who's getting jealous again!"

The three changed the subject when Jeremy returned, and they all talked about vampires, werewolves, Tanabata— the upcoming star festival—and what they would do if they had magic powers. Jeremy talked about his hopes in making the basketball team—and possibly the football team—next year. Then, Jeremy showed off his habanero peppers that he, which, according to him, were the hottest peppers on the planet.

"Just one little bite out of one of these things will set your mouth on fire!" he said. "Want to try one?"

Jeremy loved to show off, and it would appear that he wasn't afraid of anything; a closer look would tell otherwise, for Jeremy was a baby when it came to thunderstorms …

and toy balloons! On Jeremy's twelfth birthday, his little brother Ryan and sister Julia blew up party balloons right in front of him. Jeremy freaked out as the balloons grew bigger and bigger, to the point that they were just about to pop. Jeremy covered his ears and tried to run away, but Ryan and Julia kept following him all around the house with their giant balloons, hitting them against Jeremy's face. "Get those things away from me! They're going to pop! They're going to pop!" yelled Jeremy with his hands still cupping his ears. When at least two of the balloons finally burst, Jeremy nearly jumped to the ceiling!

After some fun with the hot peppers, Tamiko brought up the topic of parents.

"Do *your* parents ever send you to your room just because you're late for supper?"

"That's happened to me a few times," said Hina.

"Maybe because you were too busy fixing your clothes and styling your hair?" said Rin.

"But you have to look your best when you're sitting at the table with family!" said Hina.

"Happened to me before," said Jeremy. "And they didn't even feed me, either!"

Then, Rin shared her experience of being at the dinner table on time.

"My parents expect me to *always* come at exactly 6:00, when the sushi's on the table!" said Rin. "Or else …"

"Or else what?" said Hina.

"Or else they make me study."

"Oh, so *that's* why you get such good grades. You're always late for supper!" said Jeremy.

"Well … sometimes!"

Chapter 7
Mondays with Midori

Fuji-san—that's what the Japanese call it. The English call it Mount Fuji. The highest mountain in Japan, with its beautifully symmetrical white peak, looks like the back of a bald eagle with its wings spread out across the landscape. The mountain overlooks five lakes and three small cities— including Tamiko's hometown of Fujinomiya—and can be seen from as far away as Tokyo on a clear day. As for now, the sun announced the arrival of a new morning as it slowly beamed its golden rays on Mount Fuji and everything around it.

"It's Getsuyobi! Getsuyobi desu!" hollered Tamiko after she awoke from the buzzing of her alarm clock and saw the date.

Indeed, it was Monday; the weekend had gone by all too fast. This was one of the best days of the week for Tamiko, however, as it was when she and her older friend, Midori, went on airplane expeditions together above Mount Fuji and over its surrounding countryside.

Tamiko excitedly got out of bed and gathered her camera, binoculars, snacks, and backpack. Before going out on her next airborne expedition with Midori, though, she would have to take Butterscotch out on his morning walk.

Tamiko grabbed the dog, attached his leash, took some doggy treats and poop bags, and quietly made her way out the door.

Although it was a peaceful and pleasant morning, Tamiko felt that it had a certain matter-of-factness about it, sort of like that "back to reality" feeling kids get on the first day of school. Maybe it was the fresh, cool, humid air or the scent of lilacs and cherry blossoms. Whatever it was, it felt good. It felt secure.

Butterscotch sniffed all over the place, with his nose to the ground like an aardvark. In the distance, other dogs barked as Tamiko and Butterscotch walked by; Butterscotch barked back in reply.

As Tamiko lived in an English enclave, most of her neighbors were … well … English; the others were either Japanese or Chinese. It was a quiet, safe neighborhood, consisting mostly of smaller dwellings with a park and elementary school on its outskirts. Tamiko's street was dotted with cherry trees, maples and a few white pines; Tamiko's house had the tallest and most beautiful cherry trees on the block. It was the only one on the street with two bow windows, turquoise gables and a front door with a round top. At the end of the street and past some bushes, there was a narrow little stream where people would go fishing or just hang out. To the left of her house lived Mr. Miller and his wife, Paula, along with their two teenage sons. Mr. Miller was a tall, slender man with a somewhat snobby attitude. He spent much of his time washing his bright red sports car. If there were ever a prize for the cleanest car on the block, he'd certainly win it. To the right of Tamiko's house, there was Mr. Howard and his family of four, including a young boy and girl in their preschool years. Unlike Mr. Miller, he was plump and friendly. Apparently, his passion was his lawn and landscaping, as he always seemed to be either mowing and treating his grass to make it greener or removing weeds and planting flowers. Musoyama, an experienced Japanese sumo wrestler, resided directly across the street. He lived with his mother and was a very kind fellow. Tamiko thought of him as the "five-by-five," as he was about five feet tall and five feet wide. Like most sumo wrestlers, he wore a kimono—a colorful Japanese robe—and kept his hair in a topknot.

After walking by the older houses, the two made their way down to the new development—a dog's breakfast of smaller dwellings. This younger neighborhood was filled with small clusters of children waiting for school buses and the smells of scrambled eggs, meat, and fresh paint.

On the other side of the fences were more barking dogs—some trying to dig out the dirt to get to the other side, and some busy digging for buried bones. At least one had its snout sticking out underneath the fence, and another was nibbling on a big, white bone.

Further on, other dog snouts were busy hovering over the land in search of any form of food they could find. Many of these dogs were puppies, and, even though many were woofing at Butterscotch, they seemed to be just playfully welcoming him to their neighborhood once again. Butterscotch barked back again and made good use of his gifted little nose as he sniffed all over the deep, dewy grass and lifted his head to take in the fragrant air.

Finally, Tamiko turned around and headed back home. Now, it was time to go flying with Midori! So after a quick breakfast and a little cuddle session with Butterscotch, she and her parents hopped into the car and drove over to the placid lake where Midori's seaplane waited poised and ready to take off on yet another adventure over and around Mount

Fuji. On the dock next to the plane stood Midori, waiting excitedly for Tamiko's arrival. As the car approached the dock, Midori and Tamiko smiled simultaneously. Then, Tamiko said a quick sayonara to her parents, jumped out of the car, and ran over to Midori.

"Ohayo!" cried Midori.

"Ohayo gozaimasu!" replied Tamiko, hopping as she ran.

It was a tranquil morning by Lake Yamanaka. There was hardly even a ripple on the silvery water, and Mount Fuji shined gloriously in the light of the sun, dominating the landscape. It was as though the earth had momentarily stood still and all of life's troubles were frozen in time. Midori had Tamiko board the plane first, and then Midori untied the mooring ropes and stepped aboard. Then, Midori went over this week's expedition with Tamiko—they were going to encircle Mount Fuji as they usually did, explore the peak, and then stop at Lake Sai and have lunch. After, they would examine the foothills on the south side of the mountain in search of the shrines.

Midori revved the engine, and soon they were buzzing and skimming across the water like a dragonfly. Suddenly, they were in flight and headed toward beautiful and awesome Mount Fuji.

What a spectacular view it was! The scenery was something one would see in a storybook or movie. The foothills and valleys surrounding the mountain were a quilt of green patches, each with its unique shade and character. A few villagers could still be seen below and now looked like tiny ants scrambling around for food. The peak of Mount Fuji was a splendid white cone of shiny snow. Around the mountaintop was a thin ring of clouds that was almost as perfectly symmetrical as the peak itself.

They slowly encircled the mountain and then, as

planned, flew close to the peak and caught a magnificent view of the greatest part of the massive mountain. The actual tip was flattened and consisted of a crater resembling a volcano of snow and ice. The beauty of it all was indescribable.

After many pictures taken with Tamiko's camera, it was time to swing around and head over to Lake Sai—one of the Fuji Five Lakes. Lake Yamanaka, where they began their expedition, was actually the largest of these five lakes and east of the mountain. Lake Sai, however, was located toward the north and was the smallest of the five. They landed on the lake with a gentle splash, skimmed over to the usual dock, and made their way to their favorite tree to have lunch.

"What a gorgeous day!" exclaimed Midori.

"You can say that again!" said Tamiko.

"We'll have to bring your friends along sometime," said Midori. "But I don't think my plane's quite big enough to fit us all in."

"We could bring one friend at a time," said Tamiko. "One week me and Hina, and another week me and Rin, and then—"

"Or we could just squeeze the three of them into the two back seats," said Midori.

"They'd love that!" said Tamiko.

Then, Midori asked Tamiko to tell her a bit more about her angel friends, starting with Rin.

"Rin, she's the smartest of my team ... a straight-A student. Rin seems to know everything. You never hear her say 'I don't know' or 'What's that all about?' She's a computer whiz ... or geek ... I'm not sure which. She lives pretty close to my house."

"Then, we have ... Hina?" said Midori.

"Hina, yes, Hina," said Tamiko. "She's the fashion diva.

She's only a ten-minute bike ride from where I live. She's *always* wearing the best clothes and putting on the best makeup. I have to say that she *is* very beautiful and very—"

"Yeah," said Midori. "You showed me some pictures of her last week. They looked like they came out of a magazine or something."

"You could say so," said Tamiko. "But she's not so smart. I mean, it's not like she's stupid or anything. It's just that …"

"That she's not so smart," said Midori, laughing. "I know what you mean, though: she's just not the brightest star in the sky."

"Yeah, but she's always in a good mood and lots of fun, and she's …"

"And she's what?" asked Midori.

Tamiko, disheartened, confided in Midori that Jeremy was now going out with Hina. It was kind of obvious to Midori that Tamiko was a bit jealous. Tamiko asked Midori what to do about it.

"Tell him how you really feel," said Midori. "Just tell him all about it, and just … be yourself."

"But I'm too shy," said Tamiko.

"Oh, come on!" said Midori. "A big girl like you … shy? You can do it. I know you can! Stop thinking about it and just say it … from the heart. Stop worrying about 'What if he says this?' or 'What if he says that?'"

Midori asked more about Jeremy—his looks and likes.

"Is he good-looking?" asked Midori.

"Well … yeah," said Tamiko, "and he's very sweet. He plays football and basketball, and he likes green tea KitKats and squid ink pizza. He lives close to Hina's. He's funny and …"

"And what else?"

"Jeremy likes hot chili peppers," said Tamiko. "He has these habanero peppers and says they're the hottest in the world. I tried a little bit of one once, and it was like my mouth was on fire! The piece was only like *this* big, but afterward my mouth was burning so bad. I drank some water thinking that it would take away the pain, but it made it even *worse*! I was, like, going around in circles, and there was Jeremy just standing there laughing at me. Shame on him!"

"I know what you mean!" said Midori. "I've tried habanero peppers before too; they're even hotter than wasabi! The big mistake I made, though, was rubbing my eyes after touching them. My eyes were burning and I could hardly see!"

After a good laugh followed by a short silence, Midori talked about her latest passion—bungee jumping—and then asked Tamiko what she wanted to do when she grew up.

"I want to be … an angel that helps people in various ways," said Tamiko, "with wings so I could fly real high like your plane, Skyduck."

"It sounds like you want to be a doctor," said Midori.

The two talked some more, discussing life after death and how sad it was to think that people are born, they live, and then they die, like flowers that blossom into something beautiful only to soon wither away and die.

"It's what's in between birth and death that's important," said Midori. "So concentrate on the present; enjoy the moment while it lasts. Just be kind and have fun … and don't litter!"

Then, Tamiko told Midori about the old house, the strange man, and the girl who lost her dog.

"Poor little girl!" said Midori. "Tell me more about her."

"Well, we didn't see very much of her. But from what we did see, she's like five or six, and she's white and has black hair," said Tamiko. "She looked pretty sad, but …"

"But what?"

"I don't know," said Tamiko. "There was something very mysterious—almost creepy—about the way she looked. I just can't put my finger on it. And the man was kind of strange."

"Strange in what way?" asked Midori.

"He was … acting weird somehow. I just don't know how exactly. We're going to have to go back and investigate some more."

"Sounds like you might be a detective someday," said Midori.

The pair of explorers finished up their meal and flew again. They eagerly continued their search for the shrines over the trees of the north face. As Midori piloted the aircraft, Tamiko looked carefully below using her binoculars and took some more pictures. She searched and searched, as did Midori, but didn't find anything. All they saw were trees and bushes.

"We'll find them someday," said Midori. "Just you wait and see! Maybe next week."

Then, Midori changed course a little and headed to a region that they rarely flew over, but still there were no signs of any shrines. Before long they gave up and settled for simply enjoying the view on the way back. The craft landed on Lake Yamanaka with another splash, and before they knew it, they were back on land again.

Like their previous adventures, the joy of the search went by too fast. Happily, though, there was a new adventure awaiting them—only just a week away.

As for the elusive shrines, Tamiko thought, *Maybe they don't even exist. Maybe it's all just some kind of myth or something. Or maybe—like Midori said earlier—we'll soon get lucky. I guess time will tell.*

Then, Tamiko clenched her fists and looked the other way, as she remembered how tomorrow was going to begin. That would be a rather different kind of "adventure."

CHAPTER 8~
FROM KARATE TO PRANKS

"Block! Kick! Punch!"

These words were repeated over and over again in Japanese by martial arts instructor Kenta during today's karate class. Tamiko couldn't help but think, *Block! Kick! Punch Allan!* after all the teasing and pestering she received from Allan, the class bully, all over the fact that she was a girl, and karate just "isn't for girls." Tamiko found it hard to control her temper and was determined to someday show Allan a thing or two and rub that pompous little smile off his face.

After karate class Tamiko made her way home, where her neighbor Mr. Miller was spraying and scrubbing his car as usual. Watching Mr. Miller at work, Tamiko couldn't help but wonder if this would be the day the paint would start coming off. "It's still not clean!" said Tamiko just before entering her home. "You'll have to scrub harder."

It was now time for another tutoring session with Sakura. This time they reviewed one of Tamiko's favorite subjects—zoology. Tamiko had always loved and been fascinated by all sorts of animals, and she enjoyed going to Tama Zoo and Tokyo Sea Life Park every once in a while. She was very interested in marine life, yet her favorite animal was still the elephant.

Later, shortly after the tutoring session ended, Tamiko spent some time with her parents, who had come home from work early. The three played several games of koi-koi, a popular Japanese card game. Times like these were rather special, as Tamiko spent most of her spare hours either alone or with her friends. Nonetheless, her parents had made an improvement in being more involved in her life.

"So, how did your karate go today?" asked Thomas.

"Like usual," said Tamiko. "Allan and his mates made fun of me again, saying that I've mastered the love tap and that karate isn't for girls."

"Don't let them bring you down," said Kana. "Ignore them and they'll stop eventually."

"Easier said than done," said Tamiko.

Tamiko put the cards aside and began to set up her Japanese Monopoly game while she and her parents talked some more.

"Do I *really* need a home tutor?" asked Tamiko. "Why can't I just go to school like everyone else?"

Thomas leaned forward a little. "We've been through this before, Tamiko. Your mother and I don't think public school is a good influence—especially high school. And besides, you'll get better grades with home tutoring. Better grades mean—"

"Better jobs," said Tamiko.

"You got it!" said Kana.

"I understand that you're just trying to be good parents and all, but it would be so nice to go to school with my—"

"I know how you feel," said Thomas. "I was home tutored all the way through high school. Looking on the bright side of things, I didn't have to wait in lines, I was never bullied, the teacher never yelled at me, and I was never late for class!"

The three played for at least an hour before Tamiko eventually won the game.

"Losers pick up!" said Tamiko, laughing.

"Aaaah," cried Kana. "Not *again*!"

Tamiko helped her parents put everything away, had a quick supper, and skipped out the door to meet with her friends and discuss their next mission. Not surprisingly, Mr. Miller was still washing his car, but now he was joyfully singing some love song while he scoured his vehicle along with his sons. "You told me to scrub harder," he said at the sight of Tamiko. "In about another two hours, she'll be shining like the sun."

Tamiko hopped on her bike, which was parked at the side of the house, and cycled to the corner store, where all three of her angel friends were waiting. As usual, Jeremy had something to show off. This time it was a pair of sauce-dispensing chopsticks. All you had to do was fill them with soya sauce and then give them a little squeeze over your food. Jeremy had all kinds of chopsticks, including Star Wars lightsaber chopsticks, magnetic chopsticks, and even a two-in-one utensil combining regular chopsticks with a soup spoon.

On the outside, Jeremy appeared to be big and strong. But on the inside, he really wasn't so tough—he had a soft spot. One day he went to the cinema with some friends to watch a sad movie and was warned that he might shed a few tears. "Me … cry?" said Jeremy. "Guys don't cry!" Throughout most of the movie, Jeremy didn't shed a tear, though he had to try harder and harder the longer he watched to prevent himself from doing so. By the end of the film, Jeremy wasn't able to resist any longer; he finally let himself go and burst into tears as he used his hands to cover his face. "Maybe some guys *do* cry after all!" said one of his friends.

After a short while, Tamiko sensed that there was something a little different going on with her friends, especially Jeremy and Rin. It was almost like they were boyfriend and girlfriend now. Jeremy was all like, "Oh, you're such a *sweet* person, Rin!" as he grinned at her while she talked, and gently put his hands on her as if she were some tall, golden trophy. But Jeremy was going out with Hina!" Or at least that's what Tamiko had been led to believe. Maybe Jeremy didn't like the new blonde *and* pink streaks in Hina's hair, or maybe it was simply because she was wearing too much makeup. As for Hina's brothers, they didn't like her hair *or* her makeup and used to often tease her about it. "Plaster face!" they'd call her, and then Hina would show her usually hidden feisty side and retaliate—sometimes rather forcefully. Once she got into a fight with her older brother, Manzo, after he made fun of her hair and sprayed it with men's cologne. Hina got so angry, she grabbed Manzo by the hair and literally yanked it out. Her brother screamed with pain … and he didn't tease her again for quite some time.

"Is it my imagination, or are Jeremy and Rin more than just good friends?" said Tamiko.

"It's not your imagination," said Hina. "They're for real."

"But I thought … the last I saw you, Jeremy was—"

"*Was*," said Hina. "And now he prefers straight-A students … like Rin over there."

"It's not the marks," said Rin. "It's about love. It's about—"

"Oh, blah blah blah!" said Hina. "It's all about Jeremy's mom asking you to help him with his studies so he can get better grades."

And so it went. Jeremy was really with Rin now. But it didn't appear to be anything real serious. It wouldn't be long before Jeremy would go back to Hina … or maybe someone else.

The foursome biked around the nearby neighborhoods, and then Tamiko began having flashbacks of the spooky old house as they passed by it.

"What's wrong, Tamiko?" asked Hina.

"I'm just thinking about that old house again … where they took the dog away," Tamiko replied.

"Oh, that again?" said Jeremy.

"Yeah. I keep getting these flashes," said Tamiko. "Like I said before, there was something about that man that just wasn't right. It's coming back to me. I can feel it."

"Just let yourself go," said Rin. "Let's have some fun, and maybe afterward it'll come back to you."

It wasn't too often that Rin said this kind of thing, for a studybug like her didn't "let herself go" too often. Sometimes, though—especially when she had enough studying for one day—Rin would go into some sort of wacky "lose all control" mode. One day, after she got a series of test results back—all A-pluses with only one B—Rin started browsing the "B" test to learn of her few errors when, just like that, she threw her test papers into the air and yelled, "Let's party!" So Rin called her friends and had a big party in her basement.

"Maybe you're right," said Tamiko. "I'll just let myself go … like you said."

Then, Jeremy asked what they should do next, and Hina suggested a prank.

"How about the one where we switch the signs on the men's and women's washrooms?" said Tamiko.

And so it was decided. It was also decided, by Rin, that

the target area was going to be the Aeon shopping mall. This was a good choice because it wasn't too far away and people went in and out of the washrooms quite regularly. Hina drew the Japanese signs for "men" and "women" on white cardboard squares, and they got some of the gummy stuff that's used for sticking posters onto walls. Jeremy brought along his little digital camera to do a video of the victims' reactions. When they arrived at the mall on their bikes, they made a beeline to the public washrooms and began to put their plan into action.

With the coast clear, Tamiko walked briskly over to the each of the doors and stuck on the signs. Then she got back quickly to her fellow pranksters and the four pretended to read a magazine while keeping an eye on the area around the washroom doors as people approached.

A girl exited, then a man, then another man, and then a woman. Finally, a boy came along and entered the woman's washroom. "Unko time!" said Jeremy. The four giggled at the scene, covering their faces to muffle the noise. Within seconds, an abrupt scream was heard and the boy burst out of the washroom confused and looked at the sign … and then at the other sign.

The next victim was a woman with a young girl; they made their way into the men's washroom. Suddenly, there was a loud quarrel that could be heard from outside, and the kids put their heads in their arms as they let out more laughter. The woman and the girl bolted outside the washroom and into the other as they glanced at the two signs and gave a strange look.

Finally, it was about time to pack things up and move on; they'd had their laugh and caught it all on video. Just as they were about to take down the reversed signs, a security guard showed up and asked them what was going on. The pranksters didn't really know what to say. Finally, Tamiko answered.

"Did you see it?" she asked, facing the security guard. "Wasn't it funny? Look ... someone switched the signs!" She pulled off the signs, revealing the true ones, and then crumpled up the fake ones.

The guard gave a rather serious look as his eyes scanned the foursome, and then he spoke.

"Did you do this?" he asked, peering at Tamiko.

The four mumbled some words, not knowing exactly what to say.

"Well," began Hina, "we ... we ..."

"I saw you. From the very beginning," stated the guard with a cold expression.

"You did?" responded Tamiko.

Suddenly, the security guard broke up laughing.

"That was good ... that was ... you really made my day," he replied as he continued to laugh.

With that, the four kids joined in, chuckling along. Just then, Tamiko spotted a boy playing with an elastic band. All at once, Tamiko's bizarre observation at the old house came back to her!

Chapter 9 ~
Mystery Girl

Tamiko remembered! The man of the spooky old house—the same one the kids had seen the night the dog was removed—had, on at least one occasion, played around with some large rubber band in a rather unusual way; Tamiko had seen it all in some mirror. While the man was in the kitchen, he took the band and shot it at close range at a set of tiny glass cups or mugs, one at time, until all of them were knocked over. Then, he did the same thing to what appeared to be little toy people. Tamiko recalled the look on his face as he was shooting down his targets. The man had his tongue stuck out, wiggling it around his mouth like a vicious snake; it was almost as though he wanted to kill someone. He looked like some crazy, mean villain from a comic book.

Then, Tamiko suddenly remembered more about the girl. She hadn't seen very much of her. Nonetheless, from what Tamiko had seen, the girl didn't just look sad but also pretty scared. To Tamiko, it was normal for the girl to be frightened for the dog, but the girl's facial expression indicated that there was something more. *What was it?* Tamiko asked herself. She racked her brain for what seemed like an hour trying to figure out what it could be but failed to come up with anything. So Tamiko told her friends about the man's strange activities with the rubber band and then brought up the girl's mysterious facial expression in hopes that they would produce some explanation. Intrigued, they asked all sorts of questions, but, like Tamiko, they were unable to explain the look on the little girl's face. Tamiko suggested that they go back to the house to get some answers.

"That place gives me the creeps!" said Jeremy.

"Ditto that!" said Hina.

"When do we go?" asked Rin.

"How about right now?" replied Tamiko. "It's getting dark."

So the young group of four packed up their things, hopped on their bicycles with their walkie-talkies, and cycled toward the old house. It was getting late. The air was becoming cooler, and the sky was turning to the color of dark green tea. In the distance, Mount Fuji now appeared to be a large lump of coal. Strangely enough, the closer they got to the house, the quieter things got until nothing could be heard but the clicking sound of their bicycles while coasting. As the Japanese would say, it was very *shizuka*.

Eventually, the kids arrived and hid their bikes behind the hedge. The car was in the driveway but the house appeared to be completely devoid of life; no lights were visible and everything was silent. The branches of the maple trees in front were somehow more pronounced than the last time. They thrust upwards like giant claws ready to grasp the next bird that flew above. The grass looked like a small meadow and the hedge like a long shaggy brown dog. The curtains seemed to be all closed.

The kids crept up to the side window and peered through a medium-sized gap between the curtains. All they saw was a dim light shining through the opened door that led to the basement. The four waited impatiently for something interesting to happen ... but nothing did.

After several long minutes of inactivity, the angel gang decided to leave the premises and return the next day. Just as they were walking away, they heard a noise. It sounded like something beeping. The four froze simultaneously and then hurried back to the window. With loud footsteps, a man barged through the basement door and headed toward the kitchen; he was the same man they had seen the night the dog was taken away. The four quickly stepped to the side to avoid being seen.

After a short while, Tamiko and her friends slowly moved back to the window again and looked inside. The man was in the kitchen with the light on, his back turned to the side window; he appeared to be busy preparing something. The kids looked down the dark, narrow hallway, and, suddenly, the girl's head poked partly outside the doorway. They couldn't make out her face very clearly, but from what they could see, the girl looked sad and scared and sleepy all at the same time—much like before. She was quite slender and had messy black hair and large, round, black eyes. Something about her was very peculiar, very mysterious; it was like she popped out from nowhere like a groundhog from its burrow.

The man marched toward the girl's bedroom, and the girl quickly shut her door. He entered her room and closed the door behind him. After about a minute of silence, Jeremy decided to go to the other side of the house, next to the girl's bedroom, in an attempt to hear what was going on inside. With his ears wide open, Jeremy listened to an argument between the two occupants. Then, through the curtains, he saw what appeared to be a silhouette of the man jumping up and down. He heard noises and could see that the girl was crying her eyes out. The man yelled. Finally, using his walkie-talkie, Jeremy told his friends about the quarrel.

"I'm not sure exactly what the guy was saying, but he sounded pretty angry," started Jeremy. "It was like he was going to … I don't know."

"Why don't we just go?" said Hina. "It's just some dad getting upset at his daughter."

"Yeah," said Rin. "And what if we get caught spying like this?"

"Oh, look!" said Tamiko.

Jeremy joined his friends just as the man bolted out of the bedroom and went straight to the basement, fast as a Japanese sika. Within seconds, he returned with what appeared to be some medication and a syringe similar to the one the kids had seen during their previous visit to the house. He was also carrying some strange-looking rectangular machine with buttons on it.

"She must be sick," whispered Tamiko.

"Yeah, kinda looks like it," said Jeremy.

The man raced into the girl's bedroom, and the kids heard a scream followed by several dull thuds.

"Maybe she's diabetic," said Hina.

"Or maybe she's in some kind of pain," said Rin. "She kind of reminds me of a girl I once saw at a hospital in Fuji City."

Suddenly, all went silent, and then, after just a few seconds, the man paced into the kitchen. Just as the kids were about to move out of the way, the man caught sight of them! Like an angry bulldog, he grinded his teeth and stomped toward the window.

"Get behind the hedge!" said Tamiko.

All four angels scurried over to a nearby hedge and ducked behind it while the man tore open the curtains and quickly turned his head from side to side searching for the peepers.

Unable to find anything, the man gave up and shut the curtains most of the way. After a long pause, the curious foursome slowly got up, crept over to the window once again and noticed that the curtains were shut slightly more than before.

"That was close," said Jeremy.

The kids cautiously looked through the gap in the curtains again and saw the man bring a tray of something to the girl.

Afterward, they heard something fall to the floor, and then the man yelled. The lights flickered, and there were some strange noises like the humming of a young Buddha. The angels were all confused, for, once again, the man quickly departed the bedroom to retrieve something for the girl, and, once again, the girl watchfully peered around her bedroom doorway, showing no more than half of her face.

"Who *is* this girl?" asked Hina.

"Probably just another sick kid," said Jeremy. "But she's kind of freaky, though."

"It sort of makes you wonder," said Tamiko.

"Yeah," agreed Rin.

Finally, the man went down to the basement. Just before his descent, he pulled out his big rubber band and shot down several glasses and miniature rice bowls. After a short while, when all was clear, the girl slowly stepped outside of her bedroom door and talked into a Fisher-Price toy telephone. At first the kids thought nothing of it, but a closer look told them to think otherwise. For some time, the girl spoke into the phone as if she were really talking to someone; she was so emotional, it was almost creepy.

"Who is she … talking to?" said Rin.

"Beats me," said Tamiko. "Perhaps one day we'll find out."

The girl suddenly hung up the phone and disappeared.

"We'll be back!" said Tamiko.

Chapter 10~
Karate and Allan

At home the following day, Tamiko was finishing up her morning session with her tutor; she found it somewhat difficult to concentrate, however, as her mind was still focused on the mysterious little girl in the spooky old house.

"Tamiko!" cried Sakura. "Are you listening? You seem a little preoccupied about something."

"Oh … excuse me!" said Tamiko. "I was just thinking about yesterday."

"What about yesterday? What happened?"

"Let's just say it was a very long day, and a rather interesting one, too."

The studies continued. They were on the topic of geology, the study of rocks. This wasn't one of Tamiko's favorite subjects; her favorites were zoology, medicine, and the martial arts, especially karate and tae kwon do.

The next karate class was this afternoon. Kenta taught his martial arts in the village past the poorer quarters and several minutes north of the spooky old house. Although his school was known more for its karate instruction, Kenta continued teaching tae kwon do and began showing a bit of kung fu. Tamiko, currently a green belt, took lessons there three times a week now and the class had grown to about fifteen students. Grandmaster Shun continued to pay a visit and speak of the spiritual side of the art every once in a while—saying things like, "True strength is the flower of Wisdom, but its seed is action."—and also show some cool new moves.

After Tamiko completed her geology quiz, Sakura left and Tamiko had lunch: salad, sushi, shrimp, and pickles. It was about time to prepare her things and be on her way to karate class. Before leaving, Tamiko cuddled a bit with Butterscotch and then let him outside, in the fenced backyard, and gave him some more water. "Bye, Butterscotch, my little woof! See you later!" she said as she stroked his furry brown chin. Butterscotch let out a little whimper knowing that she was about to depart and leave him all alone.

Tamiko got on her bike and started peddling. As she passed the first house, Tamiko caught sight of Mr. Howard, who was in the process of doing something rather unusual. Tamiko stopped and watched; Mr. Howard's wife and two young children were also watching. Mr. Howard had just finished tying a thick white rope to the back of his car and was now tying the other end to one of his ugly hedges. He excitedly jumped into his vehicle and hit the accelerator, tugging on the hedge. On the second tug, the hedge popped right out of the ground. Captivated, Tamiko watched Mr. Howard's attempt to pull out the next hedge. This time, however, he wasn't so lucky; he pulled and pulled, but the bush wouldn't come out. Frustrated, Mr. Howard backed up his vehicle and thrust it forward like a dragster to the other side of the street, but instead of pulling anything out, the rope snapped at the hedge and slung toward the back of the car like a giant slingshot. It sounded as though a gun went off. The impact was so great, it put an enormous dent in the trunk of the car. Fortunately, nobody was close enough to get hurt. "Shucks!" cried Mr. Howard as he gazed at the damage.

Tamiko put her feet on the pedals again and cycled away. It was another beautiful day in Fujinomiya, though a little less sunny than the day before. The birds were singing, the flies were buzzing, and the air smelled of blooming flowers and swampy water. Before long, Tamiko passed through the downtown area and arrived at the village where she took her martial arts lessons. The village had a few boutiques and restaurants, a grocery store, a shopping mall, the karate school and various other small buildings such as gas stations and convenience stores.

Further ahead, Tamiko came across the poorer quarters, where homeless people, mainly English and Japanese, roamed the streets. Along her way, she saw the English bag lady—a homeless woman in her early fifties—sluggishly pushing along her shabby little shopping cart full of clothes and blankets and other possessions. She had brushy, black, messy hair that carried a hint of gray, and she was rather short—about four and a half feet tall. She didn't say very much—just a few words in Japanese when asking for money or food from anyone around her. Tamiko had already given her a few hundred yen, for which the poor homeless woman had been rather thankful; sadly enough, however, most people just walked by her as though she didn't even exist.

A bit further away was a spot where often stood the host of some peculiar street game. It was a game where one had the chance of winning money by "simply" karate chopping varying stacks of wood blocks, bricks, and concrete slabs. More precisely, the game began with one thin wooden block that was rather easy for anyone to break, but then it grew more and more difficult, the payout being in proportion with the difficulty level. If one managed to succeed in breaking the stack of concrete slabs in the final level, the contestant would win all the money—thousands and thousands of yen. No one to this day had ever won the jackpot.

Moments later, Tamiko showed up at her destination, where Allan McCoy stood just outside of the front door. He was part Irish and part American with dark brown hair and a medium build. He was also the oldest and tallest of all the students. Allan was a rather good fighter, almost gifted, though he had to show that he was "bigger and better" than everyone else. Sadly enough, he used his skills to bully people—especially those who were weaker and less confident. He was actually the most feared student of the entire school; even the teacher and his assistant were somewhat afraid of him. At times, Tamiko sensed that the reason for Allan's bullying was more than just self-pride. She couldn't quite figure it out; it was like he had a score to settle … with someone who had stolen something very precious from him and refused to give it back.

Just as Tamiko had anticipated, Allan began picking on yet another student just before class began.

"Hi there, Shad!" Allan cried at the other student.

Today's first victim, Roka, just kept on walking, giving Allan a sort of "I'm worried about what you're going to do next" look. Allan liked to call him Shad for "Shadow," as he would often follow or copy other students, trying to fit in with everyone else.

"Hey, I'm talking to you, Shad!" yelled Allan.

Roka stopped and turned around, thinking of something to say.

"Good afternoon!" he replied.

"Oh, how polite!" Allan retorted, laughing. "Good afternoon to you too!" he added as he jokingly bowed.

"So, show me the knee strike!" said Allan with a wide grin. "Hiza-geri—that's knee strike! Let's see what you can do, Shad!"

With that, Roka performed a mediocre knee strike, making sure he didn't hit Allan. Seeing this, Allan laughed and showed Roka a better knee strike, only that his version hit Roka hard.

"Oooooow!" yelped Roka as he fell to the ground.

"Okay, that's enough now, mate!" said Tamiko.

"Oooooh, Tamikooooo!" Allan replied. "What are you, his little guardian angel?"

"I'm his friend," said Tamiko, "something you know very little about."

"Well isn't that sweet!" said Allan. "Tamiko and Roka are good friends. Ooooooooh! And you're my 'mate' … good on you, mate!" said Allan with an Australian accent, laughing.

"Get lost," said Tamiko. "And let's hope you don't have a map to find your way back."

Roka, feeling better now, began to slowly walk away, for he thought that Tamiko's intervention would be enough to keep Allan away from him for a while. But then Allan marched in front of Roka, blocking his path.

"Hey, I ain't finished with you, Shad!"

"Do we have a problem here?" asked one of Allan's friends in a buffalo stance.

"In fact we do," said Allan. "Shad here can't do a knee strike."

"Then I guess we'll just have to show him how it's done!"

"I already did," said Allan. "So let's see it again, Shad … or do you want me to show *you* again?"

"Okay, leave him alone, Allan," said Tamiko as she gave him a light shove. "Go pick on someone your own size!"

But Allan wouldn't listen; instead, he got angrier. He pushed Roka into a hedge and insisted that he, once again, do the knee strike. Roka felt he had no choice, as he was surrounded by Allan and all his buddies.

"Let's do it! On three," said Allan. "Ichi! Ni! San!"

Just then the bell rang, and everyone shuffled inside. Once the students were all in the training room, the instructor, Kenta, entered and cried out, "Seiretsu!" to begin the session by having everyone line up.

"Today, we're going to practice last week's knee strike, and then we'll move on to the back kick and groin kick," he began. "Is there anyone here who'd like to show me a good side kick and knee strike that we learned last week?"

Allan quickly raised his hand. "I can show you a good side kick! Right here … Roka … he's my sidekick, and he's a good one, too!" said Allan, pointing to Roka jokingly.

Several of the other students laughed a little. "Very funny," Tamiko mumbled to herself.

"Yamero yo!" cried out instructor Kenta. "Let's get serious, Allan. One more smart remark from your mouth and I'm sending you home!"

Allan kept his mouth shut and then moved forward and did the two moves very well; he put on a snobby face as he walked back to his spot.

"Very good!" said the instructor. With that, Kenta pointed out a few things to the class, explaining what to do and what not to do in certain fighting situations. Later, he asked Tamiko to come forward for a demonstration. As Tamiko was one of the very few—and younger—girls in the class, some of the boys started whispering to one another, as they were curious to see what Tamiko was about to do.

Like usual, Kenta reviewed the correct way to do a back kick. As Tamiko was a girl, Kenta was rather gentle with her.

He then asked Tamiko to try out the kick on him, and Tamiko gave a fairly decent kick; according to the boys, however, this was a love tap. Then, the instructor had to leave momentarily. As soon as he left the room, several of the boys laughed a bit, especially Allan.

"Oh, Tamiko!" Allan began. "Why did you have to kick him so hard? You hurt him!" Hearing this, Allan's friends chuckled.

"Shut up!" replied Tamiko. "Or …"

"Or what?" said Allan. "Or you'll kick me? Oh, I'm shaking! I better watch out for Tamiko. She's dangerous. She'll knock you down with her angelic love tap!" Allan ran away from Tamiko like a loose chicken, pretending to be afraid.

Everyone burst out laughing—everyone, that is, except for Tamiko and some of her buddies. Whether they were laughing at Tamiko or laughing at Allan, Tamiko had had just about enough of Allan for one day.

With everybody laughing, Tamiko lost control of her anger. She went straight over to Allan and gave him a good kick in the stomach. Allan bent over, covering his belly. It wasn't clear whether he was really hurt or whether he was just faking. Then, Tamiko gave Allan a swift knee strike, and Allan fell to the floor. Just as Tamiko was about to make another move, the instructor returned.

"What's going on here?" he asked.

"Uh … just practicing," said Tamiko.

It's a good thing Allan didn't say anything with the word "reject" in it … or I would have done more to him! thought Tamiko.

When Tamiko returned home, she finished her homework, grabbed a few Bisuko Japanese biscuits, and then ran over to Butterscotch, who was barking because someone had opened the front door. It was Thomas and Kana; they had left work early to relax and spend some quality time with Tamiko.

"Let's pull out that photo album and see what we can remember," said Thomas.

The three flipped through the album randomly. They came across pictures of camping at Lake Tanuki, Tamiko playing tennis, Tama Zoo, Tokyo Sea Life Park, and several "goofy face" pictures. Then, Kana decided to go to the very beginning of the album, to a picture of Tamiko just after she was brought home from the orphanage. She was standing in front of a pile of chopped wood in the backyard. Her face was lit up with a radiant smile. Her eyes were squinting and gleaming with joy. She was eight at the time.

"I remember," said Tamiko. "That was right after you … rescued me from that awful orphanage."

"Look at you," said Kana. "So happy and so … sweet!"

"My Tamiko … our Tamiko," added Thomas. "Such a beautiful little doll."

Tamiko smiled at the picture and then gazed up at the ceiling, lost in deep thought.

"Why … why do you think my biological parents … didn't want me?"

"That's a good question," said Kana. "My guess is that they were too young and had very little money. They just couldn't afford the expenses involved in supporting a child and probably didn't know how to raise one in the first place."

"Do you think—one day—I'll ever see them?"

"Oh, we can't answer that," said Thomas. They're probably long gone. But who knows? Maybe you will see them one day. I just look at you and find it so hard to imagine anyone abandoning you the way they did. It breaks my heart."

Thomas became very emotional as did Kana and Tamiko. The latter two began to shed a few tears. As for Thomas, he did his best to restrain himself from crying. Being so analytical, he had trouble showing his true colors; he wasn't able to just let himself go and simply express his emotions. He preferred to keep some of them bottled up inside. As for Kana, she was able to express herself naturally. Interestingly enough, Kana was somewhat lacking in the self-confidence department whereas Thomas was the more-confident one. When it came to returning something to a store or filing complaints, Kana was—most often—too shy to do it alone. She either had to have Tamiko accompany her or have Thomas do the dirty work himself.

"I love you, Tamiko," said Kana. "We both do." Thomas nodded.

"I love you, too."

The family of three looked at a few more pictures and then had supper—sashimi, shrimp dumplings, and seaweed salad. Afterward, Tamiko studied a bit and then turned on her netbook and went on Microsoft Messenger to chat with her gang. To get them online, Tamiko phoned each of her friends, letting the phone ring just once to give the signal. The conversation went like this:

Tamiko: G'day Jeremy! Wutsss up!

Jeremy: Not tooooo much. My little brother Ryan is bugging me again.

Tamiko: Wuts he doing 2 ya?

Jeremy: He put toothpaste in my Oreo cookies again!

Rin: Oh man. That's bad. I can just imagine wut THAT taste like!

Then, Hina came online.

Hina: Hi gang. Konnichiwa!

Tamiko: Hi there Hina? How's it going?

Hina: Not too bad. I just had a visit with my dad. I don't see him very often, maybe once a week now. He's all right but my brothers are still taking the divorce pretty hard, and so is my mom.

Tamiko: Oh yeah? And how's your mom doing now? Did she get any help?

Hina: Yah. She's getting some help from AA. And she's drinking much less now, but she still has a little ways to go.

Rin: Good to hear! Let's hope she makes a full recovery.

Hina: Thanks. So, what do U make of the girl at the little old house? Sick? Lonely? Kind of creepy I'd say.

Tamiko: Obviously, there's something wrong with her and with that man, too. I guess the girl's real sick and it's driving the guy nuts.

Rin: Yeah. All those diabetes shots.

Jeremy: What scares me is not so much the girl, it's the house. It almost looks like haunted or something … gives me the creeps.

Hina: House IS kind of spooky looking. Could be a ghost or two in there.

Tamiko: But the girl. You see her eyes - those big curious eyes? It's like she can see right through you. And she hardly ever says anything. It's almost like she's ... maybe she's a deaf mute!

Hina: That's it! I KNEW there was something strange going on with that girl!

Rin: See the way the girl was talking on that toy phone of hers? She was so, like, into it.

Jeremy: It was just a phone but I must say she looked pretty serious about it. Makes U wonder.

Tamiko: And did you see the guy when he played with the rubber band?

Jeremy: Yeah. He was like really smiling and rolling his tongue all over the place. What a freak!

Rin: U can say that again!

Hina: So wut next?

Tamiko: Well, we can all see there's something kind of bizarre about all this. I'd say let's go back. We got 2 find out what this girl is all about. She's a mystery.

CHAPTER 11~
GARBAGE AND PRANKS

The next day the four friends sped over to the old house in hopes of learning more about the mystery girl. On arrival they saw a young Japanese boy marching from door to door with a bag in his hands across from the old house; it was obvious he was selling something. As for the little old house, there was no car in the driveway and no sign of life within the house. All was silent in the small neighborhood. In fact, it was so quiet that the angels felt as though something was going to explode, like the calm before a storm.

Just then, the boy crossed the street and made a beeline toward the mystery house. He knocked. He waited. Nobody answered. The boy moved on to the next house. After he was out of sight, the foursome crept up to the side window but didn't see very much, as the curtains were almost completely shut. Like the neighborhood, the place was as quiet as a mouse. The kids tried to get a glimpse through the other windows. Again, the curtains were shut; again, there was no noise.

Disappointed, the four decided to leave the premises. But just then, Rin got a bright idea.

"Look!" said Rin. "It's garbage day. Let's check out what's in their trash bags."

"Great idea, mate!" said Tamiko.

"Interesting," said Jeremy. "Garbage is usually collected earlier than this."

"They must be running a bit late today," added Hina.

So, the four raced over to the two bags of garbage sitting on the edge of the street in front of the house. Before they even touched the bags, they could see that one of them held several beer bottles and cans since the trash bags were transparent. Like raccoons or dogs in search of food, the kids ripped open the bags and started picking through the waste with the help of a little stick.

"Looks like this guy drinks a lot of beer," said Tamiko after having seen the many bottles and cans amongst the rubbish.

"Normally, these are supposed to be in the recycling bins," said Rin. "I guess he doesn't like to recycle."

"Not a whole lot of other garbage," said Jeremy. "And not very much food stuff."

"And no medicine stuff either," added Hina. "Let's see ... we also have here some paper, Kleenex boxes, a few KitKat wrappers, old socks, plastic packaging and stuff, a broken doll house—or more like a *crushed* doll house, some oil containers, and ... what's this?"

"That looks like ... a cassette tape," said Tamiko. "You know, one of those old audio tapes."

Just then, the garbage truck came rolling down the street. The four grabbed some crumpled papers, a partially ripped picture, and the cassette tape and then took off.

They pedaled their way over to the big tree where they stopped and began analyzing their garbage sample. First were the papers. On one of them, information about a car was written in blue ink, followed by a long cost calculation. The last few numbers were scribbled over, as though the writer made a mistake and got a bit upset because it couldn't be erased. The writing itself wasn't clean or elegant by any means—no high school teacher would have approved of it—but it was just clear enough for the young investigators to make out. On the other side of the paper was more information about the same car; only this time, the writing was in elaborate phrases as opposed to just facts and figures. The descriptions of the car matched the car they had seen at the man's house.

"Looks like he wants to sell his car," concluded Jeremy.

The next set of papers was only junk mail, and the last ball of crumpled paper turned out to be a letter from the bank asking for money. The four continued their investigation with the ripped photo. It was of a young Japanese macaque—a snow monkey. In the picture, the monkey was being fed part of an apple by some human hand over a wire fence. No person was seen—only the hand. In the background was plain green grass and bushes. The kids concluded that this was just some zoo picture.

"Cute monkey," said Hina.

"Midori would like to see this one," added Tamiko. "She loves monkeys."

Finally, the four looked at the cassette tape. It had green and white stripes with some Japanese writing printed on it. It was a bit beat up. The labels on both sides were blank.

"I wonder what's recorded on this," said Rin.

"There's only one way to find out," said Tamiko.

"Yeah," said Hina. "Play it back in one of those … cassette players, if anybody has one."

"I think my dad has one in the attic somewhere," said Jeremy. "I'll go check it out!"

Now that the garbage analysis was pretty much complete, the four discussed what they should do after supper. Tamiko suggested that they randomly pick something out of her agenda. So, without looking, she opened her agenda to the "remaining missions" page, moved her hand around in several circles and then just randomly put her finger on the page.

"And it's going to be ... the office chair prank," said Tamiko.

"Now?" said Jeremy.

"I guess it was meant to be," said Tamiko. "I put my finger right smack on OCP."

And so it was decided. The prank consisted of dressing up like a mannequin and then sitting motionless on the office chair that was on display at the entrance to the village Ito-ya stationery store. When someone walked by, the mannequin would come to life and jump up from the chair while growling like a grizzly bear.

After supper the four peddled over to the store. Jeremy brought along his video camera, Hina some makeup and gloves, Rin a hat, and Tamiko a hijab.

On arrival, they prepared themselves under an old tree outside the building. The next thing the girls knew, Jeremy—like always—pulled something from his pocket to show off. This time it was a big, ugly redback spider! There it was, in a small, glass bottle with holes at the top, running all over the place. Jeremy teased the girls, putting the bottle right in front of their faces.

"Doo doo daaaah!" said Jeremy as he shook the spider.

"Aaaaaaah!" cried Hina. "Get that thing outta here!"

"Eeeeeeee!" cried Rin.

"Jeremy, you ..." said Tamiko, "you ... freak!"

"It won't hurt you," said Jeremy as he began to unscrew the lid. "Here, take a closer look!"

"Jeremy, you wouldn't!" said Tamiko.

As for Hina and Rin, they ran away like they were being chased by an angry elephant! After some more spider fun, they started the prank. Rin volunteered to go first. She put on her hat and Hina's gloves, and the gang made their way over to the store.

Standing there in the entrance was a bright blue office chair waiting to be sat on. When nobody was around or walking by, Rin carefully sat down on the chair with the giant price tag around her neck. Meanwhile, the other two girls pretended to be shoppers as they watched with curiosity. Jeremy stood nearby with his camera positioned inconspicuously while he looked at pens and pencils.

After a minute or two, a young Japanese couple came pacing in, and the woman halted before the chair and checked out the price and began to look around Rin in order to get a feel for the quality of the chair. A moment later, her companion came beside her and scanned it too without any suspicion. Then Rin moved slightly, and the woman gave a funny look.

"Now, Rin!" cried Tamiko to herself and to Hina.

As if Rin had heard what Tamiko just said, she jumped up from the chair and let out a "Grrrrrrrrrr!" sound as she shook her hands.

"Aaaaaaaaaah!" hollered the woman.

"Hei!" cried the man.

"Good on ya, mate!" laughed Tamiko along with Hina.

Next, Tamiko took over, sitting down on the chair like a Buddha statue. After about a minute or so, a couple and their little boy entered the building. The father looked closely at the office chair as did his wife. Tamiko tried hard to keep herself from moving or laughing or smiling.

Then the two discussed the need for a new chair for their desk. They wanted to see more of the office chair, but there was only one problem—a mannequin was sitting on it. Tamiko was about to jump up when the man turned to his wife and suggested that they move the mannequin off the chair.

Hearing this, Tamiko decided to go along with them and pretend she was still a mannequin—she figured this would be funnier than popping up now. So the man, with some help from his strong wife, carefully picked up the "mannequin" and placed it on the small desk in front of the chair. Tamiko tried her very hardest to keep from cracking up. The rest of the gang was laughing hysterically.

Then, the man sat down comfortably on the empty office chair. "Aaaaaaah," he said, very relaxed after adjusting the backrest. "Feels pretty good!"

"I like the price, too!" said his wife. "That price is so low, it almost jumps out at you!"

With that, Tamiko jumped out at the man shaking her arms and yelling, "Sold, for two thousand yen!"

The man let out a sudden "Whaaaaaaah!" and flinched like he had just been electrocuted. His wife and son burst out laughing as did Tamiko's friends.

"You had me fooled!" cried the man, still giggling.

"That's a good one!" added his wife. "I don't think I've ever laughed so hard in my life!"

As they left the building, Tamiko gazed at a cashier taking money from a customer; suddenly, she had a flashback of the boy collecting money in the neighborhood of the old house before supper. Then, she had another flashback.

"I just remembered something!" said Tamiko.

"What's that?" asked Jeremy.

"The first time we went to the house, when the dog was removed, the dog pound people didn't get any money from the man," said Tamiko. "It was the other way around. Instead, the dog people paid the *man*!"

The others froze as they tried to refresh their memories of their first visit to the old house.

"What kind of dog removal service *pays* you to remove your dog?" asked Tamiko.

"Good … good question," said Hina.

"Sounds kind of strange to me," said Jeremy.

"I remember too," said Rin. "It doesn't really make a whole lot of sense unless …"

"Unless what?" asked Jeremy.

"Unless one of the dog removers wanted the dog so badly, he was willing to pay for it."

"That actually *does* make sense," said Tamiko. "Why else would he pay?"

Chapter 12—
The Formation of the Club

It was time. It was time that the four faithful friends came together as one, officially, and formed a *real* club. It was time that they sealed their friendship. So the following day, the foursome gathered at the big tree and began climbing it, one by one. Once they ascended as high as they could go, they each sat down on a thick, sturdy branch, and the proceedings began.

"We are gathered here today to—" said Tamiko.

"You make it sound like some kind of wedding ceremony," said Hina. "Why not just say—"

"Whatever!" said Tamiko. "Then how about, 'We are assembled here in this big oak tree to discuss …'?"

"Is this really an oak tree?" asked Jeremy.

"In fact it is!" said Rin.

"A sawtooth oak, I think," said Tamiko.

"No, it's actually a Mongolian oak," said Rin.

Indeed, Rin was correct. Most thought that her knowledge came from good grades that were forced upon her by her parents. However, Rin's parents weren't very severe; she was just naturally curious and had to know the answers to all of the world's questions. Often Rin would spend her spare time browsing through the howstuffworks website to find out ... well ... how everything worked.

"Whatever!" said Tamiko.

Once again, the proceedings began.

"Okay, here it goes," said Tamiko. "We are here in this ... tree to talk about what we're going to name our club ... and what the rules and roles will be."

Rin suggested something with "angels" in it and thought it would sound cooler to say the Japanese word for angel instead—*tenshi* or *enzeru*.

"Okay," said Tamiko. "Angels of what ... or the 'what' angels? And then we can say it in Japanese. Like you said, it does sound cooler in Japanese."

Jeremy came up with the Angels of Goodwill.

"That doesn't sound too original," said Rin.

"In Japanese, though," said Jeremy.

"I know ... but still," said Rin.

"Then what about the Angels of Fuji-san?" suggested Hina.

"I kind of like that," said Tamiko. "In Japanese, that's 'no tenshi Fuji-san.' Hmmm, that doesn't really have much of a ring to it. What about simply 4 Good Angels, but in Japanese? That's 'yon yoi tenshi.' That *still* doesn't sound so wonderful."

"How about we call ourselves the Fuji-san ... something?" said Jeremy. "What rhymes with 'san'?"

"San ... let's see," said Rin. "What about clan? The Fuji-san Clan!"

"Nice one!" said Tamiko. "Good on you, mate!"

"I like it!" said Jeremy.

"Catchy!" said Hina.

And so it was decided. They would become the Fuji-san Clan. Next, it was time to determine the roles that each club member would assume. After some discussion, the following was concluded:

Tamiko = Leader

Jeremy = Muscle Man

Hina = Actress

Rin = Computer Whiz

Therefore, Tamiko would be the "brains" behind the missions. Jeremy (and Tamiko with her martial arts skills) would use his strength to accomplish certain tasks—he even thought about wearing some kind of sports protective gear underneath his clothes to make himself look older and stronger. Hina would serve as a great "undercover agent," as she had a certain "actress" way about her, and Rin would have many opportunities to use her computer skills. Then the "rules" were established:

1-Be compassionate.

2-Put others before yourself.

3-Be honest.

Next, it was time to take the oath.

"Do you solemnly swear to abide by the rules of the Fuji-san Clan, and to stick together in the best of times and in the worst of times, till death do us part?" said Tamiko. "I, myself, do!"

"I do!" said Rin.

"I do too!" said Hina.

"Me too!" said Jeremy.

Then, the four placed their hands together, one on top of another, in the center.

"Isshou no tomodachi!"

All at once, they lifted their hands up. The Fuji-san Clan club was now official!

Chapter 13
Jitter Dance

For the angel gang, the city of Fujinomiya was like a giant playground. Other people, however, considered Fujinomiya to be a tourist town while others considered it to be a sleepy, bedroom town. Traditionally, the city was a market town and had a heavy emphasis on the paper industry. Now, it included many other industries such as the manufacturing of rotating equipment and chemicals. Not surprisingly, Mount Fuji was the main attraction for tourists and Fujinomiya was one of the basic starting points for climbing trips to the mountain; Shiraito Falls and Lake Tanuki were also quite popular. The city itself was a hodgepodge of little houses, parks, buildings, markets and stores; on the outskirts of the city, there were fewer houses but a considerable number of farms and fields. Most everyone was Japanese except for those who lived in one of the several English enclaves ... like Tamiko. Most adults had jobs within the city but many commuted to and from Tokyo to get to work.

During the summer, it wouldn't be the same for Tamiko, as her friends were all going to summer camp in China—no more missions and no more playing songs together. Tamiko was really starting to have a crush on Jeremy, but there wouldn't be much of a chance for her to have him as a

113

boyfriend; Hina, Rin, and many good-looking Chinese girls would certainly be spending a lot of "quality time" with Jeremy over the summer. "Oh well," Tamiko said to herself. "I just turned twelve. I've got my whole life ahead of me."

Today, Tamiko had just finished writing the lyrics of her next song, entitled "Jitter Dance." This song was about that giddy first flush of love—the crush—that makes you get so excited that you just have to break out and do a quick little happy dance or something. Eager to play her new song, Tamiko got the Fuji-san Clan together for an after-school jam session at her house. The lead singer was Tamiko, and her backup singers/dancers were Hina and Rin. As usual, Hina played the keyboard a little, and Rin did some bass. As for Jeremy, he played his drums. Hina was really dressed for the occasion, with her tight, black "punk rock suit" that included a tight miniskirt and high-cut rubber shoes, not to mention her cherry-red lipstick and flashy pink highlights in her hair. She looked like a real rocker chick.

All were ready in Tamiko's bedroom. Even Butterscotch was there waiting as if he knew that, soon, something kind of exciting was going to happen. Then, Tamiko introduced each member of the band.

"G'day, mates, I'm Tamiko B ... and this is the Fuji-san Clan, starring myself, lead singer ... and also singers, dancers, and musicians—Hina!"

Hina did a sexy pose, yelled out "Fashion, babe!" and did some cartwheels.

"And Rin!" announced Tamiko. Rin bowed and did a little dance. "Good grades, babe!" she cried, somewhat teasing Hina.

"And last but not least ... Jeremy ... on drums!" said Tamiko.

With that, Jeremy smiled, yelled "Unko dreams, baby!"

and did a quick little drum solo. "Unko dreams, baby!", Jeremy's catch phrase, was actually born several months ago—before Tamiko walked into his life—when Jeremy began adding certain Japanese words to his spoken English vocabulary.

Now, Tamiko gave the cue to begin the song.

"One! Two! Three! Four!" she cried.

But just then, Tamiko's dad interrupted by entering the bedroom.

"Tamiko," he started.

"What?" Tamiko responded as her friends waited impatiently, curious as to what Tamiko's dad was about to say.

"Just make sure you don't make too much noise. Mommy had a long day, and she's trying to get some rest," he explained.

"Don't worry, Daddy," she said reassuringly. "We'll be quiet … I mean, we won't play too loudly. And the door's going to be closed anyway, so she won't really hear us."

"I hope not," replied Thomas. "Anyway, have fun, but just keep it down a little, all right?"

"Yes, sir!" replied Tamiko happily.

Tamiko shut the door and once again gave the signal to start.

"One! Two! Three! Four!" she hollered anew.

The song began with Hina playing a somewhat synthetic sound on the keyboard. The singers were a little out of sync, Hina made a little mistake on the keyboard, and Jeremy didn't know exactly what to do. Butterscotch began barking—either because he wanted to sing or because he couldn't take any more of this painful discord. As for Rin, she hit a few good bass notes but was thrown off by everything that was going wrong. However, the band played on for a little while, rather loudly, and then finally gave up and decided to do another take, unrecorded.

"Nice try!" Jeremy cried before the second take.

"That's easy for you to say. You're not one of the singers!" replied Hina.

"Yeah," said Rin. "Let's see if you can sing and do drums at the same time."

"I don't want to sing no girl song!" Jeremy stated. "Just drums for me."

"All right then!" Tamiko broke in. "Let's try it again!"

Just as Tamiko was about to restart the song, there was the sound of heavy footsteps pounding on the stairs accompanied by an angry father yelling, "Tamiko! Tamiko! Mommy is trying to get some sleep! No more noise!"

"Sorry," said Tamiko, opening the door just a bit.

With that, Tamiko turned on her recorder, hit Record, and lead the group in once again. After "Four!" the song began with almost no mistakes, and they sang …

Whenever you're groovin', I gotta go "Ah-ah-ah-ah-ah!"
When I see you movin', I wanna go "Ah-ah-ah-ah-ah!"
Every time that you walk by. When you look my way—what can I say?
I do my jitter dance and I go "Ah-ah-ah-ah-ah!"

When I hear you call me, I wanna go "Ah-ah-ah-ah-ah!"
Say my name—you'll stall me and then I'll go "Ah-ah-ah-ah-ah!"
Whenever you say "Hi!". When you sing my song, I sing along.
I do my jitter dance and I go "Ah-ah-ah-ah-ah!"

Sometimes I just can't control it—I gotta let it all out.

So what if you see me twist and turn all about.

When I see you smilin', I wanna go "Ah-ah-ah-ah-ah!"
When you leave, I'm cryin' and then I go "Ah-ah-ah-ah-ah!"
Whenever you pass by. I see your eyes that paralyze.
I do my jitter dance and I go "Ah-ah-ah-ah-ah!"

Maybe someday I'll slow down or I'll sleep for a while.
Soon, though, you'll light my fire.

Then, Hina did a fancy keyboard solo while the others danced about the room. After that, they finished with …

Whenever you tease me, I wanna go "Ah-ah-ah-ah-ah!"
Just talk and you'll freeze me. Then I'll go "Ah-ah-ah-ah-ah!"
When you joke with me—oh my! You make me laugh and I break in half.
I do my jitter dance and I go "Ah-ah-ah-ah-ah!"

Sometimes I just can't control it—I gotta let it all out.
So what if you see me twist and turn all about.

Whenever you're groovin', I gotta go "Ah-ah-ah-ah-ah!"

The singers were dancing and shaking their heads while Jeremy banged his little set of drums as if he were trying to break open a bunch of piñatas. After the song ended, they boogied around a bit more and cheered a little.

"How about we record our songs again and put them on YouTube?" said Hina. "Maybe someday we'll be famous!"

"You wish!" said Jeremy.

"Why not?" said Tamiko. "You never know!"

"We've got what it takes!" said Rin.

Then they played a couple more songs. The last songs had a lower volume level than the first one, but they were still rather loud—loud enough for Tamiko's father to get annoyed once more. Thomas marched up the stairs again, barged into Tamiko's room, and … there was Kana, dancing around and having fun with the kids!

"What are you … what are you doing here?" Thomas asked his wife, puzzled. "I thought you were sleeping … I mean …"

"I was. Then *you* woke me up when you walked up the stairs like an elephant and yelled at the kids!" she replied, laughing.

As it was almost time for supper, Tamiko's friends had to go. Afterward, while Kana looked for the hand juicer, she said something that triggered Tamiko to have a flashback of the little old house.

"What is it?" said Thomas as Kana stared at the open drawer in the kitchen. "What's in there?"

"It's not what's there," said Kana. "It's what *isn't* there! The juicer, where is it? I wanted to make a lemon meringue pie tonight."

"That's right," said Tamiko to herself. "It's not only what's there, it's what isn't there. We have to go back … tomorrow … and find out what that is!"

Chapter 14
Home Alone

Tamiko was supercharged with energy. She had high hopes that she and her friends would soon find out more about the spooky little house, the mysterious girl, and the strange man. Today was a weekday, but Tamiko's friends didn't have school. This would give them a chance to examine the house when, likely, nobody was inside. So after Tamiko's afternoon home tutoring session, she met up with her friends at the local dairy bar to discuss their plans.

At the bar, Tamiko and Jeremy each ordered two scoops of matcha (green tea) ice cream, and the others got chocolate and strawberry. It was a rather hot spring day with almost no wind at all. Aside from a few clouds, the air was pretty clear and, from where the kids were sitting outside, all of Mount Fuji was visible. It was a great day for doing pretty much anything outdoors, especially eating ice cream. Before too long, the four finished off their cones and got down to business.

"So what do we have so far?" asked Jeremy.

"Well, we got a spooky little house with a strange man in it and ..." said Tamiko.

"A strange little girl in it, too," said Hina.

"Yeah, a sick little girl who lost her dog," said Tamiko.

"And isn't allowed to leave her bedroom."

"And talks to people on toy phones," said Rin.

"And peeks around corners … and creeps me out," said Jeremy, "like the house. "And if that isn't scary enough, check this out!"

With that, Jeremy pulled out an old Walkman—a portable audio cassette player—that he had found in his attic. It was equipped with earphones, and the cassette the kids had pulled from the garbage was inside the player.

"The tape was kind of broken at first," said Jeremy. "But my dad fixed it up and …"

"And what?" asked Tamiko. "Can you hear anything?"

"Take a listen!" said Jeremy.

One at a time, starting with Tamiko, the others listened to the playback. It began with strange hissing sounds followed by some disturbing young, crying noises that grew louder, then softer, then louder and softer again. Over the cries, there was some other deeper voice mumbling something in the background. Then, suddenly, there was a short pause of nothing and then more disturbing noises. Although similar in tone, these were quite different from the previous ones in that they were sadder and almost sounded as though the person was shivering with cold and crying with their mouth shut at the same time. Like the previous noises, the volume swelled and diminished. Altogether, it was quite a scary sound: Woo-hoo-hoo-hoo-hoo-hoo-hoo! Mmm-hoo-hoo-hoo-hoo! In fact, because it was so spooky sounding, Tamiko pulled off the earphones to take a break before she could listen to any more of it. Afterwards, several Mmmmmmms and then several clunks and clonks could be heard. Overall, it was rather difficult to make out the origin of the sounds as the quality of the playback wasn't very good.

"Could that be the girl?" asked Tamiko.

"That's what I was thinking," said Jeremy. "But it's kind of hard to say."

"That just doesn't make any sense," added Rin. "Why would the man record her like that?"

"Freakiest thing I've ever heard," said Hina. "That almost sounds like Halloween sound effects!"

After more discussion about the meaning of what they had just heard, the four didn't know exactly what to think. They finally put it aside and moved on.

"So what's next?" said Hina. "What exactly are we doing today? What are we looking for?"

"Now that—probably—there's nobody home, we can take the time to learn more about the place," said Tamiko. "There's something kind of unusual about it. Until yesterday, I was thinking about what we saw in the house so far. Now, something tells me that we should be looking for what isn't there. Something seems to be missing."

"Maybe today we'll find out what that is," said Rin.

"Let's hope no one sees us," said Hina.

On their bicycles, the curious group of four sped over to the spooky little house in hopes of getting some answers. On arrival, it started to rain a bit. Unlike the previous visits, there was no car in the driveway. Despite the rain, the kids went straight ahead with their work.

Before approaching the side window, the four scanned the surrounding area to ensure their privacy. When the coast was clear, the kids stealthily shuffled over to the window. This time, the curtains were open, providing a good view of the inside. Just as the foursome gazed through the window, a car pulled into the driveway. The four froze for a second or two.

"Looks like we have company," said Tamiko.

"That must be the man," said Jeremy. "Let's get outta here before he sees us!"

"Wait a minute," said Rin. "That's a different car than—"

"It's pulling back out of the driveway," said Hina.

Apparently, it was just someone using the driveway to turn around. The kids went back to the window and made their observations. Again, the place was an absolute mess. Stuff was scattered everywhere. On the right, in the living room, were numerous boxes stacked one on top of another in a rather unorganized fashion. Some boxes were closed, but most were open. The open ones showed some men's clothes, workshop tools, books, magazines, kitchen items, camping equipment, office supplies, an old VCR, a guitar, a small flat-screen TV, a coffeemaker, and a bunch of DVDs and video games. There were also several filled garbage bags lying around. Two of them were not completely full; those bags appeared to have children's toys in them, including several dolls, plastic ponies, toy soldiers, trucks, and a toy train. Another garbage bag revealed women's clothing and crafts. In the living room, there were also power tools and paint cans scattered all over the floor. The kitchen, off to the left, looked as though it had been hit by a tornado. Dishes and pots and pans and cooking ingredients were all over the place.

As they had expected, there were no signs of life; the man was probably at work and the girl in kindergarten. Just when the kids were about to discuss what they should do next, they heard someone from behind. The four jerked around to discover a Japanese man jogging along the sidewalk with a Chihuahua. He didn't notice the four kids, as he was too involved with controlling the dog. The curious four turned back to the window and, suddenly, there she was! At the back of the house, the little girl was cautiously peering around her bedroom doorway like she had done before. A bit more of her face was showing this time, and they could clearly see her round, black eyes and somber expression. Again, her hair was all messy and she wore old pajamas. She definitely looked sick. The four twitched in shock at the sight of her and moved out of the way to avoid being seen.

"What's *she* doing here?" said Hina.

"And where's the man?" said Rin. "It's illegal to leave a child alone like that!"

"I don't know," said Tamiko. "Maybe he's … gone out to get her some medication."

"And maybe that girl is from another planet or something," added Jeremy. "She almost scares me more than the house."

The four slowly stood up again and looked down the hallway. The girl had disappeared. Just then a blue car swerved into the driveway. The driver hopped out. It was the man!

Before the kids had much time to react, the man barged into the house and marched toward the girl's bedroom. Almost immediately, there was an argument. The four couldn't make out any of the words except for "I told you to …" and "I'm sick and tired of …" From the little the four could see and hear, the girl was being yelled at for something. Then, the four heard slapping noises.

Afterward, the man paced into the messy kitchen and grabbed himself a beer. About then, Hina saw a spider and let out a scream. The man stopped and looked toward the window, but the foursome had already ducked behind the hedge. After a short while, the kids courageously tiptoed back to the window, one at a time, starting with Tamiko.

This time they saw the man escort the girl to and from the bathroom and then give her some kind of medication. Again, like the previous visit, they saw the man carrying the funny-looking machine with buttons. The man set the machine on the floor and pressed a button. Afterward, he appeared to play with her, but in a rather unusual way, for he took some big, stuffed spider and scared the girl into her room whenever she tried to get out. Then, the man pretended to be some kind of monster and scared the girl some more. It was quite obvious that she wasn't having fun. In fact, from the few moments the kids could actually see her, she looked terrified. The man finally left, and the girl quickly raced into the adjacent bedroom and scurried back to her room with a soccer ball. Moments later, she peeped cautiously around the corner of her doorway as she held the soccer ball tight against her chest. Then she disappeared. Finally, all was calm, and the four decided to leave the premises.

On their way back home, the investigators went over the sights and sounds during their most recent visit to the old house. As much as they tried, they still couldn't make sense of everything; there was something that just wasn't there. Then, just before bed, Tamiko suddenly came to the realization of what was missing!

Chapter 15
Questions

"It came to me," said Tamiko to her angel friends the following day at the corner store right after karate class. "It came to me yesterday just before I went to bed."

"Tell us about it," said Hina.

Tamiko expressed her feeling that there had been other people living in the old house not too long ago. The others said that they had the same feeling.

"Did you see the toys?" said Tamiko.

"Yeah," said Hina. "There were some dolls and little ponies and things."

"There were also those trucks and that toy train," said Rin. "And that soccer ball and those boy clothes."

"So a *boy* used to live there," said Jeremy.

"Yeah," said Tamiko. "And it appears that …" Remembering the boxes, Tamiko made an interesting conjecture. "That they're moving out. Remember the boxes?"

"Right," said Jeremy. "All the man's stuff was there, but the mother and kid stuff was in the garbage bags along with … garbage."

"Then where's the boy and the mother?" said Hina.

"And what about the girl?" asked Rin. "Isn't she moving

too?"

"The boy's probably her brother. Maybe he died or something, and *that's* the real reason why she's so sad," said Jeremy.

"I get it!" said Rin. "The girl is going to die of the same sickness her brother had, and that's why she's not moving. But what about the mother? Did she die, too?"

"If that's what it is, then ... poor girl," said Tamiko. "First she loses half her family and then the dog. We have to go back and find out more!"

And so it went. The kids immediately sped over to the house and took another peek. The driveway was empty and the curtains were all closed. Nothing seemed to be going on—inside or out—so the foursome jumped back onto their bikes and decided to come back the next day. Just before they left, Tamiko had an idea.

"I don't know why we didn't think of it before," said Tamiko. "Let's ask the neighbors about the house. Maybe they know something."

"Good idea!" said Rin.

The four raced over to the house just north of the spooky corner house. They rang the doorbell and knocked, but there was no answer. They tried the next house down, and, within seconds, the door opened revealing a short, slender Japanese woman in her early forties. Without any hesitation, Tamiko inquired about the occupants of the old house.

"Do you know the people who live in the house at the corner, down that way?" asked Tamiko, pointing. "We're asking because we heard some strange noises coming from it."

"I didn't know them very well, but they were an English family of four, including a young boy and girl. They—"

"Were?" said Jeremy. "What happened to them?"

"I don't know. About three months ago, everything seemed fine. The mom and dad were out planting flowers while the kids were playing soccer. Then, just like that, the family disappeared. Now, there's just some Englishman living there."

"And that Englishman's not the father of the family that disappeared?" asked Tamiko.

"Oh no, he's a different man—a scary-looking fellow."

Then, Rin asked the woman to describe the girl.

"She was about six years old, black hair, big eyes, slender.

"That's the same girl," Rin whispered to Tamiko.

"You said she liked soccer?" said Tamiko.

"Oh yeah. She played it all the time with her brother."

Tamiko asked the woman what she knew about the man and the vanishing family.

"I don't really know the man; he's like a hermit. I didn't know the family very well, either. I met them once but don't remember their names. I wonder what happened to them."

Then, the woman mumbled something about a nearby dog that had just started barking. After a short pause, Rin asked the woman if she'd seen the little girl since the family's mysterious disappearance.

"No, not even once."

"Do you remember anything else—anything at all—no matter how small it is?" asked Hina.

"Not really. Well, there was one thing, come to think of it. Before the family disappeared, there were these two ambulances that went by real fast ... over toward the house on the corner. I didn't really think much of it at the time, but ..."

The woman didn't have much else to say, so the kids thanked her and took off.

"I knew it!" said Rin as the four cycled away. "Everyone in the family died of some big disease like bubonic plague or swine flu—except for the girl, the only survivor."

"Yeah," said Jeremy. "And after, the dog got infected by it too, and that's why it had to be removed and ... put away."

"But what about the man?" asked Hina. "Who's he?"

"Maybe an uncle or a friend of the girl's dad," said Tamiko.

"We have to find out more about this disease," said Jeremy.

Chapter 16~
Where Does the Expired Food Go?

Today, Tamiko called Fujinomiya Hospital to learn more about the two ambulances. Her call was transferred to the administration department, but the receptionist wasn't very willing to give any answers, as it was against policy to give information out to strangers. Tamiko tried again, this time changing her voice and speaking with greater authority, but she still failed to get anywhere. Frustrated, Tamiko slapped the phone back onto the hook. She would have to come up with another plan. Maybe Hina could use her acting skills and do better, for not only was Hina a (sometimes feisty) fashion diva, she was also very good at imitating people. One April Fool's Day, she phoned her friends—Tamiko, Rin, Jeremy, and two others—and fooled every one of them into thinking that they had won a trip to Las Vegas! That was several days after Hina had pretended to be her mom and replied to a voice message from the school principal, who had informed Hina's parents that she was late for class. "She was late because she called me and said she was feeling a bit sick. I told her to drink some water and she was okay," said Hina in her response to the phone message. The principal understood and ignored the lateness.

Just as Tamiko was about to pick up the phone to call

Hina, Kana asked something of her.

"Tamiko. Could you go to the grocery store and buy some eggs? And I'd also need some rice and tea …"

"Sure."

With that, Kana handed her daughter some money and Tamiko set out on her errand by bike. To get there, Tamiko had to pass through the poorer quarters; each time she couldn't help but notice just how little food and money many people had. Men and even women were sluggishly walking around begging for change. Some of them were fixed like statues with their palms out hoping for someone to stroll by and give them something, even if it be just a few yen. Some were sitting down like a meditating Buddha with an old hat before them. Some wore signs around their necks asking for change, and some were picking through the garbage bins for bits of food and empty cans or bottles.

These quarters had somewhat of a foul odor, and one could hear moans and groans as the beggars and vagabonds went about their work. Most of them were dressed in rather shabby and tattered-looking apparel. Their faces were expressionless and scuzzy. Their hair was twisted in knots and grimy, making them look like they had just woken up from several months of hibernation.

Tamiko always doled out some of her pocket change when she passed through. Some people, especially older ones, told her that this wasn't "solving the problem" and that the bums should just go out and "get a job." Instead of listening, she gave up the rest of her change to the old man with the hat. Tamiko tried coming up with other ways to help but felt kind of helpless, as she had a limited amount of money.

After she exited the poorer quarters, Tamiko slipped into the neighborhood grocery store to buy the eggs, rice, and tea (as her mother had asked her to do). Looking at all the wonderful food surrounding her, Tamiko felt kind of sorry for the poorer folks she had just encountered. *Wouldn't it be great if food were free?* she thought. *No,* she continued thinking, *nothing's really free in life.* Just then, an interesting question came to mind. *What happens to the food once it has "expired"? Does it get thrown out or does it get frozen or does something else happen to it?* she wondered.

After some more thought, she figured that most all of that food went to the garbage, wasted. She also reasoned that most of this expired food was still safe to eat (like her mother kept telling her) and that the only reason for the early expiry date was simply for the food companies to be "extra sure" in avoiding any complaints or lawsuits against them for any food gone bad. Therefore, Tamiko planned her next mission—to find out where, exactly, the expired food went. If it was on its way to the trash bin like she imagined, then she and her angel friends could recover it and give it to the poor. In the past, Tamiko had kindly asked the store manager if he could simply give the expired food away to the poor—but he refused.

After Tamiko returned with the groceries, she got together with her friends at the park and explained the mission.

"We go to the back of the store, outside, where they load and unload the milk and dairy stuff," started Tamiko. "Then we wait for the food truck. You know … the one that shows up every now and then. And after they load it up with all the food, we follow it to the place where they dump it or whatever they do with it—let's hope it's not too far. Once it arrives, we have to confirm that it's really being thrown away, and then … we make our move and give the food to the poor."

"And just how are we going to do that?" asked Jeremy, confused.

Tamiko explained that they could sneak into the truck and drive it away to the poorer quarters where they would drop off the food.

"What!" exclaimed Jeremy along with the other two.

"You're actually going to steal the truck and drive it?" asked Hina.

"Well … I can drive a car … somewhat … so I can drive a truck too," assured Tamiko.

"Get out of here!" exclaimed Rin.

"Oh yes I can! You just watch me!" cried Tamiko.

So the foursome turned on their walkie-talkies and put their plan in action. Hina went inside the store to confirm that any food being taken from the store and put into the truck was really expired; she would be able to do this since there was a large refrigerated room in the back where employees could be seen behind the bags of milk and other dairy items. The others went out back and waited for the truck. Since the store was about to close, Tamiko figured that the vehicle should arrive soon. Sure enough, a small white truck entered the driveway in the back within the next minute. It backed up to the loading dock of the store.

"It's here!" cried Jeremy to Hina excitedly. "The truck's backed up to the store now!"

"Roger that!" replied Hina.

New milk and other dairy products were unloaded. Then, expired food was thrown into the truck.

"They've just taken the new food out of the truck, and now they're loading it up with the old stuff," confirmed Hina. "Over and out!"

With that, Hina ran outside to join the others. The truck was almost ready to go, and the four jumped on their bikes and waited. With a slamming of the back door and an abrupt revving of the engine, the truck pulled out of loading area and into the street. The gang followed it like an eagle chasing its prey. Luckily, the truck wasn't going very fast and there were a good number of traffic lights to slow it down.

Eventually, the truck made a left turn into what appeared to be some kind of a dumping site. Just as Tamiko had figured, the truck came to a full stop next to a large bin, and the two truckers jumped out and opened the back of the vehicle. The kids kept a good distance from the scene to avoid any suspicion.

"What do we do now?" whispered Rin.

"Just wait a bit," said Jeremy. "Let's see what they do."

"It looks like ..." began Tamiko, "they're throwing it out!"

"Great. So what now?" asked Hina.

It was clear now that the food was being tossed into the garbage. But how were they going to take control of the truck and make off with the food? Tamiko had a solution.

"We need to make the men go away somehow," said Tamiko. "One of us can hide behind that building and make some sort of noise. The men will leave and check it out, and then the noisemaker can just move around to the other side of the building and meet with the rest of us at the truck. Then, we're off!"

With that, Jeremy volunteered to make the commotion to lure the truckers and hid behind the obscure side of the building. The others went to the other side of the truck, out of sight from the men. Then Jeremy made his noise.

"Heeeeey!" he yelled. "Over here!"

The two men suddenly stopped what they were doing but then gradually continued walking back to the truck to grab some more food. Just then, Jeremy made another sound.

"Helloooooooo!" he hollered.

The truckers froze once again and then scrambled over toward the outcry. As they approached the far side of the building, Jeremy crept around to the opposite side and quietly ran toward the truck. Tamiko and the others gently shut the back door, and they all jumped into the truck at once.

"I don't believe we're doing this!" Hina proclaimed.

"Me neither!" agreed Rin.

"Let's just hope she knows how to drive," said Jeremy.

"I can do this!" assured Tamiko as she shifted the truck into gear.

The truck thrust forward as Tamiko hit the accelerator. Just as she was about to turn onto the street, Tamiko pressed the brake pedal before looking both ways. However, she applied much more pressure on the pedal than necessary to stop the truck. As a result, the others—not yet buckled up—jolted forward.

"Easy on the brakes!" cried Jeremy.

"Yeah," said Tamiko. "You guys might want to buckle up!"

Meanwhile, the two men were still looking for the source of the commotion. Once it was safe to go, Tamiko turned onto the street, and just in time, too, as the men realized their dairy truck was rolling away.

"Hey!" they shouted, running after the truck. "Come back here! Hey!"

Hearing this, the foursome giggled and snorted, yet they were a bit scared. Tamiko had actually driven a bit in the country, with her dad right next to her. However, she'd never done anything quite like *this* before!

What a thrill it was! Tamiko sped down the streets, past

the neighborhoods, through the countryside, and toward the poorer quarters like a bird that just learned how to fly. The traffic signals and road signs were not much of a problem, as she had three other pairs of eyes to help her. They could hear the wind flowing over them accompanied by the low-pitched growling of the engine as lights and signs and buildings whizzed by them.

"Way to go, Tamiko!" her friends cheered.

"You're good!" said Jeremy. "I'm going to hire *you* as my chauffeur for the school dance!"

Finally, they arrived at the heart of the poorer region, and Tamiko, once again hitting the brakes a bit too hard, parked the truck alongside a backstreet.

"We made it!" everyone yelled in applause. "Yeaaaaaaaah!"

The four leaped out of the vehicle and eagerly began opening the back door. A few of the beggars noticed Tamiko when she made her exit, looking astonished to see such a young driver!

"What the …?" said one of the hobos.

"Is she the driver? But that can't be! She's only …" said another, baffled.

Once the door was completely open, there was a whole crowd of beggars and low-income folks all waiting silently and motionlessly, wondering what was going to happen next. Then, Tamiko spoke.

"Free food for everyone!" she cheered joyfully.

"Party time!" said Jeremy.

With that, the mass of poor and hungry individuals cried with joy as they went into a frenzy. They pushed and shoved each other as they made their way to the back of the truck like seagulls fighting over breadcrumbs. The kids threw out milk bag after milk bag, egg carton after egg carton, cheese brick after cheese brick, and even frozen pizza after frozen pizza (as well as some other food items that were not really meant to be thrown out). The foursome felt like heroes as they tossed the food out into the crowd. "Thank you! Thank you!" they heard about a hundred times. Then, after all the goods were gone, Hina turned to Tamiko and asked an important question.

"*Now* what?" she asked.

"Let's get a picture of all this," answered Tamiko. "Let's get further back from the truck so we can get everything."

Just as Tamiko and the gang were taking the picture, a police car arrived on the scene with its lights flashing and its siren blasting out a "Woo! Woo! Woo!" in order make a way through the crowd of happy hobos. Two police officers jumped out of the car. One of them approached a bum in the crowd, the other pointed to the truck, words were exchanged, and the bum finally pointed to Tamiko.

"Let's get outta here!" said Jeremy. "We've just been spotted!"

With that, the angel gang scampered around the corner and down a dark alley like a scurry of Japanese tree squirrels with Tamiko and Jeremy leading the way. The officers pushed their way through the mass of people and began their search with a brisk walk, followed by a light jog down the alley. With the help of their flashlights, the officers caught sight of the young thieves and picked up the pace.

"Faster!" said Tamiko, running. "They're catching up!"

But the police officers used their longer legs to gain on the teens. To make matters worse, Rin bumped her knee against a metal post and slowed everyone down. In seconds, the pursuers were only just a few strides away.

"Give it up!" cried out one of the officers.

"We've got you!" went the other.

But the young group of four kept on moving. They sped around another corner and, just in time, Tamiko led her comrades to hide behind a series of large wicker food baskets. The policemen, bewildered by the sudden disappearance of their targets, turned around in circles shining their flashlights in all directions. They decided to look behind a big, wooden sign—an excellent choice for a hideout—on the other side of the street directly opposite Tamiko and her gang. While the officers wasted their time at the sign, the younger ones climbed into the empty food baskets and closed the lids. The searchers marched over to the other side of the alley, explored the area around the wicker hideouts, and were just about to open the covers when they heard noises from the far end of the alleyway. They froze, then turned, and finally ran away. A while later, the kids slowly climbed out of their baskets and walked the other way around the corner.

"Phew!" said Tamiko. "That was close!"

Chapter 17—
The Beating

"I got a reply," said Hina the following day, "a reply from Mr. Data Analyst at Fujinomiya Hospital."

"Let's call back!" said Tamiko.

Hina picked up the phone and dialed the number and extension given in the message. Fortunately, the data analyst was in his office this time. As he was the young computer nerd of the department, he was quite easy to break and get information out of. Within seconds, he was working to give Hina all the information she wanted.

"I've got all the data right here before me," he said proudly. "I know everything. Using SQL and Visual Basic, I can determine exactly—"

"Just tell me what I want to know," said Hina.

"Okay—here—I've got it. Looks like a false alarm."

"Are you sure about that?"

"Yeah, that's what I'm getting. I know everything."

Then Hina asked if there were any other calls for that area around the same time.

"Umm, no. Nothing here. In Japanese, that's 'nanimo nai.'"

Realizing she came to a dead end, Hina quickly finished the conversation and hung up.

"Looks like we're back to square one," said Hina, disappointed.

With that, the four young explorers got together at the dairy bar again and psyched themselves up for their next visit to the old house. They had their suspicions and they had their conclusions, but they really didn't have any concrete proof. Moreover, there were still many unanswered questions. Hopefully, today's visit would tell them more.

As they were about to leave the bar, Rin had a little flashback after hearing someone complain about a dog barking nearby.

"That woman—you know, the neighbor we talked to about the mystery house—she said something about a dog that was barking," said Rin. "What exactly did she say?"

"I kind of remember something," said Hina. "She was grumbling about how noisy the dog was … I think."

"I believe she said … what was it?" asked Tamiko.

Then, Jeremy got it.

"That's right," he said. "She got upset about the barking dog on the other side of the street. She said it was always the only dog in the neighborhood, and that one was enough."

"So the girl never had a dog then!" said Hina.

"Yeah. But maybe she had a cat," said Tamiko.

Just as it was getting dark, the kids sped over to the little old house where lived the mystery girl. But before checking on the girl again, they decided to visit another one of her neighbors to get more answers. They were told a similar story as the previous one, but this time, they were also informed that the girl often liked playing outdoors with some sort of monkey—a stuffed one or possibly a real one; the neighbor couldn't really tell as she was near-sighted.

"I knew it!" said Tamiko. "The monkey … it must be the same one we saw in that ripped-up photo!"

"So *that's* what was in the bag at the start of all this," said Jeremy. "All along, we thought it was a dog when it was really a monkey!"

"Makes sense!" said Hina along with Rin.

Now, the four went over to the spooky house. It stood differently today. It appeared to possess some kind of a solemn presence that just wasn't there during the previous visits. Maybe it was the dark, cloudy, gray-blue sky, or maybe it was the unbelievably still trees and silent air. Whatever it was, it seemed as though something was about to snap.

The four carefully parked their bicycles behind the hedge and crept up to the side window. Luckily, the curtains were opened just wide enough to provide them with a decent view of the inside. However, all was dark and lifeless despite the fact that the car was in the driveway. Not a light was on, and not the slightest sound disturbed the silence.

They waited and waited for something to happen but finally came to the conclusion that the occupants were fast asleep; the kids figured that they should come back some other day but at an earlier time.

"They must be sleeping," whispered Tamiko. "Let's come back tomorrow."

"Or let's just drop the whole thing," said Jeremy, let down. "It's just some sick girl and her dad, or whoever the guy is."

"Yeah," said Rin. "What if we get caught? What if—"

Before Rin could finish, a series of dull thuds broke the silence. Almost immediately a light came on, and the action began. The man raced over to the bedroom and yelled at the top of his voice, "I told you to be quiet! Now shut up or I'll …" The kids couldn't really make out the last words, but they sounded something like "belt you one." This was followed by the girl screaming, "Please, uncle, please!" Then, the kids heard slapping sounds and an abrupt slamming of the door. Afterward, the man came marching toward the side window like an angry sumo wrestler.

"Down!" said Tamiko.

After a long pause, the foursome gradually stood up and saw the man quickly return to the bedroom. Then they heard the man yell again. The girl bolted out of the bedroom and down the hallway with lightning speed. In almost zero time, the man reappeared out of nowhere and chased after the girl like a hungry tiger. The girl ran into the living room and hid behind the television just before the man turned the corner. The monster stomped all over the living room in search of the girl. He looked behind boxes, inside boxes, behind furniture, and under clothes. At one point, the man was only inches away from the girl; all he had to do was turn his head the other way and he would have found her. Becoming increasingly frustrated with each step he took, he reached a point where it looked like he almost lost his mind.

Then, suddenly, the man stopped in the middle of the room as though he had just heard something. He shifted toward the back of the television and found the girl. The little one raced toward the front door to make her escape, but the man quickly caught up with her.

Thinking fast, Tamiko knocked on the window to divert the man's attention. Just as he was about to grab the girl, the monster turned his head toward the window and marched over to check out what had made the noise. At the same time, the kids scurried to the front door.

By now, the girl was trying frantically to open the door, not realizing that she had to unlock it first. Then, the man abandoned the window, raced over to the girl, and grabbed her. The man yelled something and dragged the girl screaming to her room. At this point, Hina and Rin had run over to the side window again to see what was going on inside. Clenching her like the jaws of a vise with one hand, the monster man slapped the girl across the face with the other. He repeated this at least four or five times as he yelled, "Get back in there! I'll feed you when I want!"

"He's beating her up like an animal!" said Hina.

"We have to stop him!" said Rin.

"But how?" said Hina.

The man gave the little girl one last blow, hitting her like a batter would hit a baseball, from the hallway to the floor of her bedroom. Moments later, the kids heard something that sounded like a door slam, and then the man exited the room, shutting the door behind him, and paced down the basement stairs. Afterward, the kids heard dull thumping noises.

Hina and Rin scampered over to the bedroom window followed by the other two angels. They peered through the slats of the window blind and saw a dimly lit room, but, to their surprise, the girl had disappeared! From what the kids could see, the room was almost empty. The door was shut, the girl wasn't hiding behind anything, and there was no sign of any closet.

"I saw the man beat her and knock her into the room!" said Rin. "She *has* to be here."

"I saw it too," said Hina.

"It sounds like she's trapped inside … somewhere!" said Jeremy.

"We have to rescue her!" said Hina.

"We will," said Tamiko. "'But not now. We have to come up with a plan first."

CHAPTER 18

PREPARE FOR BATTLE

It was pitch-black as Tamiko reached the narrow bicycle path leading to her backyard. The air was cooler and smelled of freshly cut wood, and the sound of crickets began to take over the previous chirping of the birds. Inside the house, Butterscotch was barking incessantly, as he always did when he heard anything going on outside.

Tamiko parked her bike in the back and slowly walked through the door preparing herself for another lecture from her mom and dad. As she entered the dining room, there stood two troubled-looking parents cleaning up the kitchen and one dog staring at her, wagging his little brown tail. It was as though her parents didn't even realize that Tamiko had entered the house. Then, Kana spoke.

"Finally, you're home," she said. "It's been over an hour … you're over an hour late, Tamiko."

"Sorry," said Tamiko.

"You should be," said Thomas. "When it's supper time, it's family time. You know that."

Then, Kana asked Tamiko where she was and what she was doing.

"I was just checking out that old house again with the mystery girl," began Tamiko.

"I told you before, you shouldn't be spying on people. That's an invasion of privacy," said Thomas. "Anyway ... what happened this time?"

"We saw the man ... beating her ... beating the little girl."

"Was she in any danger?" asked Kana.

"Look, I don't want to talk about it now! Okay!?" said Tamiko, revealing her angry side.

"All right, you'll tell us tomorrow then," said Thomas, playing it calm. "Well ... if that's all, then I think it's time for you to have a quick supper and go to bed."

With that, Tamiko went straight to her room, without eating, brushing her teeth, or even saying good night, and slammed the door behind her. She stood there, in the middle of her bedroom, as she thought about rescuing the lone girl. She gazed at her platform bed ... and then at the karate/tae kwon do posters stuck on her animal wallpaper. Then, instead of getting into bed, she did something quite different. She practiced her karate, tae kwon do, and other martial arts—even some fresh and original moves she had made up herself. For two long hours, she danced about the room like some kind of wild ballerina, kicking and punching and flipping and rolling all over the floor. Fortunately, her parents didn't hear much, as Tamiko had recently installed some crude soundproofing on her door and walls for musical purposes. Tamiko was now pumped up and determined to rescue the little girl. Suddenly, her martial art skills had much more meaning to her now that she was going to put them to good use.

Tamiko had an excellent sense of hearing—even through the soundproofing—which came in very handy, as she would temporarily interrupt her karate session and hop into bed each time her mom or dad came marching toward her room to check on her.

Tamiko could just imagine knocking down the front door of the little girl's house like some kind of a superhero, victoriously fighting off the bad guy, and gloriously saving the girl from the big, ugly monster. *But would I be strong enough?* she wondered. She reasoned that she couldn't do it all alone, and that even if her friends were to help her, he'd surely win. But Tamiko started thinking, *What if I were to hit him in the right place at the right time? Then, maybe, I'd stand a chance.* Finally, she figured that it would be a better plan to just slip in when he wasn't around and grab the girl as fast as she could. Her martial art skills would still come in handy in case she were to run into the bad guy himself by accident or something. She felt she must keep practicing. Yet, once again, she thought about what it would be like if she were to really go through with her big plan and find out afterward that the man really wasn't so bad after all … that he just got angry like all parents do every once and a while. She and her friends would look like fools!

She had to make a decision, and she had to come up with some kind of plan. Maybe she and her gang could record the man's yelling or, better still, film him with a video camera; then they'd have proof. *What would the police think of that?* she wondered. The man would, of course, have to get angry enough to convince the cops that he belongs behind bars. But the bad guy could probably wiggle his way out by simply making up any stupid excuse he wanted. Just before Tamiko went to bed, she pulled out her little netbook, logged onto Messenger, and began chatting with her friends.

Tamiko (to Hina): U there?

Hina: Ya. Kinda shaken up though.

Tamiko: Me 2. Did you hear the way that guy was yelling at the little girl?????

Hina: Yeah, and how he was beating her too. That guy's a monster! I think I heard her say UNCLE

Tamiko: That's right. she DID say that. And he said get back in there or something and I'll feed you when I want.

Hina: And before that he said shut up or I'll.....something.

Tamiko: And he slapped her I don't know how many times, haaard!

Hina: And that's after he had her dog ripped away from her and shipped to the pound.

Tamiko: Obviously there's a lot more to this than just some dog being taken away.

Hina: Like what?

Tamiko: I don't know.. But something's very odd about the whole thing. Makes me think of a dream I had the other day, or more of a nightmare actually.

Hina: Tell me about it.

Tamiko: In the dream, I saw the girl. Well, kind of saw her.She was locked up in this daark little room all alone. But I could hear her crying and moving all around and then banging on some wall or door. She was yelling something.

Cant remember what it was. I wanted to set her free but I couldn't do anything. Then there were footsteps. They must have been from that man, the uncle. First, they were soft..then they got bigger and bigger until they were so loud I thought the floor was going to break. The man yelled and yelled .. and that wus only the half of it

Hina: Oh yeah! What was the other half?

Tamiko: Well, then I was like zapped to outside the house, to you guys who were spying on the house from a distance with Jeremy's binoculars. Then, Jeremy saw something. So I grabbed the binocs and saw the girl. She escaped! She was running away from the front of the house. I dont think I've ever seen anyone run so fast. She kept looking behind her to see if the man was there. She looked terrified.

Hina: And what about the man? Did he go running after her?

Tamiko: Yeah. The man came out of the door and raced after her. The girl ran faster. She ran down the street, all the way past the stores and into the forest. the monster almost caught up to her. The girl climbed up a tree just as the man tried to grab her.

Hina: So, what happened next?

Tamiko: The man had trouble climbing the tree, so he turned into a werewolf and clawed his way up superfast and grabbed the girl with his teeth. He pulled her down, turned back into himself and dragged the girl to his car at the edge of the forest, while she was kicking and screaming. Then, he beat her, threw her into the car and drove away.

Hina: That's quite some dream! I get the feeling that a lot of it is true.

Tamiko: Me too. I know shes in trouble. We have to save her …

Hina: And we will! So, what R U doing now?

Tamiko: I came home late and my parents sent me to my room. I'm practicing tae kwon do now. We're going to take down that SOB!

Hina: And how exactly R we goin 2 do that?

Tamiko: We're gonna have to practice together and come up with a plan

Hina: What kind of plan? You mean like-we all jump on him at the same time or something?

Tamiko: Not really. Something smarter than that, like grabbing the girl when he's not around.

Then, Jeremy logged on.

Jeremy: Wutssssss up!

Tamiko: Hullo Jeremy. I'm doing some tae kwon do now. How bout U?

Jeremy: Not 2 much…..still thinking about the girl and that

monster, whoever he is.

Hina: The girl called him uncle I think.

Jeremy: Some uncle! He was beating her to a pulp!

Tamiko: Yeah, tell me about it.

Jeremy: All because of a dog or her sickness…..

Tamiko: I think it's more than justt. better go, parents r coming

Tamiko quickly turned off her light and went to bed, exhausted from her lengthy workout and mentally drained from all her thinking and rationalizing. Before she fell asleep, Tamiko's last thought was, *I'm doing this … we're doing this … the brave way! We're going to prepare for battle!*

Chapter 19—
Allan … Again!

The next few days whizzed by, and the summer holidays were getting closer and closer. Kana continued to sell more furniture and crafts; Thomas kept up the hard work at the Nanotechnology Research Institute. He was slowly but surely making some improvement. By now, he had increased the strength of his bulletproof vest by just over 30 percent—another 20 to go before the end of summer. He dreamed of developing a way to dramatically speed up the production process of the bulletproof coating, for if he could, then he would be able to build all kinds of things of amazing strength in almost no time at all. *It's time to get back to reality!* he would remind himself every time he began daydreaming.

As for the Fuji-san Clan, their rescue plans and "mystery girl investigations" continued. The kids went to the city hall one day to conduct a title search for the mystery house and found that it was currently owned by a Richard Powell and previously by a Kevin L. Powell. The four kids did more research at a public library and, after several hours of hard work digging through newspapers, discovered that a Kevin L. Powell and his wife were killed in a car accident on the outskirts of Tokyo just over three months ago; in the same article, the young investigators also learned that the accident victims left behind a young son and daughter.

"So *that's* what happened!" said Jeremy.

"Yeah, but ... where's the brother?" asked Tamiko.

"Good question," said the others.

As for the angels' plan of rescuing the little girl, they were just about to go out to save her when Tamiko's parents found out about it and called it off; they told her that it was time to stop peeping into other people's homes and that they had heard enough about her visits to the spooky house. Tamiko stressed the fact that they had intentions of rescuing the girl, but her parents didn't want to hear it. After all, they said, she didn't have any proof that the girl was in any immediate danger, and that for all any of them knew, the girl was just misbehaving and deserved a few spanks or slaps. As much as she hated letting it go, Tamiko knew the subject was closed. To take Tamiko's mind off her obsession with the lone girl—and to spend more quality time with their daughter—Thomas and Kana made a big effort to take time off work, and the family went on a three-day camping trip to Lake Tanuki. There, they had a great time canoeing, fishing, trekking, and sharing stories while roasting marshmallows over a campfire. "The next time we go camping, let's bring along your cousins, Yumi and Nobu," said Kana. "They'd like to see you again."

The day after the camping trip was cloudy with a bit of rain. Despite the drizzly weather, Tamiko got on her bike to go to karate class. Just as she began pedaling, she saw Musoyama, the sumo wrestler, stomp over to his next-door neighbor, who was apparently having trouble breaking an empty wooden box. Tamiko stopped and watched. Musoyama's neighbor kicked it, bashed it, and even jumped on it, but the box didn't succumb to the blows. Then, massively heavy Musoyama simply sat on it, and the box almost instantly crumbled into pieces. What a funny sight it was. "That's the way you do it!" said Musoyama.

Tamiko started cycling again and made her way to karate classes. As she biked through the countryside, the sounds of raindrops falling on leaves and birds tweeting kept her company. The wind had begun to pick up, and along with it the rain, and her face and hair were now getting rather wet. It felt kind of refreshing though, like a shower of cold water on a hot day. The landscape and distant village were a glossy dark green and brown—comforting, but a little sad and subdued because of the rain.

Soon enough, Tamiko arrived at her karate school. As usual, there stood Allan McCoy, just outside the door, with his head tilted slightly upward. If he were wearing a T-shirt, it would read "Trouble in karate shoes!" or "I'm the best!" or maybe even "#1: I'm right. #2: If I'm ever wrong, read #1!" *What is today's "thing" going to be?* she wondered. Before she could guess, several other people showed up, including Roka. Sure enough, Allan blurted out something at the sight of Roka.

"Oh hi, Shad! Konnichiwa!" he cried.

"Likewise," replied Roka.

"So where's your guardian angel?" asked Allan. "What's her name again? I think it's ... Tamiko. Is that right, Shad?"

Roka turned around a little and was about to say something, but then changed his mind and walked away. This made Allan angry, but he refused to give up.

"Where are you going, Shad? Are you looking for Taaaaamiko?" he asked.

Tamiko broke in.

"You really think you're number one, don't you?" she asked.

"What do you mean, I *think* I'm number one? I *know* I'm

number one!" Allan replied.

"Yeah, right!" cried Tamiko sharply.

"And how good do you think *you* are?" asked Allan. "Let's see … maybe number fifteen."

"Very funny," responded Tamiko. "But when it comes to being a gentleman, you're number 0!"

Although Tamiko thought Allan McCoy was a real jerk, she was—strangely enough—kind of attracted to him. He *was* sort of good-looking. Not as good-looking as Jeremy, but … Allan was a bit older and had bigger muscles. There was a certain sweetness about Jeremy that was lacking in Allan. However, Allan had this sense of humor—at times, rather unusual—that was lacking in Jeremy. For example, at a karate BBQ party where the students were selling food to raise money for the poor, Allan and his friends decided to tease Tamiko and her angelic ways by "selling" her hugs. They placed a banner above their sales table that read, "Everyone wants a hug from Tamiko! Two hundred yen per hug." As it turned out, Tamiko received many hugs and raised a lot of money!

After thinking about the several moments where Allan shined somewhat, Tamiko quickly reminded herself that he was just a bully … even if she did sense that there really was a good person underneath. "Oh well," she said to herself. "He's not my type!"

The door opened and class began. Today's lesson was all about the exciting roundhouse kick. Even more exciting was that old Grandmaster Shun was expected to pay the class a special visit and show some cool moves like he did before. Not only was the old bloke a great fighter, he was also a great speaker and storyteller; he was the kind of person who could talk about almost anything and you couldn't help but stop whatever you were doing and listen. Though he definitely had a serious/rigorous side, he was also "crazy" and comical at times. He could talk about something as silly as flying cars from outer space or peanut-flavored bubble gum and *still* keep you listening!

The instructor, Kenta, began teaching them the roundhouse kick. It looked pretty cool as he swung his leg high in a quick circle—just like in the movies! Then he showed it again, only slower this time so that everyone could see exactly how it was done. Some people, especially Allan and his friends, had already been practicing the move, as they wanted to be like Chuck Norris or Bruce Lee. Even Tamiko had tried it out a time or two before deciding it would be smarter to wait and learn to do it the right way.

As this was a rather "macho" karate move, some of the boys (especially Allan, of course) giggled while the girls practiced it. After a while, this got rather annoying for Tamiko and the other two girls, as it made them feel like they weren't really worth anything. Allan always said that karate "wasn't for girls" and that they were just wasting their time. Because of this, Tamiko was often tempted to just give up. But she couldn't; she had a purpose. She had to keep going if she were to stand any chance in defeating the monster at the spooky old house and rescuing the little girl.

After some more practicing in the training hall, Kenta had to leave the room momentarily; with the instructor gone, it was now time for Allan to do his thing.

"Ooooh, look," Allan began, using a girl's voice and looking at the three female students. "My name is Barbie, and I'm going to kick your sweet little butt. I call this the love ki … I mean the roundhouse kick. Here it comes!"

Allan spun around and did a slow-motion roundhouse kick that looked so silly and girly that even Tamiko and the other girls chuckled a bit. Driven by the attention he received, Allan did something else.

"Greeeetings, everyone!" said Allan to the class as he pretended to be the instructor.

"Oh, please!" said Tamiko to her buddy Gina.

"Tell me about it!" replied Gina.

"I'm Grandmaster McCoy, and I would like to review the deadly love strike," said Allan. "And then, the love tap. Would anybody like to show me either one, please? How about … Tamiko?"

"Oh, give it up, Allan!" said Tamiko. "Oh, excuse me. Give it up, 'Grandmaster McCoy'!"

"You're excused!" said Allan. "Now come show me the looooove strike or love tap—you choose."

"All right," said Tamiko. "As you wish."

Tamiko stepped over to Allan and prepared herself for the strike.

"I'm ready when you are," said Tamiko.

"On three," said Allan. "Ichi! Nee! San!"

Tamiko turned around swiftly and gave Allan a "love strike." Tamiko had meant to give him a hard kick in the stomach, but she missed and instead hit Allan in the crotch!

"Owwwww!" said Allan as he howled with pain. "That isn't the right way to do a—"

"Oh, I'm sorry!" said Tamiko. "I really didn't mean to hit you in the … you know."

The other students laughed and laughed.

"Good one!" said Gina.

"Nice!" said someone else.

Allan was about to do something else when Kenta returned, so he got back in his place as if nothing had happened and did his best to not appear in pain.

"And now," announced Kenta, "it's a pleasure to welcome back Grandmaster Shun!"

With that, karate master Shun entered the room, and everyone bowed in unison. Shun slowly scanned Kenta's students and smiled a little. He was a kind-looking fellow of at least seventy years. With his white hair, beard, and mustache, Tamiko couldn't help thinking he would make an excellent Japanese Santa Claus. In his karate costume, however, he appeared to be one of those old, wise martial arts grandmasters seen in the movies.

Knowing that he liked to begin his visits with some sort of story, the entire class was now waiting for him to speak.

"Hummmmmmmmm!" he began like a Buddha in deep meditation. Then he sang a droll little song about something, briefly greeted the students, and began his opening story.

Chapter 20
Elevator Problem

"Karate, kung fu, tae kwon do, jujitsu—any of the major martial arts, in the wrong hands, can be *deadly*," he began. "When you strike your opponent, you should never use full force, for it is much easier to kill someone than you think. Karate is not a game. It's not even a sport. It's an art and a way of life. A student and good friend of mine—and a great fighter, too—said to me, 'You know, this karate stuff is really cool and all, but I never got the chance to really use it.' As they say in the West, he never really got the chance to kick someone's butt!"

Everyone burst out laughing at this comment. Then, Shun continued his lecture.

"But one day an intruder, some guy on a motorcycle, broke into his house, and while the intruder was stealing my friend's treasured possessions, the two met ... face-to-face!"

Everyone was totally silent, staring at him with their ears wide open, waiting to hear the rest of the story. Grandmaster Shun carried on.

"Now, my friend had the golden opportunity to use his great karate skills—and tae kwon do skills—and finally kick someone's butt!"

Once again, everyone laughed in unison.

"As you've all probably guessed, there was a fight. The intruder threw the first punch, which my friend was able to easily block. Then he threw the intruder to the floor. The thief got up and tried to attack him once again, and the two fought for a short while, kicking and punching each other. Finally, my friend decided to get a little more serious and used his roundhouse kick to finish him off. The intruder still had his helmet on, though, so the kick was not too effective. Even though the kick didn't knock him out, it provoked the intruder and made him really angry. So the intruder pulled out some pepper spray and sprayed my friend in the eyes. As my friend squealed with pain, the motorcyclist removed his helmet and assaulted him. My friend, still rubbing his closed eyes, was able to sense where the intruder was by just using his ears. And then …"

"Then what happened?" asked one of the students, breaking the silence.

"Then my friend used a roundhouse kick on the intruder with full force. Because he was unable to see, he thought that the motorcyclist still had his helmet on!" he explained.

After a short pause, everyone started asking, "What happened to the intruder?" and Shun spoke again.

"I'm not sure," he said. "But my friend *never* heard of him again!"

The class chuckled and giggled.

"But I would have liked to have been there … to have been a fly on the wall!" he added. "I'm curious. I really wonder what his head looked like after that last roundhouse kick."

Shun was so funny! Just the way he explained the story and acted it out was better than any TV show.

"So, like I was saying, one should never underestimate the—" Shun stopped abruptly when he noticed that Allan was too busy joking around with one of his buddies to listen.

"Shut up, you little ninny!" Shun exclaimed half-jokingly. Everyone, even Allan himself, immediately burst out laughing. Shun's magical presence seemed to bring everyone together, and Allan didn't really seem so bad anymore.

As Grandmaster Shun continued his speech about "how dangerous martial arts really are," Allan once again interrupted.

"So, I'm the second-most-dangerous guy in the room," Allan said, smiling.

"Allan," replied Shun. "He's too proud of himself; he has 'elevator problem'!"

With that, everyone broke into laughter, while Allan wore only a slight grin.

Then, as Shun talked some more, one of Allan's friends spoke out of line to one of his friends. Once again, Shun said, "Be quiet, you little ninny!" and more laughter was heard. When Allan made another smart remark, Tamiko asked why he thought he was so "big." Several students immediately jumped in, giving their explanations as to why Allan acted this way.

"Because he thinks he's the best," one of them said.

"It's because he just *has* to win," said another.

"No, it's because he's just afraid of losing!" said yet another.

"It's because he has elevator problem!" said Grandmaster Shun once again.

Everybody laughed so hard that they were in tears. Even the instructor was chuckling and snorting. Too quickly class was over, and, aside from Grandmaster Shun, everybody left the room—everybody, that is, except for Tamiko. As she had during Shun's previous visit, Tamiko stayed behind to seek some advice. Today she wanted to discuss her planned use of karate and tae kwon do to rescue the girl; she also needed some guidance on how to handle Allan McCoy.

"We meet again!" exclaimed Shun as Tamiko approached him.

"Yes, indeed we do," answered Tamiko.

"I sense that something is troubling your soul," began Shun. "I suppose that is why you are sitting here before me."

"Yes, Master," Tamiko responded. "I have … I have a mission I feel I must accomplish, and … well … it's about rescuing a little girl from some big man that's being real mean to her."

"And you believe your martial art skills can come in handy?" asked Shun.

"Yeah. I mean, I know I'm much younger than he is, but if I were to hit him in just the right place, then maybe I'd be able to, like, knock him out for a short while and rescue the girl … with the help of my friends."

Tamiko had figured that, after hearing Shun talk about karate being deadly and so forth, she just might stand a chance against the monster after all. All she had to know was how to fight him.

"I admire your courage, but you're a little too young, Tamiko," replied Shun.

"But I'd have three of my friends with me," said Tamiko.

"I hear you, but you're really thinking with your heart and not with your mind," replied Shun. "I remember when I was a boy, around your age or maybe a bit older, I felt just like you one day. I was on a quest to free a good friend of mine who was kidnapped and held for ransom."

"What happened?" asked Tamiko.

Shun continued. "I set out with my friends to where my other friend was being imprisoned thinking that we could just run in there and take down the kidnapper. We broke in and confronted him; in fact, we gave him a few good strikes and blows and, together, almost defeated him. But then the kidnapper pulled out a gun, and we joined my friend as prisoners."

"How did you escape?" asked Tamiko.

Shun recalled that the police finally came and set them all free. However, his experience was rather unpleasant to say the least.

Then, Tamiko asked Shun what he suggested she do about the situation with the young girl.

"I suggest that you find out exactly who you'll be dealing with," replied Shun. "If you're sure this girl is in some kind of danger, I think it would be wiser to call the police rather than try to handle things on your own."

"But I can't prove anything!" cried Tamiko.

"I can't tell you what to do," explained Shun. "Only your heart can tell you what to do, and only your mind can tell you what not to. Anyway, I think you have lots to think about. Whatever you do, just be careful. Like somebody once said, knowing others is intelligence. Knowing yourself is true wisdom."

Then Tamiko talked about her angel missions and some of her pranks before switching to the topic of Allan.

"What do you do with a guy like Allan?" inquired Tamiko.

"Water off a duck's back," responded Shun. "All he really wants is attention, and he tries to get it destructively rather than constructively."

"But why does he act the way he does?" asked Tamiko.

"I sense that something happened to him when he was a little boy," said Shun. "The Allan you see, that we see, is not the true one. We're all good in our own unique ways ... well, not always, but you know what I mean. Sadly, though, many of us take the wrong path, which only darkens our soul, like some kind of plague, thus hiding the real beauty we possess inside."

"But what's this 'plague' he has? What kind of problem is that?" asked Tamiko.

Shun grinned slightly. "Like I said before, he has elevator problem!"

Chapter 21~
Get the Girl! (Part 1)

Tamiko and her friends had thought about it, pondered it, reviewed it, and played it out in their minds. They were going to rescue the girl today! Tamiko remembered what her parents had told her, though—to stop peeping into other peoples' homes—but this was no longer a matter of curious peeping. This was a matter of urgency, for Tamiko's gut instinct kept telling her that she and her friends had to break in and get the poor girl out of that awful place. Their strategy was simple: slip into the house when the door was unlocked and the bad guy was not around. Then they would sneak into the bedroom, get the girl, and quickly make their way out without the monster even knowing what happened. Using this strategy, they would make life easy for themselves and avoid having to fight off the villain—that is, of course, if everything worked as planned.

Just in case there was any kind of an encounter with the man, Tamiko was prepared to put up a fight with the help of her friends. Hopefully, he wouldn't be too good a fighter, but if he proved otherwise, Tamiko decided it would probably be best just to run out of the place and try a different strategy the next time around.

After Tamiko's tutoring session, she—just out of

curiosity—went on the Internet and looked up the words she had seen on the truck that had taken the little girl's dog away. Tamiko figured that maybe she could find something that would give her a better understanding of what had happened. Maybe the dog had a deadly disease or illness, or maybe it was pooping and peeing all over the place. Tamiko searched and searched until she finally found a match. She quickly called the place but didn't learn much. But then, just as she was about to hang up, Tamiko made an interesting discovery! The transportation service didn't serve the location of the girl's house. *So what was the truck doing there, and what was really in the bag?* Tamiko wondered.

Tamiko and her crew got together and started cycling over to the old house. They planned to get there before the man came home from work.

"I just found out something!" said Tamiko.

"What's that, Tam?" said Jeremy.

"I called about the dog truck, and the person I talked to told me that they don't serve this part of town."

"Are you sure about that?" said Hina.

"The guy sounded pretty sure to me!" said Tamiko.

"Then what was the truck doing there?" said Rin.

"And what was in the bag?" said Jeremy.

"I really don't know," said Tamiko. "But something's very creepy about all this!"

Hina had some startling news of her own to share. "You're not going to believe what I found out!" she said.

"Let's hear it," said Jeremy.

"Okay. I just talked to our friend Mr. Data Analyst at Fujinomiya Hospital. I asked him about the children of Kevin Powell, and he told me that both kids were declared *dead* just over a month ago!"

"But how could that be?" said Tamiko. "We saw the girl

alive … with our own eyes!"

"Now this is *really* getting strange!" added Rin.

They continued to discuss their astonishing discoveries and tried to come up with an explanation, but nothing really seemed to make any sense. The contents of the bag remained a mystery, and the "deaths" of the two kids became a new one.

Their heads still spinning with questions, the Fuji-san Clan began their rescue mission. As they were rather early, they went up to the door—as they had awhile back—and checked to see if the door was unlocked by chance; as they had figured, it was locked. Then, like they also had tried awhile back, they decided to simply knock on the door and ring the doorbell in the hope that maybe she wasn't locked up and would come running over to unlock the door. So they split up into two teams—one for ringing the doorbell, and the other for checking through the side window to make sure the villain wasn't inside.

Tamiko and Hina went to the front door and rang the doorbell. Nothing happened. Then, they knocked harder. Again, nothing disturbed the silence, and Jeremy and Rin didn't see anybody inside. Then, suddenly, a blunt thumping sound could be heard, like someone was pounding a door. "It must be the girl, locked in her bedroom!" Tamiko said. Once again they sounded the doorbell and knocked, but even louder this time, and again some dull thuds were heard in reply.

"She's trying to tell us she's there. She must be trapped inside," whispered Tamiko to Hina. "We have to—"

Suddenly they noticed a car heading down the street.

"Go over to the side!" ordered Tamiko as the car approached.

The vehicle continued on its way.

"Phhhhhhew!" sighed the rescue team in relief.

Then, Jeremy suggested trying the back door, but there was one problem: the kids would have to climb over a tall fence and be quick about it. So the gang crawled over the fence one by one as fast as they could, helping each other as they went along.

The backyard was rather square with high wooden fencing all around. The front of the yard had three windows, one on each side of the patio door and a smaller basement window through which the kids could see a desk full of papers with a computer on it. The grass was poorly maintained, and there was an old barbecue in one of the far corners, and bushes and a small tree in the other. There were also a few toys lying around, looking as though they hadn't been used for ages. The place smelled of rotten eggs and some kind of nut.

The four crept up to the door and tried to open it—no luck! Next, they hit the button for the doorbell—no sound! The doorbell must have been broken or something, so they decided to knock—very softly at first and then harder and harder. This was Tamiko's idea, for she reasoned that when the thumping sounds from the girl became audible, it would give them some indication of how isolated she was. It was only after the four knocked real hard that they heard the thumps from the girl.

"What do we do now?" asked Rin.

"I don't know," replied Tamiko.

"Maybe I can pry it open with that old screwdriver over there," Jeremy suggested.

Just as Jeremy grabbed the screwdriver and started to pry the door open, a car pulled into the driveway. It was the man!

"Let's get out of here!" whispered Hina loudly.

"We don't have enough time!" said Rin. "He's coming!"

The monster man forcefully opened the front door and marched inside. Terror-stricken, the four looked in through one of the windows fearing that the man might head to the backyard. As it turned out, he mumbled something, grabbed a beer from the refrigerator, and disappeared from view. *Did he go into the girl's room?* Tamiko wondered as they all listened silently for something to happen. Finally Jeremy spoke.

"Now's our chance to get out of this yard," he said.

Just then they heard some disturbing noises. Even though the back windows were shut, they could hear the man growling and snarling; only the sound was muffled by the closed windows and the kids couldn't really make out what was being said. This was followed by some thumps and thuds—very much like the ones before.

"It's time to go over the fence," said Jeremy. "When we get to the other side, we can make some noise to get him into the yard, and then we can go through the front door and get the girl!"

"That sounds like a plan to me!" replied the others.

The group of four had just begun to climb back over the fence, starting with Rin, when the man suddenly headed toward the backyard!

"He's coming!" cried Tamiko as Hina began her climb with the help of Jeremy.

Rin, who had already made it over the fence, waited fearfully for the others.

Chapter 22~
Get the Girl! (Part 2)

Scared stiff, Jeremy let Hina down, and the three of them swiftly scurried over to one of the far corners of the yard and hid behind the bushes. The man hurriedly opened the back door and made a beeline to the barbecue. The threesome shuffled around the bush a bit to avoid being seen. Through the bushes, they were able to get a decent view of the monster—thirty-some years old, white, about six feet tall and of a medium build with black hair and small, snakelike eyes. He grabbed some cooking utensils from under the barbecue and made his way back to the house. Just before the man reached the door, Jeremy accidentally rustled the bushes.

The man stopped and turned around. Then, he pounded toward the bushes like an angry elephant. The rescuers just stood there in dismay as they saw him getting closer. Then Rin, on the other side of the fence and just barely able to see through, tossed a rock toward one of the near corners of the yard. When it struck the ground, the man reversed his course and investigated the area where the rock had fallen. Puzzled, he went back inside the house.

"Wheeeew, that was close," whispered Tamiko.

"You can say that again," agreed the other two.

The three remained hidden behind the bush a while

longer and then rapidly climbed over the fence to join Rin.

"Good thinking!" cried Tamiko to Rin. "He almost had us!"

"No problem. You had me worried there," said Rin. "Did you see the man?"

"We saw some of him," said Jeremy.

"He's one scary-looking dude," said Hina. "He sort of looks like a snake!"

"Maybe he's a vampire," added Jeremy.

"Kind of looks like one," said Tamiko. "Now we gotta lure him into the yard again and get the girl. Let's hope he left the front door unlocked."

With their walkie-talkies on, Hina volunteered to make some noise at the back of the yard while the others waited near the front of the house. When everyone was in position, Hina banged against the fence and then watched what was going on inside the yard through a slit in the fencing.

In moments, the man raced through the door and stomped around the tree as he tried to find the source of the noise. Hina immediately radioed Tamiko and told her that "it was time." With that, Tamiko and the others barged into the house and frantically searched the place for the little girl. The inside was messy but somewhat tidier than the last time. The air was stuffy, and it smelled like burnt toast.

"Little girl! Little girl! Where are you?" they cried.

Meanwhile, the man had given up his search and was making his way back to the house. Hina made more noise, and the man grumbled a bit as he turned back to investigate the racket once more.

Inside the house, the little girl replied to the cries of the rescuers with several "clonks" and "clunks" followed by something that sounded like "Mmmmmm!" But before they could find her, the smoke detector, picking up the stench of burning grilled cheese sandwiches, went off with an ear-piercing, high-pitched buzz.

The threesome rushed pell-mell toward the bedroom where they thought the girl was located. They opened the bedroom door and shouted for her a second time. The monster man, despite Hina's attempts to keep him in the yard, ran inside the house to check out the situation with the fire alarm. Noticing his smoking meal, he rushed over and removed the frying pan from the stovetop, turned off the burner, and then turned his attention to fanning the smoke away from the smoke detector.

Taking full advantage of the chaos, the rescue team hurriedly continued looking for the girl, but there was no sign of her anywhere! Then, after barely hearing some more thuds over the incessant, blaring alarm, they scurried into an adjacent room. Again, there was no sign of any girl! *She must be here somewhere!* Tamiko thought, dumbfounded.

As the team abandoned the room, they saw the man trying to silence the alarm with his back to them. While all this was happening, Hina stood outside paralyzed, not knowing exactly what to do. Inside, the threesome briefly peeked into just one more room only to find it devoid of any human life.

"Where could she be?" Tamiko whispered. The threesome finally gave up, as they figured that their time had almost run out and they couldn't do much more anyway. Hopefully, the alarm would whine for just a bit longer and the three would have enough time to exit by the front door unheard.

Just then, the man gave up fanning the air, ripped the alarm off the ceiling, and pulled out the battery. The irritating noise stopped, and the kids could now be easily heard as they scurried toward the door. The monster spun his head around and ran after them like a bulldog.

"Hey! What are you doing in my house?" he yelled. "Get outta here before I throw you out, you little pests!"

Tamiko boldly retorted as she made her way to the door, "You won't get away with this, you beast! I'm calling the police!"

The three were almost out of the house when the man caught up to them.

"I *am* the police!" he screamed. "Now get lost! And if you ever come back, you'll be in a *lot* of trouble!"

He shoved the kids the rest of the way out and slammed the door. The three failed rescuers dashed over to the side of the house, where Hina waited looking incredibly relieved. "Oh, I am so glad you guys are okay. I was so worried!"

"So were we!" said Tamiko. "Now let's get outta here!"

With that, the reunited foursome jumped onto their bicycles and tore out of there like the devil was after them. They pedaled through the streets and over to the corner store where they eventually stopped. They hopped off their bikes. They walked and talked.

"Mission unaccomplished," sobbed Tamiko. "She's in there. We just have to get her out of that place!"

"We did our best," replied Hina.

"But where was she?" said Jeremy. "We looked everywhere!"

"I don't know!" said Rin. "How could that be?"

"It sounded like she was … inside some kind of hidden closet or something," said Tamiko.

Rin suddenly froze like a Buddha statue, horror-stricken. "Yeah!" she said. "The sound was, like … coming from inside the wall!"

"Are you serious?" said Hina. "She's being locked up in a …?"

"That's certainly what it looks like," said Tamiko.

"So *now* what do we do?" asked Rin.

Nobody was really sure how to respond. They all just stood there like a cluster of ice sculptures.

"I don't know," Jeremy responded. "But so much for calling the cops. He *is* a cop!"

"But what if he's just saying that?" wondered Hina aloud.

"Yeah," agreed Rin. "Maybe he's lying just to scare us all away!"

"I don't know," added Tamiko. "He sounded pretty sure of himself!"

Disheartened, the four slowly got onto their bikes and peddled away.

Next time! Tamiko thought. Despite the possibility that the man was a cop, she vowed that there would be a next time!

Chapter 23

Blocks of Wood and Slabs of Concrete

"Get outta here before I throw you out, you little pests! I *am* the police! Get outta here before I throw you out!"

These words played over and over again in the minds of the Fuji-san Clan, especially in that of Tamiko. Not only could they hear the beast against the dull thuds from the girl, but they could also see his face—sinister, cold, vicious, snakelike. It was like he had no heart, like he was some kind of robot that was programmed to do only harm.

The four had to come up with another plan; they had to get the girl out of her dungeon of despair—wherever it was. Like Rin said, it was like the girl was trapped inside a wall. But neither Tamiko nor her friends ever saw any kind of door or opening that might have led to the girl.

What Tamiko needed was another one of those flashbacks or sudden astonishing realizations that would point her in the right direction. Knowing that thinking too hard would only cloud her intuition, Tamiko relaxed her mind as she made her way to the village grocery store the following day to run an errand.

Just before she reached her destination, Tamiko came across the street game where you win money by successfully breaking blocks of wood and slabs of concrete.

"Come on, little girl. Give it a try!" cried the game host.

She paused for a moment and was just about to leave when something inside of her told her to stay and check it out.

"I don't think I'll really win anything, but I'll go for it," said Tamiko.

"That a girl!" the host responded. "All you have to do to win is break some wood and concrete. The concrete sounds difficult, but the bricks are very thin … and for a little one like you, I'll make them half size! It's easy at first and gets harder and harder. Let's start with the small blocks of wood. That'll be two hundred yen for the first three levels."

Tamiko paid up the first amount and prepared to chop the first block of wood. With almost no effort at all, she snapped the block in half.

"Huuuurray!" cheered the host. "I knew you could do it! Now on to level two!"

Tamiko raised her hand once again and broke the second block without too much difficulty.

"Nice one!" the host exclaimed. "Level three now."

Tamiko concentrated a bit more this time, knowing that it would be a bit more difficult. As she struck the block, she thought of the monster man and his last words again … and of Allan and his snide remarks. With a swift blow to the block, Tamiko was just able to split it in two.

The host cheered once again and asked Tamiko to make a decision.

"Way to go! Now you can either take your winnings of one hundred yen—that means I give you back three hundred yen—or you can go on to the next round!" explained the game host.

Tamiko decided to go further. The second round, like the first, consisted of a set of three more wooden blocks.

After that was the concrete. Tamiko concentrated and broke the first block just as easily, if not more so, than the previous one!

Excited, she went on to the next block. Again she succeeded but only by a slight bit. Apparently, the game host was giving her a chance by having her chop through thinner pieces of wood, as opposed to the "standard" game for grown-ups.

The third time around, Tamiko didn't break the block completely in half but ruptured it. Then, Tamiko heard a voice.

"Ha ha ha ha ha ha! You didn't break it! You're not strong enough, you little pest … you little failure!"

The voice was that of the monster! And it sounded like it was coming from behind her! Tamiko whirled around only to realize that it was all in her head, for nobody was there.

"Get lost, you meanie!" mumbled Tamiko.

Although Tamiko didn't fully break the block, the game host gave her the benefit of the doubt and asked Tamiko if she was ready for the concrete level. Tamiko decided to give it a chance and triumphed in snapping the first slab of concrete—like the host had said before, it was rather thin. In the attempt to break the second slab she failed, and the game host kept all the money.

Once again Tamiko heard a voice, but this time it was someone else.

"Ooooooh, angel Tamiko. You thought you could break through concrete with a love tap. You must think you're the Karate Kid. When will you ever learn that karate's for guys, not cutesy little girls, Tamiko!"

It was Allan McCoy this time. Tamiko felt as though Allan had paired up with the monster man somehow and the two were on a mission to break her down in any way they could.

"Shut up," said Tamiko. "Go pick on someone else."

"Are you all right?" said the host. "Don't feel bad. You did very well! Not everybody makes it to that level. Just keep on practicing and you'll do it. You know, when you chop you have to put some oomph into it—I didn't hear you scream."

"Oh well," Tamiko said to herself. "As they all say, 'Better luck next time.'"

Just as she turned away, Tamiko got the flashback she'd been waiting for!

Chapter 24
Operation "Reverse Thief"

"I have to tell them!" Tamiko told herself the next day.

She really wanted to tell them yesterday, just after her remembrance, but her friends were at an information session for their Chinese summer camp.

Today, another beautiful, sunny day with the occasional gust of warm wind, the Fuji-san Clan decided to meet at the big oak tree again to discuss their rescue attempt. Jeremy and Tamiko showed up first.

"Ever seen an Asian giant hornet?" asked Jeremy.

"I've seen them in books and on the Internet, but I don't think I've ever encountered one," said Tamiko. "Anyway, I have to tell you—"

"I saw some here the other day!" said Jeremy with excitement. "They're big … real big! Even if you're not allergic to them, you can die from their sting! In fact, each year in Japan, there are more deaths from these things than from all other animals combined!"

"You're starting to scare me now," said Tamiko. "But if one comes after me, I'll just use my roundhouse kick and knock it out! Now about what I wanted to tell you—"

"You and your karate and martial arts," said Jeremy. "It's all just an art that looks real cool. It isn't really effective or anything. It's—"

"Is too!" said Tamiko.

"To fight, what you need … is strength," said Jeremy as he showed off his biceps. Then he lifted up his shirt and showed off his chest muscles.

"Karate is all about mind," said Tamiko. "Not muscle!"

"Oh yeah? Show me!" said Jeremy.

"All right then," said Tamiko. "I take that as a challenge!"

So the two began a "playful" fight. Tamiko was determined to show Jeremy just how effective her karate skills really were.

"Come on, Tam. Show me what you got!"

"You asked for it," said Tamiko.

With that, Tamiko did a knee strike. Jeremy tried to block it but failed. He got hit in his left knee and almost fell to the ground.

"See!" said Tamiko proudly.

"Not bad for a girl," said Jeremy. "But I'm still not convinced."

Tamiko delivered another knee strike, this time to Jeremy's right knee. Once again, Jeremy nearly fell to the ground.

"What do you think now?" asked Tamiko.

"Okay. I wasn't really trying, though. I was just being easy on you!"

Jeremy, somewhat embarrassed, tried to punch Tamiko in the shoulder. Tamiko grabbed Jeremy's arm and threw him to the ground.

"You want to get tough now?" said Jeremy, smiling. "I'll show you tough."

Jeremy grabbed Tamiko and tried to throw her to the ground. He almost succeeded, but Tamiko gave him an elbow jab, backed up, and gave him a side kick. This knocked Jeremy a little off balance, and Tamiko tried another kick but missed. Jeremy sort of laughed at Tamiko and said, "Hiiiyaaa! Wooohaaa!" while at the same time moving his feet and arms all over the place like some kid trying to be Bruce Lee. Tamiko managed to hit Jeremy in the knee once again, and Jeremy started to get angry. He charged at Tamiko, and they grabbed each other like two bulls with their horns locked.

Both still standing, they wrestled it out. Tamiko tried to throw Jeremy to the ground once again but failed. She just wasn't strong enough. Jeremy, though, managed to push Tamiko to the ground, thanks to the branch of a fallen tree that tripped her. Jeremy lunged in to pin her to the ground, but Tamiko rolled out of the way and kicked him. Surprised, Jeremy tried once again and finally grasped Tamiko. They turned around in circles as they wrestled each other. At one point, Jeremy was on top of Tamiko … and then Tamiko was on top of Jeremy. Finally, Jeremy used all of his strength and pinned Tamiko to the ground, sitting on her.

"So, tell me again—just how effective is karate?" said Jeremy.

"Urghhhh! Urgh!" said Tamiko as she tried to squirm herself free.

"So tell me!" said Jeremy.

"Karate is more effective than you think!" said Tamiko, blushing.

"You know, I really like it when you …"

"When I what?" asked Tamiko.

"When you …"

Jeremy moved his face ever so slightly toward Tamiko's. It was almost like he was thinking about kissing her!

"I have to tell you something," said Jeremy.

"What? What do you have to tell me?" asked Tamiko in a daze.

"Rin ... she's just ... I mean ..." said Jeremy just as Hina and Rin showed up.

"Uhummmm!" exclaimed Hina. "What have we here?"

Jeremy and Tamiko turned their heads at the same time.

"Uhhhh ... we were just having a ... fun fight," said Jeremy.

"Yeah!" said Tamiko.

"Fun fight?" said Hina. "Yeah, right!"

"It looked like you were having more than fun, Jeremy!" said Rin.

"I was just ... look, it's not what you think!" said Jeremy. "I challenged Tamiko to a little fun fight, just to see how effective karate was, and then ..."

"And then what?" asked Hina.

"And then I ... pinned her to the ground. And that's when you came along."

As for Hina and Rin, they really didn't know what to think. The four talked about it some more and then Tamiko got down to business.

"We're all here to discuss yesterday's rescue attempt and a flashback I got yesterday."

"Let's hear it," said Jeremy.

"I was playing that street game. You know, the one down by ... okay, I'll just get to the point. Our mystery girl, we heard her make many banging noises. But ever since our second visit to her house, when the girl was sick, we've never heard her scream—except for that one time when the man was beating her."

"Yeah, you're right!" said Rin. "You'd think she'd yell for help or something, but, like you said, she never really did."

Just as Tamiko was about to say something, Jeremy

broke in.

"I get it! She's gagged!"

"My thoughts exactly," said Tamiko.

Then Rin asked a good question.

"But if she's gagged, why doesn't she just take it off. Obviously her hands aren't tied; she's beating the door."

"Yeah," said Hina.

"I think that's because she's banging the door with her—" started Tamiko.

"Feet?" said Hina.

"Bingo! You got it!" said Tamiko.

With that, the Fuji-san Clan jumped on their bikes and made a beeline to the old house. This time, they stealthily walked over to the curtain-covered window of what they thought was the girl's bedroom and knocked on it. No response. They knocked harder. Still no response.

"Could she be sleeping?" asked Jeremy.

"Maybe she's not even home. There's no car," said Tamiko.

They mustered up their courage and banged on the window but, once again, heard nothing.

"We'll be back," said Tamiko.

They finally left the premises and made their way toward the park in Tamiko's neighborhood.

"Just five more days," said Hina, "and we'll be eating Chinese food and making Chinese friends."

"And I'll be either mowing the lawn with my dad or washing windows with Mom … or picking up the dog's unko!" said Tamiko.

"That's sounds about as exciting as watching ice melt," said Jeremy.

Jeremy challenged the three girls to a bicycle race to the park. Just as the four were about to peddle away, a young

Japanese boy ran by in tears. He raced into his house and slammed the door behind him.

"What's wrong with him?" asked Tamiko.

"Beats me," said Hina. "Maybe he got in a fight or something."

"Wait a minute!" said Jeremy. "I think I've seen that kid before."

"Who is he?" asked Hina. "I didn't really see his face."

"That's the delivery boy," said Jeremy. "You know, the little Japanese kid who's always on his bike and takes all kinds of pictures with his mini camera."

"That's interesting," said Rin. "He's *always* riding his bike. I don't think I've ever seen him once with two feet on the ground until now."

"Maybe his bike is broken or something," said Tamiko. "Or maybe he's just tired of peddling all the time."

The four then raced the short distance to the park; it was a tie between Jeremy and Tamiko. As the friends rolled around on their bikes and talked, they noticed the little Japanese boy again. He was searching all over the ground in circles for something by the trees.

"Looks like he lost something," said Hina.

The boy looked and looked but couldn't find whatever he was searching for. Then, he produced a cell phone and started talking.

"I can't find my keys anywhere! What am I going to do? My bicycle just got stolen, and now I lost my keys! … I know we hardly have any money … I need a bike … Somebody stole it … Somebody stole it!" said the boy as he began walking back home crying.

"Let's see if we can find his keys," said Tamiko.

The four looked all over the place but didn't come up with anything. Then, Hina had another idea.

"Why don't each of us put some of our money together and give it to the boy so he can buy himself a new bicycle?"

"That's a great idea!" said Tamiko.

So the foursome left the park and sped over to their houses to gather money from their piggy banks. Afterward, they got together again and put their combined money into an envelope. Then, they made their way over to the little boy's house. As they were passing through the park, they spotted a little squirrel hopping around something curiously. It was the boy's keys with the mini camera attached to the keychain! They quickly peddled over and picked them up and then continued on to the boy's house.

When they arrived, it appeared as though nobody was home, so they carefully unlocked the door with the keys and placed the envelope of money on the kitchen table with the keys on top. There was only one problem now.

"How do we leave and lock the—?" asked Hina.

Suddenly, footsteps marched toward the kitchen.

"Someone's home!" said Tamiko. "Let's get out of here!"

The four scurried out of the house like a group of frightened rabbits. Although they weren't physically caught, they were seen and heard.

"Someone's been in our kitchen!" cried the mom as she entered the kitchen. "I saw them! They were at the table! My ring! My ring! They must have taken my ring!"

The terrified mother gazed down at the kitchen table and saw the keys and her untouched diamond ring. Then the boy barged into the room.

"What's going on, Mom?"

"I thought that ... I don't get it," she said. "When people break into homes, they usually steal something, but ..."

"But what, Mom?"

"Look! They gave you your keys back, and they didn't even touch my ring!"

"My keys! I've got my keys back!" said the boy excitedly as he grabbed them.

"And what's this?" said the mom, confused, when she noticed the envelope. "It says 'For a new bike' on it. Here … you open it."

The boy tore open the envelope and found enough money to buy himself a new bike! Both were stunned. "How did this happen? Who is behind all this? Why did they do it?" the mother wondered aloud.

"Yippeeee! Yippeeee! Yippeeee!" cheered the boy.

"Oh my! Our lives are back in order!" The mother cried in relief as she hugged her son. "Thank you! Oh, thank you, whoever you are!"

"Where did this come from?" asked the boy.

The mother looked upward.

"There must be an angel watching over us!"

Chapter 25
Saving Maya

"Let's go! Let's go save Maya!" cried Tamiko two days later as she and the others, including her angel friends and a special someone, made their way over to Maya's house to tell her family the wonderful news.

Maya was a ten-year-old Japanese girl with leukemia who was in great need of a kidney; one of the angels' pending missions was to find a donor for her. The days were getting fewer, and neither the hospital nor the angel gang had found a donor ... until this morning.

Her name was Taka. She was eleven years old and a distant cousin of Hina's who happened to have a blood type that was compatible with Maya's. Taka, with the consent of her parents, agreed to go along with the surgery. The angels had planned another attempt to rescue the mystery girl today, but they rescheduled that mission for the next day because of the appearance of Taka.

On the way over to Maya's house, the angels thought back on how the mission began.

It all started several weeks ago when the angels were playing around at some obscure school playground. Tamiko, Hina, and Rin were in turn swinging from bar to bar on the monkey bars while Jeremy captured the action on his new pocket camera/video camera.

"Only three more to go now," said Jeremy as he filmed Tamiko.

As it turned out, Tamiko raced to the finish but slipped on the last bar. Then the two other girls gave it try, and afterward the four watched the videos. At first, they didn't think too much of them, but then Tamiko listened to the playback with Jeremy's earbuds.

"The sound is incredible," said Tamiko. "Now, I can hear everything!"

Indeed, Tamiko was very impressed with the high quality stereo sound that Jeremy had been raving about. She heard everything from cars whizzing by in the distance to the softest bird tweets. Then, just before watching Rin's attempt at crossing the bars, Tamiko heard in the video some Japanese boy named Kannon tell somebody else that his sister was in the hospital with leukemia and in desperate need of a kidney.

"They haven't found a donor yet," said the boy, nearly crying. "Without one, she only has like a month to live."

With the boy's name and the fact that he was wearing a distinctive baseball jersey, the angels were able to track down both Kannon and his hospitalized sister. Ever since, the angels had kept an eye on Maya, inquiring about her condition and whether any Good Samaritans had volunteered to give up a kidney; sadly, no donors had come her way. Meanwhile, the angels worked hard to find a donor themselves. They searched the Internet, talked to friends and family members, called hospitals and medical clinics, and even asked people in the streets if they would be willing to donate a kidney to save the life of poor little Maya. Despite their efforts, no donor had yet been found.

Throughout the days, the angels watched over the family; they attended at least two of Kannon's baseball games and continued to check up on his sister. They saw what Maya's critical condition did to Kannon. They saw what it did to his family.

The father got angrier and angrier as Maya's days ran out, and he took a good portion of this anger out on his son Kannon.

"You can do better than that, you loser!" shouted the father to his boy after an unvictorious baseball game. "You didn't even make it to second base!"

Then, the mother would step in and try to calm her husband, but this only ended up making things worse. It finally came to a point where the angels couldn't put up with it anymore, and decided to pay a visit to the family and confront them face-to-face.

"Who ... who in the world *are* you kids?" asked the parents.

"We're simply four people who care—about you and your daughter Maya," said Tamiko. "We understand what you're going through. We all want Maya to find a donor and pull through, but that's no reason to destroy yourselves."

Then, the angels told the parents of their involvement in trying to find a donor, but the father angrily bombarded the angels with questions. The mother tried to cool him off, but doing so only worsened the situation. The kids did everything they could to calm things down, but they didn't succeed and eventually got kicked out of the house.

"Mind your own business!" said the father. "And don't come back!"

That's where things left off.

As for now, the angels were eagerly on their way to Maya's house with Taka and her parents to tell the family the good news.

On arrival, the angels rang the doorbell and hid Taka behind them to prepare the surprise. After a long wait, the door finally opened to reveal two faces that suddenly turned sour at the sight of Tamiko and her friends.

"What are *you* doing here again?" asked the father. "I thought I told you to never—"

"We have something to tell you," said Tamiko as she slowly moved forward. "It's good news."

"What's this ... good news of yours?"

Tamiko and her friends stepped to the side to reveal Hina's cousin.

"Uh ... hello," said Maya's mother. "And just who are you?"

"Her name is Taka," said Tamiko.

"She's my cousin," said Hina. "She has a blood type that's compatible with your daughter's. We told her about Maya, and she volunteered to be a donor."

Maya's parents stood there in awe with their mouths wide open, not knowing what to say.

"You see, it's kind of a long story," said Tamiko. "Let's just say that we found out about Maya's condition a while back—several weeks ago—and we have been trying to find a donor ever since."

"And now, here she is," said Rin.

"Just in time too," added Jeremy.

The parents remained frozen for a while, and then the mother raced over to Taka and threw her arms around her, crying.

"Thank you! Oh, thank you so much!"

Then Maya's parents thanked the angels and apologized for having ousted them from their house the other day.

With that, everyone raced to the hospital only to discover that Maya's condition had suddenly deteriorated. To make matters worse, the doctors said that she would have less than a 50 percent chance of surviving the operation.

"Oh, Maya! My dear Maya!" cried the mother.

The doctors immediately performed the procedure despite the dwindling odds of Maya surviving. The operation itself was a success, but Maya wouldn't wake up!

"Oh no!" cried Maya's parents. "Wake up, Maya! Please wake up!"

The doctors and nurses did everything they could to revive Maya, but it appeared that the kidney transplant was performed a little too late. At this point, nothing more could be done to bring Maya back. Then, when it seemed like all hope was lost, Maya slowly came around.

"Where am I?" asked Maya as she woke up.

"Oh, Maya! You're back! You're back!" cried the parents. "You just had surgery. You have a new kidney!"

"They did it!" said Taka, lying in the hospital bed next to Maya's.

"This is, like, the best day of my life!" said Kannon.

"The operation, it all went well? Maya's going to be okay?" the mother asked the doctor.

"No problems!" said the doctor. "She'll have to stay here for several days, but, from what I can see, she'll be just fine!"

The parents and Kannon thanked the angels once again as they shed more tears of joy. Maya was going to live!

Mission accomplished!

CHAPTER 26

DOWN THROUGH THE CHIMNEY AND RESCUE!

"Mystery girl, here we come!" exclaimed Tamiko as she peddled her way over to the house with her friends.

"Like Santa Claus!" added Jeremy.

Tonight, the four were determined to rescue the girl in a rather imaginative way. After dark, they planned to climb up onto the roof of the house, go down the chimney, get the girl, and run out. Normally, going down through a chimney would be rather difficult and kind of crazy. But it just so happened that this chimney was quite old and would therefore be much easier to travel down. Of course, they would have to make sure the man wasn't around at the time. To ensure this, one of the angels would call the man from just outside the house and conduct a telephone survey involving a few skill testing questions; thanks to Rin's computer skills, they had the phone number of the house. The main strategy was to call the man as soon as he would go down to the basement where he would be away from any noise; by asking him the skill testing questions while around his computer desk, the kids figured the man would cheat by using the Internet to find the answers. Hopefully, this would keep the man in the basement and the survey would last long enough for the others to do their job.

On arrival, the kids pulled out their equipment: two ropes, a flashlight, a cell phone, and a printout of their telephone survey. The angels, even Jeremy, were so pumped up about rescuing the girl, they put aside their fears of the house's spookiness and went straight to their work like a team of emergency technicians. As it was completely dark outside, they would be able to complete their tasks unnoticed.

Fortunately, the kids were able to look through the curtains and see the kitchen and hallway. At first, all was silent, but it wasn't long before they heard the familiar dull thumping noises. The man shot over to the bedroom with a beer bottle in his hand and roared with anger. Unsurprisingly, there were slapping sounds followed by sharp, shrill screams from the girl—it had been quite a while since they had heard her scream. Then, the man slammed some door shut that the kids couldn't see, and then the bedroom door. He walked to the kitchen, grabbed another beer, and went down to the basement.

"We're coming to get you outta here, little one," whispered Tamiko.

Now, it was time for two of the kids to climb up onto the roof. They hoped to achieve this by throwing the end of one of the ropes, equipped with a grappling hook, into the chimney—like in the movies. Afterward, they would climb the rope, as it was equipped with a series of loops.

With Tamiko shining the flashlight on the chimney, Jeremy threw the trio of hooks up toward the center of the chimney. He missed by about a foot, and the hooks came falling down. Luckily, very little noise was made as the hooks didn't touch the house. Jeremy tried once more and did better, but not quite good enough; the hooks missed by about half a foot this time and made more noise. Frustrated,

Jeremy tried a third time and succeeded! The hooks caught on the side of the chimney, and Jeremy felt like a superspy. Now, it was time for the kids to do their thing. Just to be on the safe side, Jeremy climbed a loop or two and yanked at the rope to test the grip; all was well.

Now, it was time to climb the rope and then distract the man. Hopefully, he wouldn't hear any of the noise.

With the other rope in his hand, Jeremy, followed by Tamiko, climbed the rope one loop at a time and made it safely to the top. Hina dialed the man's number while Rin stood between her and the bottom of the rope, on the lookout, to make sure everything was all right.

After the first ring, Rin and Hina saw the man open the basement door and move his head around. Maybe, he heard something—while Jeremy was throwing up the hook! For a brief moment, the man paused and then went back down to the basement. He picked up the phone.

"Good evening sir," said Hina in a mature and professional tone of voice. "I was wondering if you could spare no more than ten minutes for a survey ..."

At first, the man refused and was about to hang up, but Hina thought fast and told him that he could win some money if he answered all of the questions. She also spoke in a slightly romantic manner.

On the roof, Jeremy and Tamiko looked down the chimney—no fire. All they saw was a dim spot of light at the bottom. Jeremy hooked the second rope, also equipped with loops, to the chimney and stepped into the top loop. Slowly and carefully, he began his descent.

"Here comes Santa Claus!" Jeremy said to himself.

The chimney flue was dark and humid, and it smelled of soot. Within only a minute, Jeremy reached the bottom. If anything were to go wrong, Rin would signal Tamiko, and

Tamiko would signal Jeremy. So far, everything was going just as planned.

Through the fireplace door, Jeremy could see the kitchen in the distance and hear the continual knocking sounds from the girl. Then, suddenly, Jeremy saw the man open the basement door! With a cordless phone in his hand, the man marched over to the kitchen. Rin informed Hina of this and Hina immediately asked the man another skill testing question. As for Jeremy, he was as scared as a mouse being chased by a cat! Fortunately, the man only grabbed himself another beer from the refrigerator and went back downstairs just before Rin was about to signal Tamiko.

Now, it was time for Jeremy's next move. Frightened, Jeremy hesitated a little before trying to open the glass doors. With a little wiggling they opened, and all Jeremy had to do now was quietly step over to the bedroom and get the girl.

Meanwhile, Hina kept the monster occupied on the phone; as the kids had anticipated, the man could be heard typing away at his computer keyboard after each skill testing question. However, the survey was going faster than Hina expected: out of the total ten questions, they were at the seventh. From the way the man was answering the questions, it was obvious that he was kind of drunk.

Jeremy finally let go of his fears and briskly tiptoed over to the bedroom. Breathing heavily, he carefully opened the door. All at once, he heard the banging noises from the girl; the sound of it almost made his heart stop. He turned on the light and looked inside. Like before, the room was pretty much empty.

"Now where's the closet?" Jeremy asked himself. "It's gotta be here somewhere!"

Jeremy frantically turned around in circles looking for any sign of a closet, but … nothing! There was only a small dresser in one corner and a larger one in another along with a mirror on the far wall, a Japanese movie poster on the opposite wall, and some clothes on the floor beside the small dresser. Once again the thuds penetrated the air, and Jeremy turned toward the wall they were coming from. Jeremy gazed at the wall and came to a conclusion.

She must be in the next room, he thought. *But didn't we see her go into this one?*

Jeremy stealthily stepped into the adjacent room. Unlike the previous room, it was well furnished. Immediately, Jeremy spotted the closet and opened it—no girl! Jeremy searched through the clothes like a madman but came up with nothing. Then he heard the thuds again. They sounded like they were coming from the room he was in before!

Hina had just finished her survey and realized that she had to keep the conversation going, so she began to ask a few "bonus" questions that she rapidly improvised. By now, however, the man was getting rather impatient and was at the verge of hanging up. Somehow, though, Hina managed to get in another question or two.

As for Jeremy, he stepped out of the closet and made his way back into the other room. Knowing that he was running out of time, he moved a bit too fast and, unknowingly, made some noise in the process. As he entered the room, he glanced into the mirror, and … there was the monster in the hallway! Immediately, Jeremy shut the door, turned off the light, and hid behind the small dresser in the corner.

"Where are you, man?" muttered the man drunkenly as he opened the door and entered the room. "I'm going to get you! And wheeeeen I do …"

Sitting low in the corner, Jeremy trembled with fear as the monster stumbled around the dark room. Then, the man turned on the light and looked behind the large dresser. The man stepped over to the small dresser and, just as he was about to look behind it, he stopped—it was as though he heard a noise from outside or something. The man turned away and then started walking out of the room. Then, he froze once again just after entering the hallway. *What if he comes back?* thought Jeremy.

Thinking fast, Jeremy made a clever move; he scurried over to the large dresser, where the man had already looked, and hid behind it. In the process, Jeremy had made a little noise—just enough for the man to go back to the room and look again. Sure enough, he looked behind the small dresser and found nothing.

Thumping noises were heard again, and the monster let out a blaring "Shut up!" Then, at the top of his voice, he roared, "One more time and I'll belt you one, you ugly little rat!" The thumping stopped. Finally, he turned off the light and left the room, closing the door behind him.

For what seemed like hours, Jeremy didn't really know what to do. Like the girl, he was trapped. He was also scared stiff. Here he was, in this spooky little room of this spooky little house, surrounded by darkness. To add to this nightmare, Jeremy heard more sounds. These were much softer than the previous thuds but also much creepier, as they were more bizarre and intermittent; they sounded like howling ghosts mixed with scratching noises. Jeremy's heart was pounding with fear; he had never been so scared. Then, he mustered up all of his courage and ran to the door, opened it ever so slightly, and listened as he peered through. It sounded like the monster was mumbling something to himself. In fact, the man was staring at the fireplace doors and inquiring to himself why they were open. Now was Jeremy's chance to escape!

Meanwhile, Hina and the others were wondering what in

the world was going on inside the house.

While the monster's back was turned to him, Jeremy quickly crept over to the front door and, as quietly as possible, made his escape. The monster man still heard him and turned sloppily toward the door. At the same time, the phone rang. It was Hina, once again hoping to help Jeremy out with whatever problem he was having. The excellent timing of this call stopped the man, who picked up the phone just after Jeremy slipped out the door.

"It's my pleasure to inform you that you just won a thousand dollars," said Hina cheerfully.

The man suddenly became all happy and muttered some words of joy. He eventually hung up and paced downstairs to the basement, forgetting about the front door.

"Finally!" said Hina as Jeremy came into sight.

"What happened to you?" asked Rin. "Where's the girl?"

Tamiko grabbed the chimney rope, stepped down the ladder of loops, and met up with a terror-stricken Jeremy.

"Are you okay?" she asked.

"Yeah, but a little sh … shaken up, though."

"Did you get to the girl?"

Jeremy was still so frightened at the moment that he couldn't respond.

"Jeremy! Are you all right? Talk to me!" said Tamiko.

"I c … could hear her but … couldn't find her anywhere … sort of like the last time. She's, like, in the wall or something. She … she and that man … they really freak me out. I'm not goin' in *there* again … at least not at night!"

The four failed rescuers called it a night. They packed their things up and headed back to their bicycles. Suddenly Tamiko stopped and looked at the house.

"What?" said Jeremy.

"What about the loop ladder? How do we get *that*

down?"

Chapter 27~
Where the Birds Sing (Part 1)

It had been several days since their last encounter with the monster at the small, spooky house, and the members of the angel gang were still pretty freaked out, especially Jeremy! Aside from this mission, the gang had pretty much run out of projects, so after Tamiko finished playing tennis with her parents, and after the kids had a contest to see who could eat the most hamburgers, they talked about what to do next.

"Let's just take a break and have fun," said Jeremy.

"I guess we could," Tamiko began, "but why not … I don't know … why not just do some random act of kindness?"

"Like what?" asked Jeremy. "Like open doors for people?"

"Very funny," said Tamiko. "I mean something like … why don't we help someone out at the hospital?"

"At the hospital?" cried Hina. "What are we going to do there?"

"Oh, I don't know exactly," replied Tamiko. "I guess we'll find out when we get there."

"This could be kind of interesting," added Rin.

"Okay. Let's go check it out," said Jeremy.

So the four cycled over to the local hospital, just a short

distance away from Tamiko's karate school. It was partly cloudy with the occasional gust of cool wind. The trees shook briefly, and their large, dark green and deep purple leaves rustled with every burst of wind. Within these trees, birds seemed to be chanting a somewhat different, somewhat sad song today—as if they knew that it was going to rain soon or something.

On arrival, the foursome parked their bicycles and walked up the large hospital steps. The building was a medium-sized five-story facility with red brick walls and many windows. Though it looked rather old, it was clean and well maintained, and it featured a new section added to one side.

Once inside the hospital, the kids saw doctors and nurses walking and running in every direction. Unlike the smell of the clean, fresh air outside, the air inside was kind of stuffy and had an odor of chemicals and medicine. There was also a burst of noise, as the murmuring and chattering of doctors and patients, along with the occasional announcement from the loudspeakers, could be heard. It was a whole different world from the one outside.

The four walked down the main hall from the reception area and past the emergency ward where a crowd of people were waiting impatiently for their names to be called. In a room near the end of the hall, someone seemed to be getting a blood transfusion and another patient was lying with his leg hoisted up in a cast. Maybe they could help this young fellow with the broken leg. Just as Tamiko and her friends were about to enter the room, a nurse marched in and checked on him; he seemed to be doing just fine, so they moved on.

The kids took the elevator to the second floor, where they immediately heard sharp, disturbing cries of pain and agony; they quickly shuffled over to the room where most of the noise was coming from and peeked inside. Lying down on a bed was what appeared to be a mother in the process of giving birth while her spouse and doctor hovered over her uttering, "Push! Push! Good job!" Obviously, this wasn't the kind of situation for the four to be getting involved with.

So the four friends proceeded down the hall, where other—similar—cries filled the air. Apparently, this floor consisted mainly of delivery rooms along with a couple of rooms where groups of newborn babies were being kept. Some of the newborns were sleeping soundly, some were kicking and squawking, and others were being fed by a nurse. The foursome discussed the possibility of caring for some of the babies but decided to explore more of the hospital before making up their minds.

The kids moved up to the third floor while they still had visions of babies running through their brains. Unlike the whirlwind of discord from the floor below, floor three was almost completely silent with only the odd distant whisper or mumble being audible.

Then, as the four kids passed the first room, a nurse disturbed this silence as she spoke into a fancy-looking phone or walkie-talkie.

CHAPTER 28
WHERE THE BIRDS SING (PART 2)

"Yes … yes … I hear you!" she said as she walked out of the room. "She's dying … that's right … I'll make the arrangements as soon as I can … yes … bye!"

With that, Tamiko and her pals quickly approached the young nurse.

"She's dying?" asked Tamiko.

"Yes," said the nurse, sighing. "We did everything we could to stop the cancer. Surgery, chemotherapy—that's treatment using chemicals—even radiation therapy. But she … I'm afraid the treatments haven't worked. She may only have an hour to live. Are you her grandchildren?"

"Uhhhh, no," replied Tamiko. "We were, like, passing by and heard you say she was dying, and we were just curious."

"Well, then, I think we should just let her be," said the nurse as she got a call. She grabbed her little phone and left.

The foursome gazed into the room. On a hospital bed in the distance lay the dying woman. The place was dimly lit and devoid of any noise except for the occasional gush of wind hitting the window and a light rattling of the bed. The curtains were open, and the sky announced the looming arrival of rainfall.

They cautiously walked into the room.

As the kids got closer, the woman slowly turned her head and stared at the four youngsters, speechless, with a somewhat puzzled look on her face. She didn't look like the oldest person they had ever seen—possibly in her late seventies or early eighties. She was Caucasian, with a fair amount of gray, bristly hair, a round face with pale cheeks, and large, dreary blue eyes.

Now that the kids were close to her, the source of the rattling noise could be seen. The woman was holding on tight to the frame of her bed and trembling mildly. The group of four felt rather powerless and didn't know exactly what to say. Then, Tamiko broke the silence.

"G'day," she said. "I'm Tamiko, and these are my friends Hina, Rin, and Jeremy. What's your name?"

"M ... Marlene," the old woman replied as she slowly stopped shaking the bed.

"Marlene—that's a lovely name!" said Tamiko. "So, tell me a little bit about yourself. I have a feeling that you have an interesting story to tell. Everyone has some kind of story to share."

So the lady began.

"Well," she said, "where do I start?"

"Why not start when you were a girl ... like our age," suggested Hina.

Then, somehow, the old lady mustered up all of her remaining strength and began to talk as though she still had several years to live. *How does she do it?* Tamiko wondered. Was it some kind of magic? Was it out of fear? Or was it some last spark of energy from down deep within that enabled her to recall the story of her life ... that wanted these people to remember who she was?

"Oh, that's a long time ago," said the woman. "When I was your age, I had many friends ... and two sisters and a brother, too. There was never really a dull day with them around. I grew up in Vermont, you see—that's in the United States. The winters there were rather long and sometimes pretty cold, I tell ya. I still remember the fun we had sliding down the slopes of that big hill behind the school, just a few steps away from my house. My friends and I … we had snowball fights … amongst ourselves and with the boys, especially Peter Russell. He was a rather easy target, and we would put snow down his back … and down his pants, too!"

The four laughed as did the old woman. Then, the woman continued.

"He was kind of cute, too. Anyway, I had a lot of fond memories back then—all the Christmases and all the birthday parties. We were always doing something. When I got older and started dating, I fell in love with this Japanese fellow at the college cafeteria—Hitoshi, his name was. When I turned twenty-four, we got married, and then we had two children—a boy and a girl. We had a lot of great times together. Oh, the times we had! And then …"

"Then what?" asked Jeremy.

"Then," continued the woman, "we moved to Japan, and I became an English teacher, and my husband a carpenter. It was kind of exciting, actually, living in the big city—a different language, a different culture. We had everything."

Then, Tamiko sensed a certain sadness in the old woman; she needed to be cheered up.

"Wha … what about you?" asked the old lady.

"I … I mean me and my friends like to go around and, well, do pranks on people," said Tamiko. "Once, we did this gag where we pretended to be a radio station. We would phone people up and ask them easy, dumb questions like 'What's another word for poop?' or 'How many people can sit on a three-person couch?' Of course, they'd answer correctly, and then we'd tell them that they had won a prize and would have to go to a certain Beams—you know … the clothing store—to claim it. We told them that once they got to the store, they would need to go to the counter and ask for Yuuka … and they'd have to do this the next day at 5:00 p.m. So we went to Beams at 5:00 the next day, and all these people—at least twenty of them—showed up at the counter asking for Yuuka saying that they won a prize. The woman at the counter was all confused, saying, 'Yuuka? There's no Yuuka here. And what's this prize you're talking about?' We were there watching and laughing and …"

The old lady laughed again, as did Tamiko's friends.

"That's a good one!" she said, still giggling. "That's so funny! Keep on talking. It's so soothing, the way you talk."

"Tell her the office chair prank we just did," said Hina.

"Or how about the one where we switched the washroom signs?" suggested Rin.

"Or what about the best one?" said Jeremy. "The clock store one!"

"Good choice!" said Tamiko. "It goes like this. We go to this clock store just before they close—like ten minutes before—and it's all quiet inside because they're just about to close. While I distract the guy running the store, my friends set all the alarms of the clocks to go off at exactly 6:00— when they close! We're talking over a hundred clocks! So we leave just before 6:00 and stand beside the front window. A minute later all the alarms go off, and the guy's in there running all over the place and going insane!"

The woman laughed even harder this time—so hard, in fact, that her bed trembled like the beginnings of an earthquake. After some time Hina asked the woman about her family's whereabouts.

"And what about your husband and your two children

and your brother and sisters? Where are they? What happened to them?" said Hina.

"Well, that's … that's a sad story," the woman replied. "When my children were in their late teens, they got into a car accident. I asked my son, Andrew, to get me some groceries one night—just some eggs and flour—and so he drove to the store with his sister. And …"

"And what happened next?" asked Rin.

"On their way home, they met up with all this fog, and they flew off the side of the road and struck a tree. Both were killed. I knew it was going to be foggy that night. If only I had told them … but … it was all my fault," she said.

"Oh, I'm very sorry. But don't blame yourself!" said Hina. "It was an accident. You can't think of everything all the time. It wasn't your fault."

"You really think … you really think so?" said the woman.

"I think so, too. Sometimes things just happen and there's not really anything we can do about them," said Tamiko.

The others agreed with Tamiko and shared a few of their unfortunate experiences.

"I've never really gotten over it," the woman said. "In an instant they were gone, just like that! As for my brother, he died of a heart attack ten years ago, and my sisters are in some old folks' home overseas. My husband passed away just a few years ago. And now, I have nobody. I'm just an old wreck about to … Why me, though? Who are you people, and why would you want to be with an old hag like me?"

"Don't say that," said Tamiko. "You're a beautiful person. You're intelligent, you're interesting, you're funny, and … you have a kind heart."

"I can't ... I can't remember the last time anyone said such beautiful things about me," the woman said, sobbing. "I ... I'm dying, you know. I just never wanted to be all alone ..."

"It's okay," whispered Tamiko soothingly as she put her arms around Marlene. "It's okay, Marlene. I'm here with you ... we're here with you. It's okay."

After a long pause, the old woman muttered a few more words.

"Some ... somehow, I'm not afraid to die with you n ... next to me," she said with a restful smile. "It's about time ... it's all about ... good times. But w ... where did my family go, and w ... w ... when will I see them?"

"Soon, you'll be there—where friends and family laugh ... where the birds sing," said Tamiko, holding her.

A peculiar silence crept into the room. The light darkened for a short while and then turned bright again like a cloud passing over the sun. The old woman gently held the sides of her bed one last time and then let go. Sadly but peacefully, Marlene lost all contact with the outside world and died in Tamiko's arms.

CHAPTER 29~
RESCUE! (PART 1)

Today was the day. Somehow, Tamiko and her friends could really feel it—today was the day they would finally rescue the closet girl. After days of practice and preparation, the four were all pumped up and ready for the great challenge ahead of them. So after Tamiko's tutoring session, she snatched her walkie-talkie and raced to the door all psyched up about making the rescue.

"You seem pretty excited!" said Tamiko's mom. "And you seem a little upset about something. Are you all right?"

"Yeah," said Tamiko. "Everything's fine. I'm just going out to have some fun with my friends."

"Okay," said her mom. "Just be back for supper at 7:00."

"Sure!" said Tamiko.

"And don't forget about your special karate and tae kwon do practice tonight," her mom said. "Your cousins will be there, too … watching along with us. Even Uncle Dylan from Canada and his daughter Lily will—"

"Don't worry!"

The determined rescuer sped through the countryside and made her way to the rendezvous point—the big oak tree—where her friends were waiting. It was a sunny day with no clouds in sight, and the air was dry with barely any wind. Tamiko could already smell victory as she approached her friends. In only just a few moments, the poor little closet girl would be saved from the big, ugly beast holding her captive.

"Today's the big day!" said Tamiko as she coasted to a stop.

"Yeah, it's time," said Hina. "Are you ready?"

"As ready as I'll ever be!" replied Tamiko.

"Me too!" added Jeremy.

"Let's just hope that she's still alive," said Rin, "and that the door isn't locked this time."

If need be, Tamiko would use her martial art skills to the best of her ability to stall the monster while Hina and Rin grabbed the girl, and Jeremy, as he was the strongest, would help Tamiko.

Without any hesitation, the rescue team raced to the downtown area and over to the spooky little house. On the way there, they couldn't help but wonder why they were so sure that today's rescue attempt would be successful.

Once they reached their destination, they jumped off their bikes and quietly crept toward the side of the house. As the kids expected at this time of day, the car was in the driveway and some curtains were open. As it was rather hot outside, one of the windows was partly open. So far, everything was silent apart from the occasional chirping bird and the muffled "vrooms" from revving car engines in the distance.

Then, from out of nowhere, a couple of teenage boys walked up to the house with a clipboard and a bag of something—evidently, they were going from house to house trying to sell what was in the bag. They rang the doorbell and nothing happened. Then they knocked, and again nothing happened. However, the team of four thought they heard faint stomping sounds coming from the house. The sounds seemed to stop all of a sudden, and the four waited impatiently for the door to open. To their disappointment, the door didn't open. Instead, the stomping sounds came back again. The two young salesmen finally gave up and moved on to another house.

"Did you hear that?" said Hina. "He's there!"

"Yeah," said Rin. "That's gotta be him!"

"He won't answer … even if you knock," said Jeremy. "So whatta we do?"

"We knock harder," replied Tamiko.

Before racing to the front door, the kids quietly tiptoed to the side window to check out what was going on inside. Like before, the rooms were very untidy, and there was still that strange nutty aroma. The place was rather lifeless and dreary.

Suddenly, heavy footsteps broke the silence and got louder and louder; then the man opened the basement door and made his way toward the kitchen. The four could barely see his face, but from what they were able to make out, the man looked even scarier than they remembered. He wore the expression of a robot and moved like one too. After grabbing some food, the man went to the basement again, slamming the door behind him.

"Let's go see if the door's unlocked," said Hina. "He's in the basement. All we'd have to do is go in, get the girl, and leave."

"I have a feeling this isn't going to be quite that easy," said Rin.

"Let's give it a try!" said Tamiko.

"We better be quick!" added Jeremy.

The foursome dashed to the door and tried opening it. No luck; it was locked. Just then, the rescuers heard some dull thuds penetrate the door, only this time the noise seemed to be coming from upstairs and didn't sound like it was moving anywhere. The kids weren't sure, so they scurried back to the side window to see if the man was coming up from the basement again.

In only a short time, the previous thuds were mixed with pounding stomps—it sounded like an awkward and annoying drumbeat. The monster threw open the basement door and marched over to the room where the girl was probably being kept. He threw open the door and barged in.

Then, the kids heard the familiar roaring and growling of the monster followed by the screeching and squalling of the little girl. Now it was time for the rescue team to make their move. The foursome scuttled to the front of the house and banged on the door as if they were trying to knock it down. In no time the beast was stomping toward the door. Now was the moment the four rescuers had been waiting for; now was the moment of truth!

CHAPTER 30~
RESCUE! (PART 2)

When the pounding of the man's feet stopped at the door, it was quickly replaced with the pounding of the team's hearts. They were about to meet the beast face-to-face! The man flicked the dead bolt and pulled open the door. And then, there he was! Standing right in front of them was the beast! He had the eyes of a snake and the facial expression of a block of ice. His hair was jet-black, and he wore a well-trimmed mustache. He looked like a drill sergeant ready to give orders.

For what seemed like forever, nobody spoke; all stood there motionless, frozen in time, waiting for someone to make the first move. Something was going to happen; someone was going to snap.

"What do you want?" the man growled, looking like a rottweiler about to attack.

"Where is she?" said Tamiko.

"Where's who?" snarled the man.

"The little girl," said Hina. "The one you beat and lock up!"

"I don't know what you're talking about."

"Oh, I think you do," said Jeremy.

"Yeah, we saw you go into the room and beat her," said

Rin. "And we heard her scream!"

"You ain't seen nothin'!" said the man. "Now get outta my face before I—"

"Before you beat us up, too?" interrupted Tamiko.

"I've heard just about enough from you little punks!" said the man. "Now I said get outta here, and don't show your ugly little faces around here again! Got that?"

The man began to shut the door, but Tamiko and Jeremy forcefully grabbed it and pushed it the other way.

"We're not going anywhere!" said Tamiko.

"I said get outta here!"

The man slammed the door shut and locked it.

"Now what do we do?" said Rin.

"We're going in," said Jeremy, determined.

"And just how are we going to do that?" asked Hina.

"How about a rock through the window?" said Jeremy as he picked up a rock. "That'll get his attention."

"He's a cop, remember?" said Rin. "We could go to jail if you throw that. It's called vandalism!"

"He just says he's a cop!" said Jeremy. "He's a liar!"

"We've got to do something," said Tamiko. "But I don't think throwing rocks is the smartest—"

Jeremy pitched the rock toward the front window. The rock didn't go through, but it shattered the glass and made a pretty big noise.

"When he opens the door, we charge at him!" ordered Jeremy.

"What are you ... this is crazy!" cried Hina.

"Maybe we should just run away," suggested Rin.

"No. We've come this far, and we have to finish the job. We have to finish it now," said Tamiko as the four heard the dead bolt slide open.

"On three, we charge!" said Tamiko. "One! Two!

Three!"

"Unkoooo!" yelled Jeremy.

The man yanked open the door, and the rescuers, with Jeremy leading the way, scrambled toward the man and tackled him like a team of football players. The impact was great enough to knock the man off his feet and onto the floor. While Jeremy and Tamiko were on top of the man, the other two got up and raced frantically over to the room where the kids had first seen the girl.

"Little girl! Where are you? Little girl!" called the young rescuers.

They heard the familiar thumps in reply but couldn't find the girl anywhere. Meanwhile, Tamiko and Jeremy fought with the man on the floor for a short while, twisting and turning and hitting and kicking. The beast quickly shoved them away, though, and now it was time for Tamiko to try out her martial art skills on him. She kicked him and punched him and jabbed at him. The man seemed rather surprised at her courage, and Tamiko was able to stun him a little while his guard was down. With that, however, the man got even angrier and thrust himself toward Tamiko.

Jeremy blocked the attack and fell on impact. Tamiko got another couple of good punches in, and the man retaliated by grabbing her and throwing her to the floor. Jeremy lunged at the man, and the two fell onto the coffee table, knocking over several dishes. The man got up, and Tamiko gave him a knee strike that sent him back onto the coffee table, knocking even more stuff over. As for Hina and Rin, they could clearly hear the bumping and thumping along with some muffled yelling from the girl, but she was still nowhere to be found!

The man got up and slapped Tamiko. Jeremy grabbed the man from behind, and the monster elbowed him sharply.

Somehow, Tamiko imagined the man calling her "reject" and her anger pumped up. Now, Tamiko lost her temper and used her best roundhouse kick against the man—it was kind of effective, seeming to hurt him somewhat, and he almost fell to the floor as he was banged against the wall. The man now flew into a rage, knocking Tamiko to the floor once more and yelling, "Get lost, you bratty little punk!" Then, Jeremy made a move, and the man knocked him down, too.

Meanwhile, as the others searched for the girl, they accidentally brushed against and tore the large poster on the wall of one of the bedrooms revealing a small, curious-looking door recessed into the wall. As the door trembled with each thump, Hina and Rin instantly realized that this was where the girl was trapped! Hina was just about to unlock the door when the man marched into the room, grabbed the two rescuers, and threw them into the hallway. "You get outta my house, you little brats—once and for all!"

Outside the bedroom, he grabbed them again and shoved them out the front door. Then, Tamiko got up, ran over to the bedroom, and unlocked the little door. Just as the girl stepped out, the man burst into the room, hit Tamiko from behind, and dragged her out of the house.

"You bratty little twit," the man said to Tamiko. "You think you're some karate star, don't you? You're just a wimpy little girl. You'll never beat a man!"

As for Jeremy, he pulled himself up off the floor only to find himself immediately struggling with the man, who grasped him and tossed him out the door and into the arms of his three teammates. Hina and Rin were shaking and coughing. Jeremy squirmed around sluggishly as if he had just been drugged. As for Tamiko, she just sat down with her face in her hands, crying.

"I failed," she said. "We failed. It's all over."

"Are you okay?" asked Jeremy, worried.

"I'll … I'll be all right," said Tamiko.

"Let's just call the police!" said Hina.

"But he *is* the police!" said Tamiko along with Rin.

Tamiko's friends put their arms around her and provided her with more words of comfort. The four slowly got up, got back onto their bikes, and peddled away.

Chapter 31-
I Quit!

When Tamiko got home, she didn't feel like eating. She didn't feel like talking. She didn't feel like playing. She didn't even feel like cuddling with Butterscotch. All she felt like doing was knocking out that poisonous snake and finally freeing the closet girl from all her misery and torment.

"Tamiko, what happened to you?" said her dad.

"I'll be all right," Tamiko replied.

"But your face ... your hair ... your ... Did you get in a fight or something?"

"Sort of," Tamiko responded.

"Tamiko, you have karate class in only—" Her mom froze. "Tamiko! You look like you've just been ... what happened?"

Tamiko didn't have much choice but to explain what happened. After hearing the story, Tamiko's parents were shocked. They immediately called the police. Afterward, Tamiko was somewhat relieved; within hours or minutes, the girl would be free and the monster would be behind bars where he belonged. Calling the police was something that she and her friends really should have done from the start, for doing so would have saved the girl some suffering.

With the knowledge of everything Tamiko had been

through, her parents said that she should skip the special karate session and go to a medical clinic instead to check for any internal damage.

"That's okay," said Tamiko, brushing her hair. "I quit!"

"You what?" said her dad. "You're not a quitter! You're a fighter!"

Despite the attempts of Tamiko's parents to stop her from quitting, Tamiko didn't change her mind. So her parents drove Tamiko to the medical clinic near the karate school. On the way, they dropped by the school so Tamiko could pick up her things and inform Kenta of her decision to quit. And of course she had to run into the great Allan McCoy.

"Oh, it's Tamiko!" he said. "And what happened to her? Did she get into some kind of a fight?"

"Shut up!" cried Tamiko.

"I hear that you're some kind of angel going around town helping people. Well, isn't that sweeeeet!"

"Get lost!" said Tamiko. "And get a life!"

"Oh, Tamiko!" said Allan. "That's no way for an angel to speak to someone! Where are your good manners?"

"I said shut up!"

But Allan didn't stop. He took great pleasure in teasing Tamiko in any way he could.

"Oh, and I can just imagine you … flying from place to place, fighting off the bad guys with your girlie little karate skills," Allan said as he and his friends started laughing.

"Not another word!" said Tamiko. "I've heard enough of you, and if it makes you feel any better for your royal self, I'm …"

"You're what?" asked Allan.

"I'm quitting!" said Tamiko. "Go tell Kenta!"

"Well, hurray!" said Allan, clapping his hands. "Finally,

you see it—girls weren't made for fighting!"

Allan and his friends laughed and chuckled once more.

"Way to go, Tamiko!" said a friend of Allan's.

"Nice knowing you!" said another.

"Who knows?" said Allan. "Maybe we'll meet again someday ... in your dreams!"

"Yeah, right!" said Tamiko on her way out.

With that, Tamiko left the building with her belongings and the last of her thoughts of "Allan and friends." At the clinic, the doctor gave her a quick examination and took a few x-rays. Fortunately, Tamiko had no internal injuries and just a few scrapes and bruises, so she was given a clean bill of health. Tamiko knew better, though. She actually *did* have some "internal injuries"—from failing to rescue the girl and giving Allan the opportunity to say, "I told you so!"

Chapter 32
Heart, Strength, and Mind

The next day Tamiko woke up to the sound of Butterscotch barking and looked back at yesterday's events as if they were just some bad dream. Now, it was all over; the beast was surely arrested and thrown in the slammer, and the girl was probably in the hospital being treated for all her wounds— both physical and psychological.

Now, it was time for that snake to feel what it's like to be locked up and powerless. Tamiko still felt like a loser, though. She wanted to be the one to save the day along with her friends, but they'd failed. Although Tamiko was a rather good fighter for a girl, she just wasn't of the same caliber as a boy, let alone a man.

As for her quitting karate, *Is this the right thing to do?* she wondered. *Should I change my mind and continue lessons?* Like her dad said, she was not a quitter. She was a fighter. *Oh well,* she thought. *Maybe I should have another talk with Grandmaster Shun. Maybe he can work things out and make me feel better somehow. He's a good listener, and he always has that magical way about him whenever he talks.*

That afternoon, after her tutoring session, Tamiko decided to hop on the bus and pay Shun a visit at his temple across town. But just before she left, she decided to call her friends, starting with Jeremy, and tell them that she had told her parents everything and that they had called the police.

"Hi, Jeremy," said Tamiko.

"Oh, hi, Tamiko," he replied. "How are you doing? Did you get any sleep?"

"Oh, enough I guess," she said. "It feels like a bad dream now—like it really didn't happen or something."

"Yeah, tell me about it!" said Jeremy.

Then, Tamiko began telling Jeremy her story.

"Well, I ... like ... told everything to my parents," said Tamiko. "I didn't really have much choice. And they called the police. So it's all over now. I just wish that—"

"They what!" said Jeremy. "Did you say they called the police?"

"Yeah," said Tamiko. "But like I said, I really didn't have—"

"When? When did they call?"

"Last night, right after I got home."

"Then I don't understand!" said Jeremy. "I just walked by there again, right after school—I didn't get too close, though—and I saw him with my new binoculars. And I could even hear the girl screaming again. I saw her this time. She—"

"What!" cried Tamiko. "My dad told everything to the cops—the girl being locked up in that small room, the beatings, the fight yesterday, the guy's address—the whole thing!"

"Then I don't get it," said Jeremy. "I saw what I saw, and I heard what I heard, and I'm telling you—"

"Yeah," said Tamiko, interrupting. "It's all about proof! We don't have any!"

"Either that or this guy's, like, above the law or something," said Jeremy.

"Or maybe he really *is* the law! He even said it himself!"

"Right," said Jeremy. "Anyway, I better go. Dad's telling me to do my homework. We'll talk later!"

"Yeah!" said Tamiko, still in shock.

Tamiko stared at the wall.

How could this be happening? she thought, feeling powerless. *The police told my dad they'd get on it right away! It's just not fair! How could the police let that monster off the hook and allow him to go back and beat the girl? What am I going to do now?*

With that, Tamiko phoned the police herself to ask what was going on. Once she was transferred to the appropriate person, she received some rather interesting but disturbing news.

"I'm sorry," said the officer. "They searched the place but found no girl!"

"But I know she's there!" said Tamiko. "I heard her! She's in a little secret room—"

"Sorry!" said the officer as he hung up.

Now what? Tamiko thought.

Maybe Shun could help her out somehow. So Tamiko wrote a note to her parents, caught the next bus, and made her way over to the temple where Grandmaster Shun lived. On arrival, she slowly walked toward the temple. It was a majestic-looking building of red, green, and brown that was beautifully ornamented with three doors. The center door was slightly open. Tamiko quietly tiptoed over to the door and found Shun sitting down, meditating with his back turned to her. Then, he suddenly turned around, as he "magically" sensed Tamiko's presence.

"Tamiko!" he said. "What a surprise! It's a pleasure to see you. What brings you here?"

"Konbanwa!" said Tamiko respectfully.

"I sense that you have much on your mind," said Shun.

"And I suppose there is something I can help you with?"

"Don't you find that the world is just ... so unfair sometimes?" asked Tamiko.

"There are times," said Shun. "But life is made up of the yin and the yang—or as we'd say here in Japan, the *in* and the *yo*. One can't exist without the other; it's a package deal."

"Yeah, I know all about that, but that doesn't mean we have to accept the bad things people do."

Shun asked Tamiko where, exactly, all of this was coming from. Tamiko told Shun everything: the failed rescue attempts, her parents calling the police, her most recent conversation with Jeremy. Then, she disclosed her decision to terminate her lessons in the martial arts.

"You quit?" said Shun. "That's no reason to quit."

"But I'm a girl, and karate is for guys," said Tamiko. "And I failed to save the girl from that—"

"Heart, strength, and mind," said Shun.

"'Heart, strength, and mind'? What do you mean?" asked Tamiko.

Shun led Tamiko over to the meditation room, lit some incense, and began to sing! The song he sang was all about heart, strength, and mind. Once he finished, he chuckled a little and stood up.

"You have a good voice—even better than I thought," said Tamiko. "And the song ... did you write it yourself?"

"Well, thanks! And, as a matter of fact, I did write that song," said Shun, smiling. "You have a good heart, Tamiko. Someday, you'll be a great fighter. I can feel it."

"Really?" said Tamiko. "Me?"

"Really," said Shun.

Then, the two shared some stories with each other. Tamiko talked about her missions and pranks. Shun recalled some early chapters of his life when he was learning to fight.

Shun even gave Tamiko some private karate lessons. "You have the strength of an eagle and a heart of a lion," Shun told her.

During her practice, Tamiko got a very special feeling. A feeling that, someday very soon, her life was going to change dramatically in one way or another. It felt like something fantastic was going to happen but only after something very tragic. Tamiko tried to figure out what it could possibly be, but didn't come up with anything.

After her thought had faded away, Tamiko asked Shun an important question.

"But what about the girl? What do I do now?"

"Well, you have heart and strength; now, let's look at mind," said Shun. "Like Plutarch once said, the mind is not a vessel to be filled but a fire to be kindled. Now, imagine you're the bad guy. What would be the first thing you'd do just after you had an encounter like yesterday's? Think about it—you threw the kids out of the door, just after everything they saw and heard. What's the first thing those kids are most likely to do?"

"Tell someone. Call the police," said Tamiko.

"Right," said Shun. "So what do you think the bad guy would probably do then?"

"Um … he would … of course! He would move the girl somewhere else, outside of the house!" said Tamiko, amazed at what she just said.

"You got it!" said Shun.

Chapter 33
Turning Point

It was a new day, and there were many things on Tamiko's mind. How were she and her friends going to outsmart the bad guy and *finally* rescue the girl? What about her karate classes? Should she change her mind and go back? And what was she going to do this summer while her friends were gone at summer camp in China? What Tamiko needed was a change in scenery.

Suddenly, Tamiko realized that it was Monday—time to go out on yet another exciting plane ride with Midori and look for the elusive shrines. So Tamiko ate a quick breakfast and walked the dog with her parents, and then the three drove off to Lake Yamanaka to meet Midori. It was a great day for flying—sunny and warm, with just a bit of wind. Like always, the scenery was magnificent; it was like Tamiko had just stepped into a storybook. Tamiko kissed her parents good-bye and got out of the car to join Midori.

"Have fun, Tamiko!" said her parents.

"Oh, we will," said Tamiko. "And I'll take lots of pictures."

"You have to find the shrines this time!" said Kana.

"I can't make any promises," replied Midori. "But who knows? Maybe today will be our lucky day."

"Ganbatte kudasai!" said Thomas.

With that, Tamiko and Midori ran to the plane.

Unlike the last time they went flying, there were a few ripples on the water today because of the gentle summer wind. Mount Fuji stood there in the distance like a giant snow cone that someone had just taken a small bite out of at the tip.

"So, today's the big day, right?" said Midori.

"You bet!" said Tamiko.

"It's a perfect day for flying," said Midori. "It doesn't get any better than this!"

The two good friends jumped into the sea plane, and, within seconds, they were gliding across the water like a speedboat. Then, the plane lifted above the water and soared into the sky like a great bird. The plan today was to fly over to Lake Sai, like they usually did, have lunch, and then explore new ground on the way back. On the way to Lake Sai, Tamiko took some pictures as usual—especially of majestic-looking Mount Fuji. Every trip was a new adventure. The sky today was full of birds, wispy clouds, and rays of sunshine. On the way to the lake, both looked everywhere for the shrines but, like before, found nothing but trees, a few odd houses or shacks, and more trees. As they approached Lake Sai, their stomachs began to growl for lunch; they gently landed on the lake and paced over to their favorite tree.

"Well, last time you asked *me* what I want to do when I grow up," said Tamiko. "How about *you*?"

"I want to be a trail guide ... a mountain guide!" said Midori with energy. "It may sound like I'm exaggerating a little, but someday, I'm going to climb to the top of Mount Fuji. Just kidding; Mount Fuji is just a four-hour walk. I mean Mount Everest, the highest mountain in the world.

Someday I'll do it. Just you wait and see!"

"But isn't that kind of dangerous?" asked Tamiko.

"Yes, but I'm up for it. I'll risk it," said Midori. "Of course there'll be some heavy training to do, and I'll have to bring an oxygen tank for the final part of the climb, but … I'm going to do it."

Then, Midori talked about her other thrill-seeking pleasures and aspirations, like bungee jumping, sky diving, zip lining, surfing, and even parasailing. When Midori's mouth finally took a break from opening and closing so much, Tamiko made a suggestion.

"You know," began Tamiko, "wouldn't it be nice if we could just stay here for several days and throw all our troubles away?"

Midori suggested that the following week they go camping and do a little hiking.

"That's a plan!" said Tamiko. "My home tutor is off next week! I'm sure Mom will say yes!"

"One condition, though—don't pull any pranks on me," said Midori, "like putting a frog in my sleeping bag or something!"

"Good idea!" said Tamiko, giggling.

Then, Midori recalled a fond memory of when she babysat Tamiko for the first time.

"What's that thing you did with your hair when I was babysitting you?" said Midori.

"Oh, that was when I took rice and put it all in my hair, and then I walked up to you and went crazy, moving my hands all through my hair and screaming, 'I have a lice attack!' Rice was flying all over the floor, and you actually thought it was real. You were running all—"

"I remember now!" said Midori. "I went insane! I was going to call 911 or your mom. I'm serious!"

"You finally figured it out, though. It took you a while, but you finally got it!" said Tamiko, laughing along with Midori.

"So no pranks when we camp next week, deal?" said Midori.

"Deal!" replied Tamiko.

After lunch and some light trekking, the two got back into the plane and set out once again to search for the ancient shrines. They flew over to the south side of the mountain but traveled a new route this time. They looked everywhere but failed to find any shrines. Then, Midori turned the plane around and flew just above the tree line and toward the mountain. They looked to the left, they looked to the right, they looked in front, but still no shrines! Eventually, the two gave up and called it a day.

"Once again, better luck next time!" cried Tamiko over the noise of the engine.

Even though Tamiko felt somewhat like a failure once again, finding the shrines was no big deal—there were more important things in life to deal with. As before, Tamiko thought these ancient shrines holding all sorts of "treasures" were probably just a legend anyway. As Midori checked the time, Tamiko yawned a bit and rubbed her eyes. She was starting to feel a bit tired.

Midori began to slowly turn the plane back toward their starting point while Tamiko took one last picture of the mountain. All that was above was clear blue skies without even a single cloud now, and all that was below were beautiful green trees. As Midori continued her gradual turn, Tamiko settled her sleepy head against her headrest and glanced once more at the beauty of Mount Fuji.

Then, as she looked down and to the right, something caught her eye. *What the ... could it really be?* It was! There, right before her eyes, were some of the ancient shrines, standing like old trophies!

"Look! Look!" cried Tamiko, pointing. "To the right! The shrines!"

Midori turned her head.

"Jackpot!" she cried as the two gave each other a high five. "Way to go! We did it!"

They looked exactly like Midori had described them— some like miniature white courthouses that only had their pillars and roof structures remaining, and others like strange brick-red lighthouses with boxlike bases having two small windows in the front and one big, doorless, round-topped entrance. Tamiko could almost hear a symphony of strings play as she gazed over the relics. Finally, they had succeeded in finding them!

"I told you today was the big day!" said Midori with pride as she lowered the plane to get a closer look.

"You got that right!" said Tamiko.

"They're gorgeous!" said Midori. "Gorgeous like you, Tam—"

Suddenly, there was a loud "Bump!" and the plane jolted as if a giant had kicked it like a football. Midori had gone too low, and the plane had struck a tall tree! Now, they were spinning around like a pinwheel with almost no control! "Aaaaaaah!" screamed Tamiko. Then, the plane stabilized a bit and swerved back and forth.

"Mayday, Mayday, Mayday!" yelled Midori through her headset. "This is Skyduck, Skyduck, Skyduck! Mayday, Skyduck. Position 35 31 North 138 72 East. My plane is out of control. I require immediate help. Two people on board. Over!"

The plane did another spin and lost altitude. In the cockpit, lights were flashing and things were beeping and buzzing. The plane brushed against the treetops and then somersaulted in the air. Parts of the wings were falling off and flying through the air.

"We're going down!" yelled Tamiko. "We're going to crash!"

"Hold on!" yelled Midori.

The plane kept getting closer and closer to the ground. Smoke filled the air as Midori struggled to make the craft go back up. Then Skyduck scraped the ground on an open patch of bush, somersaulted once again, and whirled into the trees ahead, beating and banging the ground in a frenzy of noise.

Finally, the plane came to a stop within the trees. All that remained of the craft was a mess of metal debris. From above, it would have looked like someone had walked all over a model airplane, crushing it into so many pieces that nobody would have ever known it was an airplane in the first place. Smoke rushed out of the wreckage, and the engine hissed like a snake. Tamiko and Midori lay there motionless inside the wreckage like a pair of crumpled crash test dummies.

Part 3—
The Invisible Gifts

CHAPTER 34
AFTERMATH

Within minutes, a rescue team in a helicopter zoomed toward the south side of Mount Fuji and hovered around the coordinates Midori had blurted out earlier. It wasn't long before they spotted the smoke and landed on an open space close to the wreckage. The rescuers jumped out of the chopper and tramped through the woods toward the smoke. Finally, they arrived at the crash site, where the engines were still hissing and the plane was on fire. The rescuers walked through the debris and over to the cockpit. They extinguished the fire outside and then worked hard to pry open one of the doors, letting out more smoke. Inside they had to put out even more fire. The occupants were unconscious, still buckled into their seats; they were almost unrecognizable.

Meanwhile, Tamiko's mother, Kana, was waiting impatiently by the lake for the arrival of the sea plane. She pulled out her binoculars and scanned the skies for the aircraft—nothing in sight. *Maybe they're just taking their time*, she thought. But Midori was *never* late—in fact, she was always at least fifteen minutes early. Then, Kana saw a couple of planes buzzing toward her in the distance, but they weren't sea planes. Beginning to worry, she pulled out her cell phone and called Midori at least twice. No answer. She waited and waited. Finally, she called Thomas and informed him of her concern.

"Moshi! Moshi!" said Thomas, who was driving, on his way to pick up his wife and daughter.

"Hi, Tom. I'm still waiting for Tamiko to come back with Midori. Has she called you at all?"

"No, nothing," replied Thomas. "That's strange, though. Midori's always on time … usually a bit early even."

"I know. Look, I'll call you back if I hear anything," said Kana. "Bye!"

"Okay, see you soon!"

The rescue team carefully removed Tamiko and Midori from the wreckage, quickly carried them over to the helicopter, and flew off toward the hospital. Having found their wallets, the rescuers were able to identify the victims. They were still alive, though unconscious; the rescuers were busy giving first aid.

Kana paced for about another fifteen minutes until her husband showed up.

"They're *still* not back?" said Thomas.

"No!" said Kana. "Where are they? Where could they be?"

"I don't know!" said Thomas.

"It's not like they had any special plan for today. Wait a second! Maybe they found the shrines!" said Kana. "But they would have called … or at least answered my calls!"

"Maybe they found all kinds of treasure in the shrines and got so excited that they just forgot about it."

"Come on," said Kana. "They would have heard the

phone!"

"I guess all we can do now is wait," said Thomas. "They'll be back. Don't worry!"

During the next hour, Thomas and Kana waited and called and waited and called—no sign of them whatsoever! Finally they called the police and told them their predicament, but that wasn't much help; all they could say was, "We'll look into it."

By now it was getting dark, and the two were really worried. Then, Kana had an idea.

"Maybe she left a message at home," she said.

So Kana phoned home to check for any messages on the answering machine and found that there was one new message. She put the cell on speakerphone so they could both listen to it.

"Hello. I'm Officer Haga. I'm calling to inform you that your daughter, Tamiko Brown, has been involved in a plane crash. She and the pilot have been taken to Fujinomiya General Hospital. I'm ... really sorry to have to tell you this."

With that, Kana burst into tears and Thomas sobbed in grief. Both stood there in shock.

"Not our Tamiko! Not our Tamiko!" cried Kana. "This can't be happening!"

"We have to think positive here. Midori's a good pilot," said Thomas. "Everything's going to be all right!"

"But you don't *know* that!" replied his wife.

The two then jumped into the car and rushed over to the hospital.

When the anguished parents arrived, they made a beeline for the emergency ward and begged to see their daughter.

"Tamiko Brown? Yes, she's one of the two in the plane crash. She's just been admitted, and she—"

"What's her condition? Is she still alive?"

"She's in critical condition … in room 5. Follow me."

Thomas and Kana marched over to room 5 and gradually peered into the room, afraid of what they were about to see.

"Oh my!" said Kana, horror-stricken. "Tamiko!"

"My Tamiko!" said Thomas. "My baby! My Tamiko!"

There she lay, severely burnt and almost unrecognizable. It was almost like something out of a horror movie, only this was no movie—this was real. For Thomas and Kana, it was almost unbelievable, as though this was one big bad dream they would soon wake up from.

"Tamiko, can you hear me? Tamiko!" cried Thomas.

"She's unconscious now," said the doctor. "But we're doing everything we can to bring her back."

"Does she have any broken bones?" asked Kana.

"We don't know at this point," said the doctor. "We'll be taking x-rays soon and doing some other tests. I'll let you know as soon as we find anything."

"This can't be happening," cried Kana. "This can't be … Tamiko … my baby … my little girl!"

"We're right here with you, dear," said Thomas. "We're right here, Tamiko!"

"And what about Midori, the pilot?" asked Kana. "What's her condition?"

"We tried everything we could," said the doctor, "but I'm afraid she didn't pull through."

With this news, Kana's eyes filled with even more tears, as did the eyes of her husband.

"No!" said Kana. "No … not Midori!"

"Oh man!" said Thomas.

"Midori … she … she was still so young," said Kana, crying. "She had her whole life ahead of her."

"I still don't believe all this is happening," said Thomas.

Thomas and Kana went over to see the late Midori while the doctors and nurses worked on Tamiko. Like Tamiko, Midori was burnt, beaten up, and almost unidentifiable.

"Oh, Midori!" cried Kana as her eyes dripped with tears. "How could … how could this happen to such … to such a beautiful person like you? How? You were like a sister to me."

"That goes to show just how fragile life really is," said Thomas.

"You can't be dead! You can't be!" said Kana. "You have so much … energy … so much to live for!"

"Here … it's okay dear," said Thomas, holding his wife.

"She didn't deserve to die. Not like this," said Kana.

After spending some more time with Midori, the saddened parents walked back to Tamiko's room and then to the waiting room. While they waited and hoped, the doctors and nurses worked to bring Tamiko back to the real world. Then, after several hours of waiting, the doctors finally had some news for Kana and Thomas.

Chapter 35–
What Happened to Me?

"I have some good news. Your daughter opened her eyes. But only for a second or two."

Thomas and Kana eagerly followed the doctor to Tamiko's room.

"Tamiko, can you hear me?" asked Thomas. "Please say something."

"Can you open your eyes, Tamiko?" asked Kana.

Tamiko didn't respond. Thomas and Kana asked their daughter a few more questions and gently stroked her face, but Tamiko still didn't react. Finally, the parents gave up trying to wake her and just talked to her for a while before leaving.

Just after they got home, the distressed parents received a call from the hospital.

"Good news," said the doctor. "Tamiko opened her eyes again—longer this time—and she can speak, but just barely."

The excited parents sped back to the hospital and rushed into Tamiko's room.

There she lay, very much like before but with her eyes slightly open this time. Just the fact that she was still alive and conscious filled the parents' hearts with hope and confidence. Despite the good news, they were still very

238

disturbed at the sight of her numerous burns and bruises.

"Tamiko," said Kana, crying. "It's Mommy. How … how are you doing? How are you feeling?"

Tamiko slowly scanned her parents, and then she took a deep breath and spoke.

"H … hi, Mommy," she said. "I'm … feeling … not too good. You're … you're wearing that ugly necklace again. You need a new one."

With that, Kana and Thomas chuckled and shed a few tears of joy. Tamiko hadn't lost her sense of humor!

"That's good," said Kana. "And yes, I do need a new necklace. This old one is awful. I'll buy a new one!"

"Hi, dear," said Thomas. "You remember me, don't you?"

"You're that crazy scientist," said Tamiko. "You're my dad."

"Yes, dear!" cried Thomas. "I'm your dad, and I'm staying right here. Everything's going to be all right, dear. Everything's going to be all right!"

"The doctor said … I was in a … a plane crash," said Tamiko.

"That's right," said Kana. "You were. But that's over now, and soon you'll be home again."

"What … do I look like?" asked Tamiko. "Not so pretty … I guess."

"You're … as beautiful as you always were," said Thomas. "I mean … your skin's a bit different, but it's really what's inside that counts."

"And where are my friends … my three friends?" said Tamiko.

"They're not here right now," said Kana. "They'll come see you tomorrow."

Thomas and Kana stayed with Tamiko all night and

called her friends the next day. They were stunned when they heard the news and couldn't help but drop their heads and cry. Later that day, the three entered Tamiko's room not knowing exactly what to expect.

"Tamiko!" said Hina. "You were in a plane crash. How did this happen?"

"Not sure," said Tamiko, all bandaged up.

"You look like a mummy," said Jeremy. "At least you're still alive—that's what counts."

"But can you move at all?" asked Rin.

"Just a little bit," said Tamiko.

"You … like … have to get better soon," said Hina. "We need you back."

Then, there was a short pause; Tamiko's friends didn't know what to say next.

"You won't die on us, Tamiko!" said Jeremy, worried.

"You're strong," said Rin. "You've always been. You're going to get through this. You hear?"

"Yeah, you're going to pull through," said Jeremy. "And then we're going to rescue the closet girl. Are you still in?"

"If I could … if only I could get to her … if I could save that little girl from all her pains … I wooooould," said Tamiko sadly.

"You will. We all will!" said Hina. "If it's the last thing we do."

"Yeah!" said Jeremy. "We're going to kick the unko out of him!"

The four talked for a few more minutes before being interrupted by another visit from Thomas and Kana. Just before Tamiko's comrades made their departure, Jeremy had some last words to say to Tamiko.

"I … I don't really know how to say this … but before when we were …" Jeremy whispered to her. "Okay, I'll get right to the point. I love you, Tamiko. Unko dreams!"

After Tamiko's friends left, her parents took over, and the family of three discussed Tamiko's recovery, along their plans for the summer, and even shared a few laughs. Thomas and Kana tried to be as positive as possible, as they didn't want to drain Tamiko's energy. However, Tamiko gradually drifted off to sleep as she muttered a few last words.

"All I ever wanted to do was ... be an angel that helps people."

"I think we'll just let her sleep," said Kana.

"You're right," agreed Thomas. "It's been a long day for her."

Later, a nurse came in to check on Tamiko. To the nurse's surprise, Tamiko wouldn't respond.

"Tamiko!" she cried. "Tamiko, can you hear me? Tamiko!"

Despite the nurse's attempts to rouse her, Tamiko continued to lay there in a trance. Tamiko had fallen into a coma!

Chapter 36
My Tamiko

Tamiko lay there in bandages and hooked up to a life support system, unconscious once again and unresponsive; the room had never been so quiet. Once the nurse and doctor confirmed that Tamiko really was in a coma, it was time for the parents to learn of the bad news.

"In a … coma?" said Thomas.

"For how long?" asked Kana.

"Normally, it doesn't last any more than two to five weeks," explained the doctor.

"And what are the chances of survival?" asked Thomas.

"The chances are different for every patient; it depends on a lot of factors. But, on average, the chances of her pulling through are about 60 percent."

"Sixty percent!" said Kana.

"The odds are in our favor, Kana. We have to stay positive and give Tamiko all the love and support we can!" said Thomas.

As if this bad news were not enough, the doctor had more—the x-rays showed several bone injuries that were rather serious. Heavy with worry, Thomas and Kana made their way over to see Tamiko.

Like the first time that Tamiko was unconscious, the

room was very quiet. But this time it wasn't just quiet, it was dead silent. In addition to this quietness, Tamiko was absolutely motionless and lifeless—it was as though she were a mannequin or dummy wrapped up in oodles of gauze. The two parents stood there, helpless, powerless, unable to do anything to reverse the situation.

"Tamiko," said Thomas, "I know you can hear me. You have to get through this. I know you can get through this. You're a fighter, remember?"

"You have to come back to us, Tamiko," said Kana. "We need you, baby. We need you to come home, where you belong. Please, Tamiko, please!"

"I ... I know that ... we haven't spent as much time together as we should have lately," said Thomas, trying hard to prevent himself from crying. "I've been ... too much into my work lately. I know, I'm a real crazy dad working some really crazy hours sometimes, and I just ... I just want to tell you how sorry I am for treating you like ... a time slot. I'm so sorry. Just know that I'm going to change all that, dear. Things are going to change. I love you, Tamiko."

"Me too," said Kana. "I've been too much into my store, and have been kind of ignoring you lately. I realize now—we realize now—that life's too short and fragile. Family's most important. So from now on, it's family first—you hear, Tamiko?"

The couple talked for a while longer and eventually left the room. It was getting late, and they both needed to try to get some sleep of their own. It wasn't easy, though, for almost all they could think about was Tamiko awakening from her coma, and being able to remove her bandages and bring her home. They also had Midori on their minds—her untimely death and approaching funeral.

After a rather short sleep, Thomas and Kana woke up to

a new day. The weather just happened to match their moods, as it was quite dark and rainy outside without even a peep of sun. The parents drove to the hospital once again only to find Tamiko exactly the same as before.

After an uneventful visit, Thomas drove Kana to her store so that she could wrap up a few things. On arrival, Kana discovered that she had lost her store keys—all except the one for the front door, as it was on her main keychain. Shortly after the two entered the building, the phone rang. It was Kana's father, who already knew of Tamiko's condition, as Kana had informed him the day before.

While Kana was on the phone, Thomas decided to go back to the hospital in hopes of retrieving her keys, as he seemed to remember seeing them in Tamiko's room. As for Kana, she wouldn't be without company while her husband was gone, as talks with her dad would sometimes go on for hours.

When Thomas entered Tamiko's room, he stared at her once again and talked to her, hoping that she would suddenly awaken from her long sleep. He found the keys in the corner of the room and spoke to Tamiko again.

The silence was almost driving him crazy. He paced around the room like a zombie with his hands clasped behind his head. He moved faster and faster, turning in circles as he went from one corner of the room to the other. Finally, he stopped in the center of the room and just fell down and cried.

"Nooooooo!" he screamed at the top of his voice over a clap of thunder.

Gradually, he picked himself up, and he stood there with his eyes fixed on his frozen daughter. He slowly walked toward her with his head down, and he sang ...

Tamiko, my dear,
Why are you now lying here?
I just fail to see,
How you could abandon me … so suddenly, my dear.

Tamiko, awake,
Through these walls of sleep and silence you must break,
We've so much to say to you. If you only knew,
Come back to us for goodness sake.

Someday soon, the shining sun will come out,
And you'll be home at last.

Till that day, there'll be rain and more doubt,
We just have to get past!

Tamiko, my dear,
Listen now if you can hear,
You don't have to fear,
I'm right here … I'm standing near,
Don't cry a tear, my dear.

Soon, though, I must go,
Before, there's one thing that you should know,
I love you so, my Tamiko. My heart's aglow,
Come back to me, my doll, my dear.

For losing you like this I fear.

Chapter 37
Life without Tamiko

Life without Tamiko just wasn't the same. Thomas and Kana couldn't eat, couldn't sleep, and couldn't work. They even had trouble talking. Even Butterscotch could sense Tamiko's absence, as he occasionally yelped and yowled. It really wasn't long before the two understood the meaning of the expression, "You don't realize how precious someone is until you've lost them."

The parents made frequent visits to the hospital and even brought over some of Tamiko's favorite belongings to "keep her company." Each visit began with new hope and ended with heartache, as Tamiko remained stationary and lifeless. In fact, Tamiko seemed to be in exactly the same position every time, and it appeared as though she wasn't even breathing. While impatiently waiting for Tamiko's revival, minutes seemed like hours, hours seemed like days, and days seemed like weeks.

If Tamiko's situation wasn't sad enough, the fourth day brought even more grief. It was Midori's soshiki—her funeral. The ceremony took place in Midori's hometown of Oyama, not far from Kana's country store. The air was still and odorless, and the silence was broken only by the sad cooing of mourning doves. A good number of people were present, including Tamiko's home tutor, Sakura, and Kana's father and brother Makoto along with his wife Hiroko. Men in their black suits, white shirts, and black ties alongside women wearing their black dresses or black kimonos gathered in mutual mourning. Some carried prayer beads or juzu, and most guests brought condolence money in fancy black and silver envelopes, which is a traditional part of the Japanese funeral.

The wake began with a Buddhist priest chanting part of a sutra and ended with an offering of incense on the incense urn. In the casket on the altar was a charred version of Midori. Dressed in a white kimono, Midori was as still as Mount Fuji itself; her face was partially covered with a veil, and her arms were folded gently upon her chest. Also in the casket were some things that represented activities that Midori was particularly fond of, like mountaineering guides, trail maps, model airplanes, Pocky sticks, wasabi peas, microscope slides, little toy animals—especially Japanese macaques, and even tiny bungee cords. Afterwards, the funeral ceremony was held, and it was quite similar to the wake except that Midori received a new Buddhist name written in Kanji.

At the end of the ceremony, loved ones placed flowers in the casket around Midori's head and shoulders before the casket was sealed and carried to the hearse. Many tears were shed, bows exchanged, and questions asked about the plane crash and Tamiko's condition. Finally, the crate was taken to the crematorium where Midori's body, like most deceased Japanese, was cremated. Some of the ashes were buried in the family grave and the rest were scattered over the foothills of Mount Fuji.

"It wasn't her time," said Kana, sobbing and unable to silence the thought of Tamiko possibly being next on the funeral list. "Midori was so young ... and so full of energy."

"I know," said Thomas. "Midori was such a good person. Sometimes, life just isn't fair."

"I really loved her," said Kana. "Midori will always be in my heart ... and she will be missed."

Thomas looked to the sky.

"And may she finally rest in peace."

It had already been "only" a week, and the two parents still didn't see any change in Tamiko's condition whatsoever. At least she was still alive, though, looking on the bright side. Every time their phone rang, there was a moment of extremely mixed feelings—was it going to be someone from the hospital or someone else? If the call was from the hospital, were they going to receive good news—that Tamiko had finally awakened—or bad news? Thomas and Kana did everything they could to extinguish any thought of the latter; they had to stay positive and just pray. The most frustrating part of all was that there was nothing they could do to bring Tamiko back; all they could do was wait.

Week two was under way, and the parents had to turn on the TV at night and even during the day sometimes to "fill in" Tamiko's absence with at least some semblance of life. Often, Thomas would gaze at the television and a few other electronic things around the house and think back on how "valuable" they seemed before Tamiko's plane crash. Now, however, they appeared almost worthless. Unlike the first week, which was cloudy and rainy, the second was quite warm and sunny. This certainly helped lift the spirits of the lone parents, giving them some illusion of hope or faith that Tamiko would soon pull through.

At work, Thomas struggled to speed up the process of creating his carbon nanotubes—not so much for work purposes, but for Tamiko! If he could create the right kind of nanorobots, he would be able to produce many different kinds of material rapidly and fix up Tamiko's skin in almost no time. In fact, he was already able to do skin repairs using his nanotechnology, but, as always, it was a very time-consuming process. He had already put so much time and effort into his work, and was so close to making a breakthrough—it was like doing a puzzle and finding out in the end that one or two pieces were missing. He worked and worked till late at night, trying to find the missing piece.

As for Tamiko's state of hibernation, up to this point in time, Thomas and Kana had done some research on comas and asked the doctors many questions. They learned that although many coma patients recover full awareness, some may never progress beyond the most basic of responses. They also learned that regaining consciousness is not immediate, and that, during the first few days, the patient is awake for only minutes but then gradually stays conscious longer as the days go on. Some patients may awake in a deep state of disorientation and may also have disabilities, such as dysphasia—an inability to speak or understand words that is caused by a brain lesion.

During this second week, it seemed as though Tamiko was trying to say something to her parents when they came to visit—a faint, distant murmuring of words. It wasn't clear what she was trying to say, but her voice sounded both somewhat creepy and somewhat comforting.

After what seemed like months now, it was week three, and Thomas and Kana were beginning to lose a part of their sanity. Every phone call was now like a fire alarm, and every day was another long challenge of hope mixed with despair.

"What do we do now?" said Kana. "How long can we go on like this?"

"I understand," said Thomas. "I feel the same way. But

all we can do is wait. She will come back. Believe me … she will!"

Thomas's positive attitude seemed to help Kana somewhat, but it was still far from easy for them to withstand the emotional strain.

During week four, they seemed to, somewhat surprisingly, accept that Tamiko was really disconnected from the world, and they kept telling themselves that she'd wake up "when it's time." However, it wasn't necessarily this cut-and-dried, for there were still moments when one or both parents would go crazy for a bit and have a conniption only to quickly remind themselves that they had to stay focused on being positive. Finally, after all the waiting, they got a call from the doctor, who spoke in an optimistic tone of voice.

"I have some great news for you," said the doctor. "Your daughter just awoke from her coma!"

Chapter 38
Big Bears, Flower Cards, and Little Toy Magnets

Even though Tamiko had only roused for a few minutes, this was music to the ears of Thomas and Kana! They jumped up and down with excitement and cheered as though they had just won the lottery. Butterscotch even ran around in circles and wagged his tail as if he understood the news. The parents just happened to be finishing up the dishes when they got the call, so they left the kitchen and zoomed to the hospital to see Tamiko.

On the way there, they quickly stopped off at a toy store to get her the big teddy bear she had always wanted; they would put it beside her on her bed as a token of hope and good fortune. The parents ended up buying two bears—one from Thomas, and one from Kana.

When they got to the hospital, they raced to Tamiko's room and found her sleeping, but in a different position than the one they had seen a thousand times before. They placed the big brown teddy bears next to her, one on each side, as if to guard her somehow.

"Hi there, Tamiko!" said Thomas excitedly. "It's Daddy! I hear you're starting to wake up!"

"You can do it," said Kana. "You have to, baby!"

Then, the doctor walked into the room.

"Oh, isn't that sweet!" said the doctor, looking at the bears.

"They'll keep her company," said Kana.

"So, you heard the good news then?" said the doctor.

"We certainly did," said Thomas. "But we have a few more questions for you, though."

"Go ahead."

"Did she talk at all when she woke up?"

"She grumbled a little bit and then said, 'Where is everyone?' We asked her if she knew where she was, and she asked if she had been in a plane crash. Just moments later, she realized that she was in a hospital. Then, she went back to sleep."

"Do you think she'll wake up again soon?" asked Kana.

"There's a good chance she'll wake up again within the next twenty-four hours. And when she does, it'll most likely last longer."

So the parents waited all day long, but Tamiko lay there like a statue. The next day, the two went to work with only their daughter on their minds. As Thomas sat at his desk filled with anxiety, Kana found it difficult to perform her duties, as she moved around in slow motion, waiting for the phone to ring with good news.

Then, Thomas got a call from the hospital. Apparently, Tamiko had roused again—for five minutes this time! Moreover, she even "had her mind," as she was able to answer a few simple questions. But it would take a very long time before the bandages could be removed, and years before Tamiko could ever walk or run again—if ever. Thomas quickly told his wife of the good news and finished up a few things in the lab and in his office. While sitting down at his office desk, Thomas reached into his pocket and pulled out some of Tamiko's belongings that he had previously taken from the house to decorate his office.

First he took out some flower cards—the ones Tamiko used when playing koi-koi—and then he produced a set of little cylindrical toy magnets. With the cards, he began making little houses as he racked his brain trying to figure out the "secret ingredient" to speed up his nanotechnology; he was just on the verge of throwing in the towel.

When he started constructing the third floor, the card house suddenly collapsed, and Thomas began building another. Soon, the second house tumbled as well, and Thomas pushed the cards aside and began playing with the toy magnets. By now, he had pretty much given up on finding the solution to his nanotechnology problem, as he was tired, frustrated, and stressed.

To waste some time, he spaced each of the little magnets, like miniature wheels standing up, about three inches apart from one another; for some odd reason, he imagined planting apple trees in a certain pattern. With his head hanging low, he was about to complete his "apple orchard" by laying down the last magnet when he got a phone call.

"Hi, Tom," one of his colleagues said. "I'm sorry to inform you that the Japanese government won't be funding our nanotechnology project anymore. The results are just not impressive enough, so they're pulling the plug. Sorry, Tom. I know how much time and energy you put into this."

With that, Tom threw his papers against the wall in anger and then just lay his head down and cried. After all that hard work, he ended up a failure. Moreover, Tamiko would have to stay in bandages like a mummy for ages. With his face almost touching the desk, Thomas took his last magnet and gently sent it rolling toward the other magnets. As it approached the nearest one, the two attracted and clicked together. These two magnets, now stuck together as one, rolled even further because of the initial momentum, and another magnet stuck to the rolling magnets ... and then another and another in an accelerating chain reaction of magnetic attractions—"Click! Click! Click! Clickety click click click!"

Finally, all of the magnets were stuck together, and the resulting big "single magnet" rolled to the edge of the desk and into the hands of Thomas, as he snatched it just after it rolled off the edge. Thomas stared at the table, frozen and with his mouth wide open, in utter amazement of what he had just seen. After a few more seconds, he sprang up from his chair.

"I've got it! I've got it! Eureka! I've got it!" he yelled as he ran out of his office and jumped around like Archimedes did when he discovered the law of buoyancy.

He danced around and jumped some more and even did a few somersaults! He was so excited, he even hugged and kissed his colleagues.

"What is he, crazy?" one said.

"What's with you, Tom?" said another. "Are you feeling okay?"

And so it went. Thomas had now discovered the secret ingredient!

Chapter 39 —
Reconstruction!

Thomas really got it! Just after he saw the magnets click together, he realized that he could use a "chain reaction" of magnetic attractions in his nanotechnology to piece together the necessary atoms and produce pretty much anything he wanted. Therefore, he would be able to fix up Tamiko's skin and other body parts in almost no time! First, though, he would have to run a few tests.

Over the next few hours, Thomas and his colleagues made some adjustments to his machines, did some computer programming, and "sprayed" a thin layer a carbon nanotubes on a test dummy that Thomas named "Jun"; before, it would have taken him days or weeks, but now it only took him a few seconds!

Then, the team did some tests on Jun and found a few imperfections, so they reconfigured the machines and computers over and over again until they succeeded in producing a layer of "perfect" carbon nanotubes. Thomas didn't like the fact that the new substance conducted electricity, so he tried to think of a way to get around this. After a few more hours of work, he was able to produce carbon nanotubes that were resistant to electricity. He ran more tests with his team members and sprayed a layer of these new and improved nanotubes on Jun.

Afterward, they tested Jun's new "skin" in various ways; they poured acid on him and many other kinds of chemicals—the skin remained intact, like nothing had happened to it. They also tried penetrating Jun's skin by stabbing him with knives—they were unable to cut through it! They did tests with electricity and found that Jun was, in fact, resistant to it. They even fired bullets at Jun and found that they were able to penetrate his skin at close range. This wasn't really a problem, though, for Jun's new skin was extremely thin; by making it thicker and also more "rubbery," Jun would be virtually indestructible. In fact, only two or three millimeters of thickness was hundreds of times the strength of steel—no bullet would ever be able to penetrate it. So Thomas and company sprayed a thick coat of the substance on Jun's chest and fired bullets at it. Like Thomas had thought, the bullets—even at close range—did absolutely nothing to Jun. Finally, there were other obstacles to be taken into consideration, such as allowing the protective substance to be flexible and "breathable."

As a final test, they threw fire on Jun, and, as they had anticipated, the skin didn't burn or melt whatsoever. Now Thomas was ready to fix up Tamiko! After doing all these tests, Thomas suddenly realized that he hadn't informed his wife that he would be running late, so he called and told her the wonderful news. Although both were very happy with the breakthrough, this would not guarantee the full awakening of Tamiko from her coma.

Later they raced to the hospital only to find Tamiko, once again, in a deep sleep. Thomas asked for her to be transferred to his lab, but it wasn't quite that easy. There were questions to be answered, papers to be filled out, and arrangements to be made. Thomas tried hard to get his daughter moved to his lab, but the hospital wasn't willing to fulfill his wishes. Thomas, however, was a fighter like Tamiko—he just wouldn't give up.

After a whirlwind of activity and hours of discussion, Tamiko was finally transferred to the lab, where Thomas would now dedicate all of his time to fixing her. With the help of several highly skilled doctors and his teammates, Thomas proceeded in the reconstruction of Tamiko. First, she was given a special anesthetic and her bandages were carefully removed. Then, Tamiko was operated on. Her muscles, especially those in her arms and legs, were dramatically improved. In addition to this, many of Tamiko's bones were greatly strengthened with the nanotubes. They even added some very special "nanorobots" to her blood that would kill off virtually any kind of disease and rapidly repair any internal wound. Then, a very thick coating of the new carbon nanotubes was applied all over Tamiko's body.

Finally, her face was completely redone, and carbon nanotubes were applied to it too; however, her face was now Caucasian rather than Japanese. The reason for this was twofold: first, Thomas accidentally programmed the wrong skin shade because the computer monitor wasn't color-calibrated correctly. He immediately saw the problem just after he applied the first coat of nanotubes, but Thomas figured that this was normal and that the color would darken as he added more layers. He thought about spraying the top layer with the correct color, but he was afraid that doing so might corrupt the lower layers somehow.

Secondly, Thomas had inadvertently selected the wrong face from among the several faces of Tamiko that were programmed into the computer database. There was a story behind this: In the past, Tamiko had made several sketches of what she thought she would look like if she were an angel.

Just out of curiosity, Thomas had programmed a sketch of her as a fair-skinned blonde angel, in addition to her real likenesses. When it came time to reconstruct her face, he dropped his eraser on the Enter key with the angel face selected. Rather than stop the process halfway through and try to revert, Thomas played it safe and went ahead with it. Besides, the angel face went along much better with her white body.

The entire process of reconstructing Tamiko would take several more days to accomplish. Thomas worked day and night, hardly even getting any sleep at all. He had never worked so much in his life.

Finally, after all the hard work, the rebuilding of Tamiko was complete. She was now virtually indestructible in practically every way! All she had to do now was simply wake up. Hopefully, she would still have all of her mind.

CHAPTER 40–
THE SPARK

Now that Tamiko's skin was very thick, the team had to greatly increase the sensitivity of the heart monitor in order for it to do its job. For now, her heart was still stable. Thomas and Kana, along with some of the doctors and nanotechnology people, waited with impatience for Tamiko to finally awaken. They anticipated, though, that she would probably wake up for only a few minutes and then fall back to sleep again—it would take some time before Tamiko would stay awake normally. There was also the question of her mind—would she have all of it? Time would tell.

As they waited longer and longer, they became more anxious. Finally, after several days, Tamiko moved a little. Her parents were so excited, and they encouraged her to wake up.

"That's it, Tamiko, that's it!"

Suddenly, the heart monitor went dead with an awful-sounding "Beeeeeeeeeeeee!" There was nothing more that could be done—this was the end of Tamiko!

"Tamiko! Tamiko!" her parents cried helplessly. "Oh … Tamiko!"

Thomas wrapped his arms around his daughter and burst into tears as he held her tight.

"You did everything you could, Tom!" said Kana, crying along with her arms around her husband. "You really tried."

"Tamiko," Thomas cried softly one last time with his arms still wrapped around his daughter. "I just needed ... that last ... spark."

In Tamiko's mind, everything was black. Then, suddenly, she saw a kaleidoscope of colors dancing all around her like quiet fireworks. Then, the colorful fireworks turned into strange kinds of birds and butterflies. Things got brighter and brighter until Tamiko could see the most beautiful landscape she had ever seen. It was full of lovely flowers and tall trees. Above her was a sky full of birds merrily singing. In the distance, there was a large, placid pond with ducks swimming all around in it. Tamiko was either flying or walking without feet down a path toward the pond when, suddenly, a familiar figure appeared right before her eyes. It was Grandmaster Shun!

"Hi, Tamiko," he said, smiling.

"Grandmaster Shun! G'day. What are you doing here?" asked Tamiko. "And where are we?"

"Well ... those are good questions," said Shun. "And for every good question, there's a good answer! I'm on my way to paradise. You see, my time on Earth has come to an end. My days in the sun and around the beautiful Mount Fuji are over now. But you, Tamiko ..."

"What about me?" said Tamiko.

"I'm afraid you won't be joining me ... or at least not now. It's not your time, Tamiko. You see, where my life has ended, yours has just begun."

"But I don't understand," said Tamiko. "Right now, I'm ... like ... dead or something."

"You've been given a gift, Tamiko," explained Shun.

"You have a heart of great compassion that very few people possess. It shows in everything you do, like always trying to help others in any way you can … like trying to rescue that poor little girl and comforting that dying woman in the hospital … like sharing your own heart with her on the darkest day of her life and giving that poor boy enough money to buy a new bicycle. And as for asking for absolutely nothing in return, that is a gift that you were born with, Tamiko. I have another gift; I have the gift of great fighting ability. Well, I *do* have compassion, too. It's just that I'd have to say that fighting is my number one thing. I have dedicated my life to learning and mastering virtually every form of martial art known to man—even street fighting. I want to give this gift away—to you. It's not of very much use around here. As I know you, Tamiko, I know you'll use it wisely."

"But when am I going to see you again?" asked Tamiko.

"I don't know," said Shun. "That's not something I can really answer. But just know that I'll be watching over you from time to time. And I'll be rooting for you!"

"But I'm going to miss you," said Tamiko. "You're such a great person. And you're funny too."

"You're kind of funny yourself," said Shun. "All those pranks you did …"

"Yeah, well … sometimes," said Tamiko. "You should check them out on YouTube. My friend Jeremy just put them there. I mean, there must be computers around here somewhere."

Shun laughed. "Well, I think there should be at least one not too far away from here. Anyway, I better be going now, Tamiko."

Strange but beautiful music began to play. The colorful butterflies came back, and the sky got brighter and brighter as Shun stood there almost like a statue.

"To accept my gift ... my gift of great fighting abilities ... touch me. Touch the light!" said Shun.

With that, Tamiko slowly put both of her hands forward, and a burst of sparkly dust or something plunged into her and swirled all around her like a miniature tornado making a "Whoooosh!" sound. Tamiko had never felt anything like it. It felt wonderful! In the background somewhere, or possibly from Shun, Tamiko heard muffled words that sounded like "Heart, strength, and mind." After the mini whirlwind of light and stardust was finished, Shun gently raised one of his arms and, with a slight grin, pointed to Tamiko.

"Good-bye, Tamiko!" he said with a somewhat sad tone of voice.

"Good-bye," replied Tamiko. "And thank you."

A blue streak of electricity then shot from Shun's pointing finger and zapped Tamiko like a Taser gun. In reaction to the jolt, Tamiko suddenly twitched on her bed, and the next thing she knew, she was lying on a bed with joyful people looking down on her making all sorts of noise.

"Tamiko!" yelled Thomas as the heart monitor sounded a healthy "Beep! Beep! Beep!"

"Tamiko, you're back!" cried Kana. "You're back!"

"She just woke up!" shouted Thomas to the doctors and other people nearby. "She's back! Tamiko's back!"

Tamiko was now wide awake and staring at her parents. Thomas and Kana expressed more words of joy as they hugged and kissed their daughter. They were now happier than the luckiest lottery winner, for Tamiko was alive and well!

Chapter 41
Welcome Back, Tamiko!

"Tamiko," said Thomas, "do you know who I am? Do you know who we are?"

Tamiko looked at the two, somewhat confused. Then, her puzzlement slowly disappeared.

"I'm not dreaming?" said Tamiko. "Daddy, Mommy, is that really you?"

"Yes, dear, you got it!" said Thomas. "Mommy and Daddy are right here. This is no dream. It's really us!"

Thomas and Kana cried tears of joy. Even the doctors, who had just come over, shed a few tears.

"We missed you so much! We missed you *so* much!" cried Thomas and Kana.

"I missed you too!" said Tamiko. "It's like I went on a trip for several years and now I'm back!"

"Yes, you're really back! We love you, Tamiko. We love you so much!"

"Where am I?" said Tamiko. "This is like a *Star Trek* movie or something!"

Her parents laughed.

"Yes, it does sort of look like *Star Trek*, doesn't it?" said Thomas as he continued to laugh.

"How do you feel?" asked Kana. "Are you feeling sleepy

at all?"

"I'm feeling ... I don't know. Not really sleepy, but ... I feel great!" replied Tamiko.

Her parents uttered some more words of joy and then squeezed, hugged, and kissed her.

"Can I get up?" asked Tamiko.

"I think ... sure!" said Thomas. "Just be careful, though!"

"This is incredible!" said one of the doctors. "Coma patients don't normally recover that quickly. I'm amazed!"

Tamiko, with some help from her parents, slowly got up from her bed and stood up. Hung up in the corner next to her was a light pink yukata dress that Thomas and Kana had recently bought for their daughter. Tamiko put on the dress and then slowly walked around.

"This place ... do you, like, work here?" asked Tamiko.

"That's what I was going to tell you," said Thomas. "This is my lab. I had you transferred here from the hospital so I could ... I'll explain later. It's just so great to have you back!"

"I feel like ... I don't know how to describe it! I feel like a brand-new person!" said Tamiko. "It's so weird! I like it!"

Tamiko continued to stroll around the room curiously eyeing all the funny-looking machines and chemicals and equipment. Finally she stopped in the center of the room.

"What ... what do I look like?" she asked.

Her parents exchanged a look that made her worry, and then they brought over a tall mirror. Just before they put it in front of Tamiko, they spoke some works of "preparation."

"Tamiko," Thomas began, "what you're about to see may ... come as sort of a shock. You see, you were in a plane crash and ... let's just say your face is not exactly what it used to be. Here. Have a look."

Kana gently turned the mirror around to face Tamiko.

"Woooooooow!" exclaimed Tamiko in utter amazement. "I thought I was going to look …"

"You like it?" said Kana.

"I … I love it!" said Tamiko. "It's awesome!"

"I'm glad you think so!" said Thomas.

"How did you do it?" said Tamiko. "I thought I was Japanese. Is this, like, makeup or something? "

"No, it's … something else," replied Thomas.

"You're beautiful!" cried Kana, hugging Tamiko. "You're so beautiful!"

"And your voice is beautiful too," added Thomas. "It's a bit different, but I'd say it's even nicer than before!"

Tamiko had the face of an angel—her previous Japanese face now replaced with a white one. Her eyes, still blue, were no longer slanted; though sleepy, they gleamed with wonder as she continued to gaze into the mirror and slowly run her hands through her long golden blonde hair. Tamiko's build was considerably larger than before; it looked as though she'd put on a good number of extra shirts and pants—a moderately puffed-up version of a Barbie Doll. Although Tamiko appeared different in many ways, one thing hadn't changed: her smile.

Some of the other doctors and lab people came over to see the living Tamiko; it wasn't long before phone calls were made and the good news spread around like wildfire. In less than an hour, everyone who had worked on Tamiko came over to witness her extraordinary recovery. Of course, everyone in the room knew of Tamiko's "super abilities"— everyone, that is, except for Tamiko. Little did she know that she was over hundreds of times stronger than steel, that she was resistant to fire, and that she had incredible strength and agility.

While everyone was yakking, chattering, and asking all sorts of questions, Tamiko was trying to understand where, exactly, she "came from." She was told that she was in a plane crash, but she couldn't really remember anything about it. She knew who her parents were, and was able to speak normally and understand what was going on around her, but most everything else was just one big blank. It was as though she had just been zapped to Earth not knowing exactly where she came from, but she had no bad feelings of any kind, no "baggage." It was actually a very warm and peaceful feeling.

Quickly, the noise level of the chattering went from loud to quiet; it was time for a speech.

"I would like to express how happy I am … how happy we all are … to see that Tamiko has made a full recovery. Congratulations to Thomas and Kana, and to their daughter, Tamiko!" said a colleague of Thomas's. "Now, I think it's time for our good friend Tom to say a few words!"

"Thom-as! Thom-as! Thom-as! Thom-as!" everyone chanted.

"I … I can't even believe this is happening!" said Thomas. "I really don't know what to say. I've gone through so much lately. My life, and my wife Kana's life too, has been a real roller-coaster ride during the past few weeks. I'm sure it's been quite a ride for Tamiko, too. Right now, I'm just plain overjoyed—and also a little tired, I must say—but I'd like to thank everyone here for all the hard work and long hours you put into my daughter's recovery. Thank you all so much!"

Then, glasses of champagne were poured, and another one of Thomas's colleagues proposed a toast.

"Here's to Tamiko and her full recovery … and may she stay in good health. Welcome back!"

"Welcome back, Tamiko!" everyone cheered.

Chapter 42
Back to Reality

After the "welcome back" party had pretty much ended, Tamiko was transferred to the hospital, where she spent a few more days to fully recuperate. Not only did Tamiko get more rest but she also took time to walk around, do some light exercise, and get used to her new body. When it was finally time for Tamiko to be discharged, the doctors ran some final tests just to ensure her a clean bill of health.

"It looks like everything's in order!" said one of the doctors. "I'd say this girl's going home!"

"I still can't believe she made such an amazing recovery!" said another.

"Thanks again for everything," said Thomas. "You don't know how much I appreciate it."

"Domo arigatou gozaimasu!" said Kana.

So the happy family of three hopped into the car and made their way home. When they arrived they saw Butterscotch at the window, barking as he always did when anything exciting was going on within close proximity.

"Do you remember who that little guy is?" asked Thomas, pointing to the dog.

Tamiko looked at Butterscotch, confused. The dog looked familiar, but she just couldn't put her finger on the name.

"That's ..." Tamiko began. "That's ... what's the name again? I think it starts with a 'B.'"

"You're right!" said Kana. "Now, think of an ice cream topping. Butt ..."

As soon as Thomas opened the front door, the dog came running at them with his tail wagging excitedly.

"Hi there, Butterscotch!" cried Tamiko, not realizing that she just said his name.

"You got it!" said Thomas. "You said his name—Butterscotch!"

After they all played with the dog some, Thomas opened the door all the way to reveal a big sign reading "Welcome Back!" surrounded by balloons and streamers.

"Oh, that's beautiful!" said Tamiko.

"You're beautiful!" said Kana.

Next, it was time for Tamiko to try to remember the rooms of the house; however, her parents were careful not to pressure her too much. First, they went upstairs to Tamiko's bedroom, where, with some time and a bit of help from her mom and dad, she slowly remembered her furniture and belongings. On her way out, Tamiko accidentally slammed the door, for she wasn't yet used to the extra muscles that were now starting to kick in.

"Sorry," she said. "I didn't mean to."

"That's okay," said Thomas. "You're just kind of excited, that's all."

As Tamiko went from one room of the house to another, she gradually remembered little pieces and fragments. It was sort of like trying to do a puzzle for each room—each puzzle was only partially completed. Not only was Tamiko somewhat disoriented, but she also felt a bit different somehow, but in a good way. Tamiko asked more questions about her past and the plane crash; her parents only gave a few simple answers in order to be easy on Tamiko.

Soon it was time for Tamiko to go to bed, so her parents brought in her big teddy bears, along with the other items that had kept watch over her at the hospital, and placed them around her bed. They read Tamiko several stories and kissed her good night.

"Get some good sleep, my dear," said Thomas. "I love you."

"I love you too," said Kana. "It's so wonderful to have you back."

After the two gave Tamiko another kiss good night, they calmly left the room and then exchanged worried looks.

"What if … what if Tamiko doesn't wake up?" asked Kana.

"I know," said Thomas. "I thought about that myself. We're just going to have to keep our fingers crossed."

So the family slept through the night; however, Thomas and Kana got up at least twice during the night to check on Tamiko. Everything seemed to be fine. The next morning, the parents got up first and let Tamiko sleep in a bit. Then, they crept into Tamiko's bedroom and shook her a little to wake her. Tamiko lay there immobile but only for a second or two. Then she squirmed a bit and got up. "Phew!" went both parents.

For the next several days Tamiko took it easy—not only physically but mentally. Thomas and Kana didn't ask her too many questions, as they didn't want to push her memory beyond its limit; they felt that the best treatment for now was simply spending quality time with her and talking to her. So the parents put work aside and dedicated all of their time to Tamiko: they read books, played games, walked the dog, and slowly caught up on old times. The previously distressed parents were now overjoyed to finally have their daughter back in their lives.

As for Tamiko, she still felt as though she were zapped to Earth from another planet. She felt good. She felt secure … without any concerns or worries or negative emotions of any kind, just the simple love of life and love of family.

Having extra strong muscles, Tamiko would often use excessive force when doing simple things like closing doors, washing dishes, wiping counters, and making her bed. Tamiko's memory was gradually improving. She remembered more about the rooms of the house and her belongings; she remembered more about her neighbors and the times she had with her parents.

Of course, Tamiko's neighbors were puzzled when they first saw her; they just couldn't understand what was going on. Tamiko's parents had told Mr. Miller and Mr. Howard about her airplane accident while she was hospitalized; the neighbors had seen the sheer agony Thomas and Kana went through. What a surprise it was for the neighbors to then see Tamiko's parents return home, as happy as could possibly be, with what appeared to be another girl! It wasn't long, though, before Thomas "explained" Tamiko's new look.

It had now been a week since Tamiko's release from the hospital, and Thomas and Kana felt that it was about time for "the big day."

"Sleep tight, my dear," said Thomas. "We have a big day ahead of us."

"A big day?" asked Tamiko. "What's happening tomorrow?"

"It's kind of a surprise," said Kana.

"You'll see," said Thomas. "Let's just say that tomorrow's going to be kind of interesting."

Little did Tamiko know what the next day had in store for her. Her parents were tempted to tell her all about it, but they resisted, thinking it would be best to let her mind rest overnight.

The next morning the three woke up to another beautiful day. Somehow, Tamiko sensed an upcoming change in weather, a certain excitement in the air.

"Are you ready for the big day?" asked Thomas.

"As ready as I'll ever be, I guess," said Tamiko.

After breakfast, the threesome drove over to some kind of facility just outside of Tokyo. From the outside, it looked like a hospital or a research and development building similar to the place where Thomas worked, only it was bigger and more modern looking. When the family of three entered the building, they had to go through a gauntlet of high-tech security checks—it was almost like something from a James Bond movie. The air smelled of sweet chemicals and scrambled eggs. Everything was very modern looking—the ceilings were tall, the hallways were wide, the paint was of vibrant colors, and the floors were sparkling clean. Throughout the building, there seemed to be an odd silence—it felt as though a whole crowd of people might jump out at any second and yell something.

After Thomas swiped his pass card, entered a secret code, and did a fingerprint scan, the three were finally escorted to an elevator and lowered to a large room below. Here there were machines and gadgets of all sorts. It reminded Tamiko, once again, of James Bond—it looked like the place where all of Bond's cool toys and weapons were tested.

"Thomas!" someone said. "What a pleasure! I see you

brought the whole family!"

"Indeed I did!"

"And how is Tamiko feeling today?" asked the mystery man. "By the way, I'm Kinji. I'm a friend of your dad's. I'm sure you're wondering what this place is all about."

"Oh, she's been asking some questions on the way here," said Thomas. "But I didn't give in."

"She's one curious kid," said Kana.

"Well, curiosity's a good thing," said Kinji. "You can never ask too many questions. So, shall we get started?"

Tamiko's curiosity was building even more now. *Where am I? What am I doing here? Are they going to do more tests on me or something? What is this all about?* she thought.

Chapter 43—
The Truth about Tamiko

"Tamiko," said Thomas, "what you're about to learn is … going to be somewhat of a shock to you."

"A shock to me?" said Tamiko.

"First, let me introduce you to Jun," said Thomas.

In the distance, at the far side of the room, a white curtain lifted off what appeared to be a crash test dummy sitting on a chair wearing some sort of vest.

"Now it's time to have some fun … with Jun," said Thomas.

Suddenly, a loud burst of bullets were fired at Jun from some sort of machine gun.

Kinji removed the vest to reveal that Jun's plastic "skin" had not been damaged whatsoever.

"DCN—dielectric carbon nanotubes!" said Thomas. "Hundreds of times stronger than steel, and resistant to electricity."

"Wow! That's … that's really cool!" said Tamiko. "But I don't quite understand, though. What does that have to do with me?"

"As a matter of fact, it has everything to do with you," said Thomas.

"Everything?" said Tamiko. "What exactly do you

mean?"

"You, Tamiko, you are—" began Kinji.

"Let me explain," interrupted Thomas. "You see, Tamiko. After your plane crash, you were ... you were so severely injured that you were nearly unrecognizable. After you were rushed to the hospital, you were almost totally wrapped up in bandages. Many of your bones and internal organs were damaged, and ... something happened to your nerve sensors too. Although you still have some sense of touch, you can't experience any pain. Well, we worried that you wouldn't make it. Then you fell into a coma, and I had you transferred to my lab at work. At first, I wanted to fix up some of your cuts and scrapes using my nanotechnology, I couldn't do much because the work process was so slow. But then I made an amazing discovery ... a breakthrough. This breakthrough enabled me to speed up the process enormously, and now I can quickly produce almost any material or substance I want using my superfast nanorobots."

"Nanorobots?" said Tamiko. "What's that?"

"Oh, those are just microscopic little robots that actually do the building of the substance," said Thomas. "Anyway, I used these nanorobots to create my dielectric carbon nanotubes—not only for Jun, but for you too."

"You did that for me?" said Tamiko. "What exactly do you mean? In what way?"

"What I'm really trying to say here is that ... I fixed your skin using these carbon nanotubes. You're covered, from head to toe, with a very thick coat of them. Tamiko, you're hundreds of times stronger than steel—you're basically indestructible! You're even resistant to fire!"

"Are you ...?" said Tamiko. "Is this ... some kind of a joke?"

"No, Tamiko," said Thomas. "This is no joke. And there's more."

"That's not all?" said Tamiko, startled. "Then tell me … tell me what else you've done to me!"

"We've also greatly improved your muscles. I've always wondered how a common cat can easily jump several times its own height and how a simple ant can carry over twenty times its own weight. I, along with some other colleagues of mine, discovered the secret behind those wonders a little while back, but, like I said before, I was unable to speed things up. So, because of my new discovery, you … well … you should be able to jump like a cat and be as strong as an ant!"

"This is … I still don't believe this is really—"

"Here," said Kinji. "Here's some fire."

Kinji lit up a torch nearby and invited Tamiko to come over and test out her resistance to fire.

"Trust me," said Thomas as Kana showed a somewhat worried look. "Remember, you can't feel any pain."

Tamiko walked slowly over to the flaming torch, lifted her right hand, and waved it through the flame. Tamiko didn't really do a very good test, though, as she moved her hand too fast; any "regular" human being could have easily done the same thing.

"Slower," said Thomas. "Don't worry … trust me."

With that, Tamiko swiped her hand through the flame once again but slower this time. Like before, she felt nothing. Then, Tamiko got a bit more daring and passed both hands through the fire at such a slow speed that any ordinary person would have been screaming with pain. Tamiko felt nothing; it was like the burning torch was just a toy or something.

"Woooow … that's unreal!" said Tamiko. "I can't …

that's incredible!"

Just to be certain, Tamiko simply stuck her hands smack in the center of the flame for several seconds—no pain, no burns, nothing!

"How?" said Tamiko. "I still don't believe what I just did!"

"Amazing, isn't it?" said Thomas. "And you can even hold your breath for twenty minutes. Now, let's see how high you can jump!"

Tamiko was led over to a structure about five feet high—it resembled a hydraulic lift that outdoor painters often use. Thomas and Kinji, along with a lab technician, showed Tamiko the best starting position from which to jump. On the count of three, Tamiko sprang from the floor like a grasshopper and landed on top of the ledge without any difficulty.

"Hurray!" everybody cheered.

Then, the people raised the ledge from five feet to ten feet. Again, Tamiko had no difficulty in reaching the top, and the people applauded once more. Then, the ledge was raised to fifteen feet; Tamiko was barely able to make it. At twenty feet she failed and landed on the padding below.

"It's okay, Tamiko," said Thomas. "It just takes a bit of practice."

Tamiko tried again and again. The third time around she succeeded, and everyone in the room burst into applause. This was absolutely amazing to watch; nobody had ever seen anything so incredible! Now, it was time of test out Tamiko's strength. She was asked to break five wood blocks, starting with the thinnest and working up to the thickest—it was very similar to the street game Tamiko had once played with the pieces of wood and concrete. Tamiko concentrated on block number 1 and gave it a quick blow; it was rather easy for her to break. So was the second. Block 3 was more difficult to break, but Tamiko succeeded nonetheless. As for block 4, a wooden stick that only a very strong and highly trained martial artist could rupture, Tamiko was barely able to break it.

"Way to go, Tamiko!" everyone applauded.

Now, it was time for wood piece number 5—the most difficult of all. Tamiko tried to cut through it but failed.

"Concentrate, Tamiko," said Thomas. "You can do it!"

So Tamiko focused all of her attention on the block, gathered up all of her energy, and quickly busted the wood in two.

"I did it!" said Tamiko.

"Hurrrrray!" cheered the others.

"That's absolutely … that's awesome!" said Kinji.

"You can say that again!" said Thomas and Kana.

"You're dangerous now, my little Tamiko," said Thomas.

"The force necessary to break that last piece is several times what it would take to crush a human skull!" said Kinji.

The final test was of Tamiko's reflexes and fighting skills. In what appeared to be a boxing ring in the distance, there stood a rather experienced martial artist ready to "do battle" with Tamiko. He was a Japanese fellow in his twenties and stood about six feet tall, weighed around 200 pounds and looked fairly muscular. He wore a karate gi. And he also wore a somewhat arrogant smile. Little did everybody know that Tamiko had already "inherited" the great fighting skills of the late Grandmaster Shun—everything from karate to street fighting.

"Go get him, Tamiko," said Thomas.

"Don't worry," said the other fighter. "I'll be easy on you. We just want to test your reflexes."

CHAPTER 44
BATTLE ROYAL

Tamiko stepped into the ring, and the two bowed. Then, they danced around a little, like a pair of ballerinas out of sync. Finally, the other fighter swiftly, but gently, let out a few kicks, but Tamiko easily dodged out of the way.

"You're a fast little one!" said the nameless fighter.

The anonymous fighter kicked some more and was finally able to hit Tamiko at least twice. Then, Tamiko did some kicking of her own and almost knocked down her opponent. The latter swiftly got up and made an attempt to throw Tamiko down. Instead, it was Tamiko who threw down her adversary, and without very much effort.

"Take that, white belt!" said Tamiko.

The spectators laughed a bit and cheered for Tamiko. By now, her rival was getting somewhat embarrassed, for he was a karate black belt in his late twenties, and he was just thrown down by a twelve-year-old girl. Actually, he more or less let himself be thrown down, as he was still being a bit light on her.

"I was just being easy on you," said Tamiko's adversary. "Now, it's time to put on my spurs."

So, the nameless martial artist fought his best and managed to punch Tamiko a few times. Tamiko blocked one or two of them and then retaliated with a knee strike, half-dropping her opponent. Her rival answered with a few kicks and made Tamiko fall at least twice. Despite the fact that her opponent was defeating her as the fight progressed, Tamiko still looked like a very decent fighter for her age. However, Tamiko didn't seem to be very "into it" for some reason; she got hit and knocked down a few times and didn't really do anything spectacular. Where were the great fighting abilities that Shun had given to her? Maybe they had to be "activated" somehow.

"Hmm ... not bad for a green belt," said her opponent. "Maybe someday you'll be as good as me."

Then, her opponent made a silly mistake, as he let his guard down and got knocked flat on his stomach while everyone, including Tamiko, laughed at him. At the same time, the anonymous fighter's two older brothers walked into the room; they, too, were karate black belts.

"Well, I think that's enough for one day," said Kinji.

"Good on you, mate!" said Thomas.

Suddenly, Tamiko's adversary shifted toward her with a cold look.

"I want a rematch!" he said.

"Oh, I think I'll call it a day," said Tamiko. "Maybe later."

"Anytime, Barbie Doll!"

"Did you just call me Barbie Doll?"

"I think I just did ... and you fight like her, too," replied the anonymous fighter as his brothers laughed a bit.

"You have your rematch!"

So Tamiko jumped into the ring for a second match with Mr. Wise Guy. Unlike before, Tamiko appeared to be very focused, like an olympic diver concentrating intently just before jumping off of the platform; she wasn't the same person at all.

For a short while, Tamiko's adversary stared at her as if to say, "Is this some kind of a joke? There's no way you're going to beat *me*!" Tamiko stared back. Then, after a quick bow, the two stepped back and slowly took their fighting positions. Tamiko's opponent smiled. "Ko-I," he said, meaning "Come on." For a short while, the two stood there like a couple of statues, frozen in time. Tamiko could feel the tension in the air build as the room became deathly quiet and as her competitor's smile grew wider; Tamiko remained calm, but her body was catching fire. Now positionned in what is known as a horse-back stance, Tamiko finally made her move. She lunged forward and did a quick fake to the right. Her opponent twisted slightly in that direction and then Tamiko grabbed his left hand, forced it down, stepped to the side and, with her other hand, delivered a sharp blow to his unprotected chest. With that, Tamiko's adversary stumbled backwards in rapid, little steps, nearly falling to the floor as he gasped for air.

"Suddenly, you've ... you've really improved!" said Tamiko's rival, still huffing and puffing.

Frustrated and a bit embarrased, Tamiko's opponent tried some kicks on her, but she quickly avoided almost every one of them. Then, the fighter did a series of fancy punches and roundhouse kicks, and, again, Tamiko rapidly danced and dodged her way out of most every strike.

"How did she ...? She's so fast!" said the fighter's brothers.

Afterward, Tamiko did a knee strike and immediately sent her opponent flying to the floor.

"Oh ... are you okay? I didn't mean to hurt you!" said Tamiko.

The latter, really starting to get angry now, slowly picked

himself up.

"That's for calling me Barbie Doll!" said Tamiko.

"So you must think you're a real black belt. I'll show you black belt!"

"Show me!" said Tamiko.

He sent a series of karate punches toward Tamiko, and she swiftly blocked each and every blow. Now, Tamiko started looking like a champion. Her opponent charged at her, and Tamiko threw him to the floor as if he were just a little boy. Now, the fighter was getting quite humiliated, and he grabbed a pair of batons and threw one over to Tamiko.

"Okay, you little … let's see how good you are with the jo!"

The enemy swiped his baton as cleverly as he could and tried to hit Tamiko, but Tamiko was so fast in blocking his strikes that he hardly even touched her. Finally, as fast as lightning, Tamiko grabbed the end of her rival's stick and threw him to the floor.

"Okay, that's enough!" yelled Kinji.

"Don't worry," said one of the brothers. "I'll stop her!"

So, the brother joined in, and it was two against Tamiko. The brothers punched, jabbed, and kicked in every way they could, but Tamiko was so incredibly fast and agile that the two just couldn't keep up with her. Tamiko was a completely different fighter than she had been at the very start. Thomas and Kana were absolutely stunned at how good she was.

"Tamiko! Tamiko!" cried Thomas. "I never knew you were this good!"

Within seconds, the two brothers were on the floor, and the third brother joined the party. Now, the fight was getting wild, and the foursome moved out of the ring and along an aisle of machines and gadgets like a miniature tornado.

"I said, that's enough!" hollered Kinji. "You've gone too

far. We just wanted to test her reflexes!"

"What have I done?" Thomas thought to himself. "Tamiko's strength with her anger management issues spell trouble! She could really hurt someone!"

But the fight went on. The three brothers did everything they could to take down Tamiko, but she just kept on blocking and striking her opponents at just the right places at just the right time. Tamiko had now reached the point where she was fighting like Shun! Thomas and Kana just stood there frozen, not believing their eyes and not knowing what to say.

"I thought you said Tamiko was a green belt!" said Kinji. "This is ... I don't know what this is, but it's certainly far beyond a green belt ... or a black belt. This is unreal!"

Just when everyone thought it was all over, the three brothers grabbed some swords off the wall, as did Tamiko. The three brothers fought furiously as they tried to defeat Tamiko. Despite their attempts, Tamiko stopped every strike. She was a real whirlwind of energy as she spun, jumped, flipped, and danced all over the place. "Ting! Ting! Ting! Ting! Ting!" the swords sounded as they clashed against one another. By now, things had really gone out of control, and the four were banging into all sorts of things and knocking them over as they slowly swept across the room like a cyclone.

Finally, Tamiko hammered away each of the others' swords, one by one, did an ultrafast twirl, and gave each of the brothers a roundhouse kick. The brothers were almost literally knocked out and were lying on the floor like half-dead bodies. It was a good thing that Tamiko wasn't too offensive or forceful, for if she had used her full strength in her roundhouse kicks, she would have done some very serious damage to the brothers. Just then, Kinji's superior walked into the room, looking startled as he glanced at the fighters and the mess of debris all over the floor.

"What in the world!" he said. "What happened here? How did Tamiko do?"

"Well," said Kinji, "she passed the test."

After a long pause, everyone just burst out laughing and called it a day.

CHAPTER 45—
THE CAUSE OF THE CRASH

On the ride back home, Thomas and Kana were almost speechless; they had a hard time trying to digest their memory of the battle royal. They had seen Tamiko fight a bit before during karate/tae kwon do practice and small competitions, but never in their lives had they seen anyone fight like she just did. It was like something out of a Bruce Lee movie!

"So, how did I do?" asked Tamiko.

"You were … you were spectacular!" said Thomas.

"My little Tamiko, that was incredible!" said Kana.

"But how did you learn to fight like that?" asked Thomas. "That was … out of this world!"

Tamiko hesitated; she didn't know how to respond. As she didn't remember her last encounter with Shun, she didn't have any idea where her great fighting abilities came from.

"I don't really know," said Tamiko. "I'm still pretty surprised myself!"

"You really … how do you say it?" said Kana. "You kicked butt!"

"One thing's for sure," said Thomas. "We better not call you Barbie Doll!"

"Only you two can," said Tamiko. "But nobody else!"

Thomas lectured Tamiko some on anger management and how to use her strength wisely so that she wouldn't cause serious damage to anybody. After a long pause, the conversation continued.

"Man, what a day!" said Thomas.

"You're telling me!" said Tamiko. "I'm actually indestructible! And I can jump like a cat! And I can fight like … I don't know!"

"You're one amazing girl, Tamiko!" said Thomas. "Not too long ago, we thought it was the end of you. And now … here you are, like I've never seen you before! I love you, Tamiko. We love you!"

"You are awesome!" said Kana. "You're not a little girl anymore! You're … a superhero!"

"Just a reminder, though, Tamiko," said Thomas. "Your new abilities … we don't want you telling anyone about them. That's top secret!"

As Tamiko continued to rejoice over her newfound abilities with Kana, Thomas couldn't help but think of the one thing that was harmful, if not deadly, to his daughter. This "thing" was a toxic gas composed of several highly potent chemicals—one of the many gases that was tested on the artificial respiratory system of Jun the test dummy, version 2. It just happened to be the only one that was harmful to Jun. The release of the gas was brought forth by adding water to a mixture of the chemicals in the form of a powder. As it was the only substance able to defeat Jun, it was dubbed "Junpowder." If Tamiko were to inhale this toxic gas, she would be severely weakened for several minutes, and a high enough dose could prove fatal. Luckily, the effects wouldn't cause any permanent damage, and, if the dose were low enough, Tamiko would soon return to normal. Thomas didn't feel that it was necessary to inform

Tamiko of this weakness; he figured that such information was simply useless to her, as the gas didn't present any real threat.

When they got home, not only was it time for Tamiko to relax a little but it was also time for her to remember a few things about the airplane accident.

"Tamiko, I have some important questions to ask you about the plane crash," said Thomas.

"What kind of questions?" replied Tamiko.

"Well … about how the accident happened in the first place," said Thomas. "Do you remember anything about the accident … just before it happened?"

Tamiko hesitated.

"Not … not really," she said. "It's like one big blank."

"Let's see. You were flying around Mount Fuji, and I think you were also looking for something," said Thomas.

"The shrines … you were searching for the ancient shrines!" said Kana. "Midori was with you, remember?"

Tamiko scratched her head as she tried to remember who Midori was.

"Midori?" said Tamiko. "The name sounds kind of familiar.

Tamiko tried harder.

"Is she a neighbor? Or … no … she's a cousin or a friend."

"Yes," said Thomas. "She was a good friend of yours."

"So, I was flying with her?" said Tamiko. "Then Midori is—I remember!"

"What's that?" asked the parents.

"She's a pilot!"

"Very good!" exclaimed Thomas. "Now think. What actually happened just before the crash? Were you looking at the mountain? Were you looking for the shrines? Were you—"

"The shrines," said Tamiko. "I don't know what … but there was something about the shrines."

"Let me show you something," said Kana.

Kana and Thomas looked for the printout of the ancient shrines but couldn't find it, so they turned on the computer, and Kana went to a website that displayed the ancient shrines—in fact, this was the picture that Tamiko had printed out and taken with her on the plane trip. Tamiko gazed at the picture and shook her head a little. Suddenly, she stopped and experienced a flashback. It was of the shrines; they were the same ones in the picture, but they were moving by her somehow. Tamiko could also hear some loud noise like an engine or something.

"That's it!" said Tamiko. "I found the shrines!"

"You found them?" said Kana. "That's good, Tamiko. Keep on going!"

"What happened after that?" asked Thomas. "Do you remember anything … anything at all … even just something small?"

Tamiko continued to stare at the ancient shrines on the computer monitor while she racked her brain to recall what happened next.

"I … I … that's right! I found the shrines, and then I got real excited and … yelled something," said Tamiko.

"What exactly did you say?" asked Thomas. "Do you have any idea what you said?"

"I … just can't remember," said Tamiko. "All I know is that I got real happy."

"Anything else?" asked Kana.

"Yeah. It was kind of strange."

"What was strange?" asked Thomas.

"I don't know. It was like the shrines were … like …

getting bigger and bigger or something," explained Tamiko. "Maybe Midori can explain. Where is she? She's alive, right?"

Her parents sat there motionless and expressionless.

"Midori ... where is she? Is she still in the hospital? How is she?" said Tamiko.

"I'm afraid she ... didn't make it," said Thomas.

"She's dead?" said Tamiko. "No, not Midori! She was one of my best friends."

"She died within minutes after arriving at the hospital," said Kana, sobbing.

"No, this can't be happening," said Tamiko, weeping. "She didn't deserve to die. She was a good person!"

Just then, Butterscotch found an old chocolate bar in the corner of the room and started chewing it.

"Look! Look!" said Kana. "To the ... over there! Butterscotch is eating a chocolate bar! Chocolate is poisonous to dogs. Take it away."

Suddenly, Tamiko had another flashback.

"I remember now!" said Tamiko. "It's all starting to come back to me now; it was almost like what you just said. Just after I saw the shrines, I said, 'Look! Look! To the right! There are the shrines!' or something. That's what I said ... and then ..."

"And then what?"

In yet another flashback, Tamiko saw Midori turn her head toward the right, smiling. Then, Tamiko heard the word "jackpot" and some other words followed by the clapping of a high five.

"Then, Midori turned her head around and looked at the shrines all excited, and she said, 'Jackpot!' I think. She just stared at me and said something else, and then I think she gave me a high five and looked at the shrines again, and ..."

Suddenly, Tamiko burst into tears, realizing what really

happened.

"It was me!" she cried.

"You?" said Thomas. "What do you mean?"

"It's my fault! If I hadn't found the shrines, none of this would have happened!"

"But it's not your fault, Tamiko!" said Kana.

"It was just an accident!" said Thomas.

"But I told her to look at the shrines and she did ... and she forgot about controlling the plane. It's all my fault! I killed Midori!" said Tamiko, crying with guilt.

"She would have looked at the shrines anyway ... even if you hadn't told her to," said Thomas.

"But I'm the one who found them in the first place!"

"And Midori was the one who was responsible for flying the plane safely, not you!"

Tamiko stopped and thought about it for a while. She told herself that Midori really was the pilot and therefore responsible. Tamiko reasoned that if she were to be riding in a car, with Midori at the wheel, and suddenly pointed out some fancy restaurant they were looking for, Midori would still be responsible for keeping her eyes on the road. If there were an accident, Midori couldn't blame her for finding the restaurant. That wouldn't make any sense!

Although saddened by the bad news, Tamiko didn't feel so guilty anymore. The three hugged and hugged as they shared their tears. Even Butterscotch yelped a little. Then, Tamiko asked some more questions about Midori.

"So, where's Midori's grave? Is it in ... where did Midori used to live again?"

"Oyama," said Kana. "That was her hometown where she grew up—it's close to where I work. After she was cremated, her ashes—most of them—were scattered over Mount Fuji."

"But don't they usually put the ashes in a … you know … that jar and bury it?"

"It's called an urn," said Thomas. "You're right. That's more common."

"But Midori always said that she preferred to have her ashes scattered instead—Mount Fuji was very special to her—but a few of her ashes were buried in her family grave," said Kana. "She must be in heaven now, looking down on us."

Once again, Tamiko's eyes filled with tears.

"Why do people have to die? Good people, like Midori. I loved her."

"It's … it's just part of life," said Thomas. "Whether you die from an accident or illness or just plain old age, it's nature, and there's nothing we can really do about it. That's just the way it is."

Tamiko wiped her tears, and the three embraced each other once again. Somehow, they felt Midori's presence in the room. It was like her spirit radiated through their hearts and almost spoke to them in some way or another. It was soothing. It was love.

Finally, Tamiko knew what happened to her friend Midori.

Chapter 46—
Retrospect

Now that Tamiko knew the truth about the accident and remembered the main things—like her parents, house, and dog—it was time for her to try to recapture the other things that had been important to her. She already had little pieces of memories floating around in her brain, but they were just not put together yet; it was sort of like several unfinished puzzles, each with just enough pieces missing to not know what the picture was. The next day, just before supper, the family of three sat down, and Tamiko attempted to finish some of the "puzzles."

"Let's start with Sakura," said Kana. "Do you remember her?"

"Sakura ..." said Tamiko. "She ... was she a friend of mine?"

"Well ... sort of," said Kana.

"Umm ... she's ... Mrs. Claus. You know ... the wife of Santa Claus," said Tamiko.

"Very funny," said Kana.

"Yeah," said Thomas. "You have Santa Claus and "Sakura" Claus—cute, Tamiko, very cute!"

Then, Kana gave her a hint. Tamiko hesitated a bit and remembered. After briefly filling Tamiko in on her karate and tae kwon do lessons, Thomas asked her about her angel friends.

"Now ... what about Hina, Jeremy, and ... there's a third one ... Rin? Who are they?"

"They're ... the names sound familiar. They're ... of course! They're my friends!"

"Well done, Tamiko!" said Kana. "And what kind of things did you do?"

Tamiko thought about it for a moment or two. Then, Kana gave her a clue.

"You played ... something ... on people," said Kana.

"What's the 'something'?" asked Thomas.

"We played ... it's coming back now ... we played ... like, pranks and things on people."

"You got it!" said Kana. "And you helped people too, like angels."

"And sometimes you played music and sang songs," said Thomas. "Remember that last song you played here in the house with your friends? It think it was 'Jitter Dance' or something."

Thomas tried singing a bit of it—from what he could remember—and the other two had a good laugh.

"I think I ... yeah ... I remember. We were, like, singing real loud, and you got mad because you thought we'd wake up Mommy!"

"Great, you remember!" said her parents with joy.

"Where are they now? I want to see them!" said Tamiko.

"Oh, I don't think they're here," said Kana. "You told me before that they were going to some summer camp in China."

It was now time for a late supper. Kana asked Tamiko if she could run to the local grocery to fetch some potatoes and cream for their clam chowder but then decided that would be pushing her too far.

"You don't have to go," said Kana. "Just stay here. I'll go instead."

"I can do it," said Tamiko. "The grocery store can't be too far. Where is it again?"

Kana refreshed her daughter's memory, and Tamiko made her way down the street toward the local grocery.

Outside, it was already dark and kind of foggy, but the sky was clear and starry, with a full moon. The only sounds to be heard were the distant revving of car engines, some train horns, and the humming of streetlights. Tamiko felt rather calm strolling down the streets all alone. It was as though she owned the night or something. It was a rather special feeling. Though some of the details of her life were coming back to her, she still didn't really know where she came from. Because of this, she felt as though she were living in a mysterious dream.

As Tamiko continued her walk, she encountered the smells of other "late suppers"—tomato soup, sushi, chicken teriyaki. These scents seemed to blend in somehow with the peaceful, cloudy light from the streetlamps. Even though there were hardly any other people in sight, Tamiko didn't feel alone; there were cats wandering around—some meowing and looking for food, some playing, and some fighting with other cats. The fights emitted some strange noises into the air. One cat was busy chewing through a garbage bag; when it finally succeeded in freeing whatever morsel it was after, some bottles and empty tin cans also spilled from the bag, banging and rattling as they fell to the ground.

The dreamlike quality of the night helped Tamiko think more clearly and enabled her to remember a few more bits and pieces of her past. For some reason she couldn't really put her finger on, Tamiko felt as though she had to be somewhere … as though someone really needed her. Confused, Tamiko wandered into the darkness and started dancing around. As she danced, she sang.

Why am I here? Where did I come from? I just need to know.
I'm feeling kind of lost and lonesome everywhere I go.

Slowly, I'm seeing more and more … bits and pieces of then.
But something's missing I can't ignore. The worries stir me again.

Who was I then, before I fell asleep? I just don't recall.
And even when I search the ocean deep, nothing's there at all.

But I am starting to see some light … through the dark, foggy air.
Yet, still there's something that isn't right, and I just have to be there.

Who is calling me … across the meadows and streams?
I keep falling free. Someone's ailing it seems.
Who is calling me … through the fog and the darkness?
I'll keep on chasing these flashes I'm racing until I know why I'm here.

Is this a dream, or am I really here … dancing to and fro?
It may seem at times I disappear as I search to know.

I keep getting these winks of light … sparks and flashes of yore.

But something's weird in the air tonight that I just have to explore.

How much time will I keep wandering? How long will I last?
It feels like I'm a ghost that's looking for pieces of its past.

But day by day I see clearer skies … fresher is that of the air.
Then I hear echo the distant cries of someone who's in despair.

Who is calling me … across the meadows and streams?
I keep falling free. Someone's ailing it seems.
Who is calling me … through the fog and the darkness?
I'll keep on chasing these flashes I'm racing until I know why I'm here.

Soon, I will fly. Like an eagle, I'll soar up high.
Then, I'll see all there's to know as I glide over the hills below.

Who is calling me … across the meadows and streams?
I keep falling free. Someone's ailing it seems.
Who is calling me … through the fog and the darkness?
I'll keep on chasing these flashes I'm racing until I know why I'm here.

Finally, Tamiko bought the food and returned home, and then she helped Kana make supper. While working close to the stove, Tamiko accidentally moved her hand onto an open burner.

"Tamiko!" cried Kana. "You—"

"What happened!" yelled Thomas.

"Mom!" said Tamiko, showing her unburnt hand.

"Oh, that's right!" said Kana. "I forgot."

Then, while the clam chowder was simmering, Thomas called Tamiko over to the coffee table for some family fun.

"Say, Tamiko ... how about an arm wrestle?"

"I think we know who's going to win now," said Tamiko.

"I wouldn't be too sure," said Thomas, smiling. "You're just a little girl. You'll never beat a man."

Tamiko just sat there as if she was off in another world; she had just had another flashback.

"So what do you say? Tamiko? Tamiko, are you all right?"

"I just remembered something," said Tamiko.

"What's that?" asked Thomas.

"Some guy ... a real bad guy."

"What does he look like?"

"He's ... like a snake, and he's at a door or something."

"Anything else?"

"Yeah ... there's a young girl screaming. I ... I remember! The closet girl ... I have to save the closet girl!"

Chapter 47 –
Home Alone ... or Almost

"Oh ... you remember her!" said Kana. "That's good. That's very good. You're really starting to get your memory back!"

"I have to go and rescue her ... and this time, I won't fail!" said Tamiko. "I have to go now!"

"But you're forgetting something, Tamiko," said Thomas.

"What's that?"

"When you came home the day you tried to save this 'closet girl,' you were pretty beat up, and we asked you what happened. You told us all about it, and then we called the police," said Thomas. "Remember? It's all over now. The police have already taken care of it. That monster's finally behind bars."

"You mean that ... wait a minute ... it's coming to me now. That's right. I told you about what happened, and then you called the cops and told them everything."

"You got it!" said Thomas. "So ... how about that arm wrestle? Are you still up for it?"

"You bet!"

So Thomas and Tamiko sat across from each other at the coffee table, placed their elbows on the table, and cupped their right hands together; Kana assumed the role of referee as she placed her hand on top of those of the two competitors and counted to three in Japanese.

"Ichi! Ni! San!" cried Kana.

And the game was on. Thomas tried to push down Tamiko's hand but could hardly even make it budge.

"Ooooh … watch out for Tamiko!" said Kana. "She's strong now!"

Then, Tamiko gave Thomas a chance, as she let her hand go weak. Thomas was close to winning, just an inch or two from the table, when Tamiko suddenly used her full strength and won almost instantly.

"Hey! You were just letting me … and now you do it!" said Thomas.

"Loser! Loser!" sang Tamiko as Kana laughed.

"You're strong!" said Thomas. "That's amazing! I turned you into Supergirl!"

"Want to try again?" said Tamiko. "Let's do the other hand."

So the two battled again. This time, Tamiko just kept her dad's hand at the starting position and smiled.

"Come on, Dad! You can do better than that! You're not trying hard enough!"

Thomas strained and fought, but there was no way he could pin down Tamiko's hand. Finally, Tamiko slammed her dad's hand down on the table once again and laughed.

"Hurray!" cheered Kana.

"That just isn't fair," said Thomas. "I'm no match for Supergirl here!"

After a great supper and a good sleep, morning came quickly. This new day was "fix the roof" day, as Thomas had decided to replace some worn shingles that were the cause of a few leaks. The weather was fully cooperating—warm, sunny, with only a gentle wind. As Thomas was working near the center of the roof, Tamiko suddenly appeared out of nowhere—just like that!

"What in the ... where did you come from?" said Thomas, surprised.

"From down there, silly," said Tamiko.

"But the ladder's on the other ... you jumped!"

"Of course! The ladder would have taken too long!"

"Very funny!"

The two completed the roof and put away the tools. Just as they finished everything, a phone call came in. Some people in the scientific community were, understandably, quite interested in learning more about Thomas's astonishing discovery in nanotechnology.

"Yes, we would like you come give a lecture early next week at Nanobiotix and speak of your amazing 'découverte'!" said an excited French scientist. "It's just for three days, maybe four. And bring your wife! Paris is a 'ville' very romantique!"

Thomas accepted the invitation, even on such short notice. After everything the family had been through, it was about time for Thomas to finally get away on a romantic trip with his wife and just relax for a while. As for Tamiko, her home tutor could keep an eye on her, just in case anything happened. This would also be a perfect opportunity for Sakura to help Tamiko remember her studies. So, Thomas told his wife and daughter of the plan, and the two parents packed their suitcases and made arrangements for Sakura to come the following week. Before their departure to Paris, however, Tamiko's parents took advantage of their time off work and had more good times with her. The days went by quickly, and soon Paris was only a day away.

"Before I forget, I'll give you a little money in case you need to buy more food or something," said Thomas. "Wait

… I don't seem to have … I just have a few coins. Well, here! Here's my second credit card; try not to spend too much!"

"What about my face, though?" said Tamiko. "Sakura's going to freak when she sees me!"

"Don't worry," said Thomas. "I told her all about what happened—fixing you up and all—but I didn't say anything about your indestructible skin or abilities."

"So you don't want me to tell her about … you know?"

"No! That's top secret information, Tamiko. You don't tell anyone. Got that?"

"Got it!"

The next morning Sakura arrived on time, as she always did. Even though she already knew about Tamiko's face change, she was still stunned when she saw her.

"Tamiko! I don't know what to say! You were beautiful before, but now … you look stunning … anata wa utsukushii!"

"You think?"

"Why, yes! I mean, you were beautiful before too, but now you're like an angel or something!"

"She's my new Tamiko!" said Thomas. "Same smart girl, different face!"

"She's mine too!" said Kana.

"You take care now, Tamiko," said Thomas. "I love you!"

"Good-bye, Tamiko!" said Kana. "If you have any problems, you know where to reach us."

"Stay out of trouble," said Thomas.

"Bye!" said Kana.

So the parents hugged and kissed their daughter good-bye, got into their car, and drove away to the airport. Now, it was just Tamiko and Sakura … as well as Butterscotch.

Chapter 48—
The Real McCoy (Part 1)

"Well, it's just the two of us!" said Sakura.

"Actually, we're three!" said Tamiko.

"Oh? Who else?"

"Butterscotch! We can't forget him."

"Ah, right!" said Sakura. "Well, I still can't believe it's really you! You're absolutely gorgeous!"

"Thanks!"

"So, tell me about everything that happened to you. I was so worried when they said you were in a coma. I wasn't sure what to think; I wasn't sure if you'd ever wake up! And now, you're here … more beautiful than ever!"

So Tamiko recounted everything she could, from the plane crash to her amazing recovery—everything, that is, except for her indestructible skin and extra strong muscles.

But then, Sakura and Tamiko went into the kitchen to prepare lunch and Sakura searched for the large Chef's knife—the sharpest knife in the house—to cut a watermelon. She looked and looked but couldn't find it.

"I think it's on the top shelf of that cupboard over there," said Tamiko, pointing.

Sakura opened the cupboard, reached for the knife and touched its handle. But before she could grab it, the knife toppled down like an arrow from a speargun. Before it touched the floor, Tamiko seized it by the blade with her right hand. It almost looked as though she had caught a fly without a chance of escaping.

"Tamiko!" cried Sakura. "You caught it! How did you … but your hand! Oh dear, you must have really cut yourself! Let's have a look."

"Oh, I … I'll be all right," said Tamiko, still holding the knife and pretending to be in pain.

"Now let's have a look," said Sakura as she gently took hold of the knife's handle. "Open your hand."

Tamiko let go of the blade and opened her hand so only she could see her palm. No cut. Not a spot of blood.

"Oh, it's not as bad as you think. Hurts a bit, though. But … I don't want you to see it. It's kind of gross. Just get me a bandage and I'll stick it on."

While Tamiko rinsed her hand with water, Sakura got the bandage. Tamiko snatched it and quickly pressed it on her "cut".

Phew! Tamiko thought.

Strange! thought Sakura staring at the knife while Tamiko went to get the watermelon. *The blade doesn't have any blood on it. Oh well!*

After lunch and a brief recapitulation of her previous studies, Tamiko decided to take the dog out for a walk while Sakura napped.

"Here, Butterscotch! We're going outside! Come on now, let's go!"

"See you later!" said Sakura.

"Jaa mata wani!"

And the two were off on yet another magnificent day. Walking, Tamiko led Butterscotch through the streets and down toward the village where her karate school was. What began as a walk quickly turned into a jog, and, before long, they were passing the karate school. At the back of the school, Tamiko could see an open yard where students were roaming around in their gis—some were playing, some were practicing their kicks and punches, and some were just standing there, waiting for something to happen. This place looked kind of familiar. Tamiko felt as though she had been there before, but she wasn't sure.

Off in the distance, a cheerful, electronic beeping tune—the kind that is heard from a cheesy video game—was playing. Looking toward the backyard, Tamiko noticed that one of the older students was pushing another around somewhat and seemed to be chuckling at the same time. The student that was being pushed around looked younger than the laughing one, and he appeared to be sort of fighting back. From where Tamiko was standing, it wasn't really clear whether they were fighting or just playing around with each other.

Tamiko moved on and jogged once again, this time down the street with all the shops and restaurants. Tamiko felt free, as though she could do anything she wanted to without a single obstacle in her way. The only thing bothering her was a little voice down deep inside that was calling for her; Tamiko felt that it was the same voice as before—the voice of the closet girl. Tamiko could still feel that she needed her somehow and that she had to be there—even though the monster was gone.

Tamiko looped around the village and headed back toward the karate school. As they passed by it again, Tamiko scratched her head, trying to figure out what this building was all about. She decided to take a closer look. The place looked deserted; peering through the side window and looking at the yard, it was clear that everybody had left.

Tamiko decided to go back home. She gave Butterscotch a swift little tug on the leash, and the two started to walk away from the building. Then, suddenly, Butterscotch began to bark.

"What's that, Butterscotch?"

Tamiko listened closely between barks. From the corner of the yard, just behind a small structure, came the sound of some kind of dispute. As Tamiko walked closer, Butterscotch's barking picked up.

"Butterscotch, no bark," said Tamiko in a loud whisper as she stepped quietly forward.

Two boys were now visible. Both were obviously karate students, as they were wearing gis. Tamiko quickly realized that they were the same two that she had seen playing together earlier. The older fellow had his back to Tamiko, and the younger one looked scared, like he was trying to escape. There were some pushes and shoves, and, unlike the last time, it was clear that they weren't having fun. As more words were exchanged, something about the way the older student referred to the other as "Shad" struck a nerve in Tamiko.

"What's that, Shad?" said the older student.

"I just thought it was ... I wasn't laughing at you, man!" said the younger one.

"You think I'm funny? I'll show you who's funny! Let's see you do a back kick. Can you do that ... Shad?"

Shad did a half-descent back kick, and the bully grabbed his foot and yanked him to the ground.

"Way to go, Shad! You know the back kick now! Yeah! Yeah!"

The younger student, humiliated, finally reached his limit and lashed out at the bully, and with that, the fight was in full swing. The bully, who was obviously the more experienced fighter, began to really put a licking on Shad.

Though Butterscotch barked and barked as they fought, neither of them really took notice of Tamiko or the dog.

"So, you think I'm funny now, Shad? Huh? Huh?" said the bully as he trapped his victim in a headlock.

"Okay, that's enough!" yelled Tamiko.

The bully shifted his head toward Tamiko and looked at her as though she were from outer space.

"What do you want?" he said.

"I want you to give it up and pick on someone your own size!"

The bully let go of the victim and shoved him away.

"And just who are you? Some kind of angel or something?"

"Never mind who I am!" said Tamiko. "Think about who you are!"

The victim, confused, quickly slipped away.

"I'm the best fighter in the whole school. The best! That's who I am!"

"Oh yeah?" said Tamiko as she tied Butterscotch to a nearby post. "Prove it!"

"Wait a minute. You … want me to fight you or something? What, are you joking?"

"Does it look like I am?" said Tamiko as she pushed the bully.

"You're really asking for it, angel face!"

"Come on! Show me what you've got, tough guy!" said Tamiko as she pushed the bully once again even harder.

The bully slipped and fell. In his book, this was just enough for a fight.

CHAPTER 49~
THE REAL MCCOY (PART 2)

"Boy or girl, you're going down!" said the bully after he got up and stared at Tamiko with venom.

Suddenly, Tamiko recognized the bully by his unforgettable, cold eyes—it was Allan McCoy! With that, Tamiko remembered the building and yard as her karate school, and Allan McCoy as the class bully. Angry, Allan attempted to push Tamiko, but he was thrown to the ground. Allan popped up and charged at Tamiko, and found himself being thrown to the ground once more.

"I thought you were the best!" said Tamiko. "You can't beat a girl?"

"Why, you little …!" said Allan.

The bully tried some karate on Tamiko, starting with a few punches, but Tamiko blocked them easily and delivered a blow to his stomach followed by a chop to his back, and Allan was down like that. Tamiko was amazed at just how easily she was able to defeat the "great" Allan McCoy.

"You want karate?" said Allan as he picked himself up. "I'll show you karate!"

Allan did a series of front kicks, side kicks, and roundhouse kicks, but with her catlike reflexes, Tamiko avoided every one of them. More bits and pieces of Allan flashed in Tamiko's mind—his teasing, his bullying, and his quest to "be the best." She even remembered him laughing at her when she quit karate. Then, Tamiko felt a certain grief from Allan on top of his anger; it was like he was fighting because his heart had just been broken or something. Suddenly, Tamiko recalled what one of her karate buddies had said to her about Allan, not long before her accident— that all of his bullying was out of anger ... anger from the fact that, years ago, his kid brother died and he never got over it.

"He's gone, Allan!" said Tamiko. "No amount of fighting is ever going to bring him back!"

"What are you talking about?"

For a moment, Tamiko questioned her memory. Even if it was correct, this could have been just a rumor. Tamiko took a chance.

"You know who I'm talking about!" said Tamiko. "You lost him years ago, and you've been crying inside ever since!"

These words struck a nerve, and Allan's face changed from just an angry person with angry eyes to someone with the eyes of a vicious snake; Allan had a score to settle! This change in expression was proof enough that Tamiko's assumption was indeed correct.

"Okay ... now you're really starting to piss me off," said Allan.

With that, Allan used some of his best fighting skills on Tamiko. He tried punching her. He tried kicking her. He tried throwing her. Allan had the appearance of a well-seasoned fighter, and he managed to get in a little hit or two, but he wasn't on par with Tamiko by any means. Tamiko, with the skills of Shun, and her extra-fast reflexes and extra-strong muscles, was fighting in a completely different league. Despite the fact that Allan knew he was losing, he didn't give up, for the great Allan McCoy wasn't going to be beaten by a little girl!

"I don't want to hurt you!" said Tamiko. "But there are things you need to hear!"

"Hear what!?"

"That being a bully is not the way to let out your anger and sorrow!"

This made Allan even angrier, and he flew into a rage.

"Shut up! Just shut up!"

"You'll never get over it until you see what you've become!"

"I said shut up!"

"Your brother wouldn't want to see you like this; he wouldn't be proud of you!"

With those words, Allan lost all control. He simply went crazy, doing everything he could to eliminate Tamiko. Yet, no matter how hard he tried, Tamiko defeated him. Exhausted, Allan mustered up all of his remaining energy and delivered his best roundhouse kick.

"It wasn't fair!" Allan yelled.

With lightning speed, Tamiko dodged it, spun around in several quick circles like a figure skater, and threw a side kick at Allan.

The bully picked himself up once more, this time like an old man, and tried to make another move, but it was no use, as pretty much all of his energy was drained. Suddenly, Allan just leaned against the tree next to him, put his hands over his face, and burst into tears, letting out all the pain and sorrow that he had kept inside of him for all those years.

"It wasn't his time! It wasn't his time! It wasn't his …" he said as he continued to cry.

Tamiko went over to Allan and threw her arms around him.

"It's okay," whispered Tamiko into Allan's ear. "I'm here for you, Allan. It's okay."

"I ... I miss him sooooo much!"

"You really loved him ... I understand."

"Do you really?"

"In fact, I do. Not too long ago, I lost a very good friend of mine in a plane crash; she was like a big sister to me. I know it's not quite the same thing, but I must say that I do know what it's like to lose someone you love."

"My dad, when I was young, he told me ... not to cry when it ... happened. He was hit by a car. My dad said that crying ... was for babies, and I was afraid that ..."

"That what?" asked Tamiko.

"That if I started ... I'd never stop."

Allan shed more tears.

"It's okay, Allan. Let it all out. You can cry on me all you want," said Tamiko as she hugged Allan once again.

After most of the teardrops had rolled off his face, Allan felt better, as much of his heartache had finally escaped from him. Then, Allan looked at Tamiko in a strange way.

"You just called me Allan again. How do you know my name?"

"It's kind of a long story," said Tamiko. "Let's just say we've met before."

The two talked some more, until Butterscotch barked and signaled that it was time to move on. So Tamiko untied the dog leash and wished Allan farewell.

"So long, Allan. Take good care of yourself."

"You too and ... thanks. Thank you for turning my life around."

"Do itashi mashite."

"By the way, what's your name?" asked Allan, as his "angel" looked somewhat familiar.

"Tamiko."

Allan stood there confused and speechless as Tamiko turned and started walking away.

"Tamiko?" Allan mumbled to himself. "There's something about her eyes ... and her voice too. But it can't be her! The Tamiko I knew was Japanese and couldn't fight like that."

The two wanderers made their way home, where Tamiko fed Butterscotch and washed him up a bit. Then, she ate, she read, and she slept.

CHAPTER 50
Jackpot!

The next day, Tamiko caught up on some more studies with Sakura; this time, it was zoology and medicine—Tamiko's favorite subjects. Sakura kept on commenting on how beautiful Tamiko's new face was. She was also quite impressed with how fast Tamiko was remembering her schoolwork.

After her second lesson, Tamiko strolled around town again with Butterscotch. As she walked, she couldn't help but hear the voice of the closet girl inside of her again, telling her to "be there" in some way or another. Maybe she was now living in an orphanage and couldn't handle being locked up anymore. At least her nightmare of being held prisoner by that big monster was all over now and, like her dad said, the bad guy was finally behind bars where he belonged.

As Tamiko approached the main street, she noticed a little game where you win money by breaking blocks of wood and stuff; it looked kind of familiar.

"Come on, girl. Give it a try!" said the game host.

"Oh … why not," said Tamiko.

"That's what I want to hear!" the host responded. "All you gotta do to win is break some blocks of wood and concrete. I know the concrete sounds real hard, but the

312

bricks are very thin ... and I'll even make it a bit easier for ya! It goes from easy to hard. First, the small wood blocks—that'll be two hundred yen. That's for the first three wood levels."

Tamiko paid and easily split the wood in two.

"Huuuurray!" cheered the host. "I knew you could! Now it's level two!"

Tamiko snapped the second block just as easily as the first.

"Right on!" said the host. "Level three!"

Tamiko struck the block with a swift blow and cut through it like butter.

The host cheered again and then asked Tamiko if she wished to continue.

"Good one! Now you can either leave with your winnings of one hundred yen ... or you can go to the next round!"

Tamiko decided to continue. The second round was a set of three more wooden blocks, thicker than the previous ones. Afterward, it would be a round of three thin concrete bricks. With very little effort, Tamiko broke all three blocks of wood. As for the concrete level, Tamiko quickly snapped the first brick ... then the second ... and then the third as if they were just thin pieces of wood.

Impressed, the game host set up the real concrete slabs in front of her for the next level, for the previous ones were intentionally thinner in order to give Tamiko a better chance. Tamiko agreed to continue.

Using a bit more effort, she ruptured all three bricks. The host was surprised.

Just then, an old homeless man walked by begging for money. He approached everyone he came across but with little luck. The man turned around to watch the game. Then the man asked the game host for money and was turned down. Tamiko was about to donate a few coins when, suddenly, she came up with an idea.

"I'll go straight to the last round. If I can do all three, then I win the jackpot, and I also get … another ten thousand yen," said Tamiko, as she noticed that the current "jackpot" was only just a few yen and figured that the game host had some more money in his pockets.

"You're crazy! I'm not going to—"

"And if I lose, you get … these coins," said Tamiko as she showed her "lucky" coins—rare Japanese collector coins that were worth a lot of yen.

"You know, you're quite the kid. All right then. Deal!"

The homeless man stood there frozen with excitement, waiting to see how this was all going to turn out. So the game host set up three stacks of concrete bricks for the last round; once again, he made things a bit easier for Tamiko by using thinner bricks. As Tamiko didn't want to give her secret away, she only used moderate strength and was "just able" to rupture the first two stacks of concrete. As for the third and final stack, she only cracked the concrete. The game host was amazed, as was the homeless fellow. After a long, silent pause, the game host gave Tamiko the benefit of the doubt and paid up. Instead of keeping the money for herself, Tamiko gave it all to the homeless man!

"Oh, thank you! Thank you! God bless you, girl!"

"No sweat!"

As Tamiko walked away, she chatted with the happy homeless man.

"Wow … you're good! You really showed *him*!" said the man.

"I guess I did!" replied Tamiko.

Then, the homeless man babbled on about the game

host—the other games he hosted in the streets and how he cheated.

"These street games are illegal, you know," said the man. "I saw him do three-card monte once, and I'm sure I saw him cheatin'. And even when the cops were around, he just kept doin' his game. The cops didn't do nothin'. Some don't believe me. But I saw what I saw. It's like he's above the law or somethin'. I mean—"

"What did you just say?" asked Tamiko with a serious tone of voice.

"I said I saw what I saw. That guy's a dirty little. Are you listening to even a word I'm sayin'?"

These words—"I saw what I saw" and "it's like he's above the law"—sounded very familiar; Tamiko tried to think of where and when she had heard them before. Then, Tamiko had some flashbacks of the last conversation she had with one of her friends just before the plane crash. She recalled Jeremy's voice over the telephone telling her something about the closet girl. Stunned, Tamiko suddenly realized what the conversation with Jeremy was really all about!

Part 4

The Rescue of the Lone Girl

CHAPTER 51~
LIBERATION (PART 1)

Tamiko now remembered that, the day after her parents called the police to report the crimes against the closet girl, Jeremy told her that nothing had changed … that he walked by the house and saw the monster loose in his house and heard the little girl screaming again! He had said that the bad guy was "above the law." Tamiko had led herself to believe that it was all over after her parents reminded her that they told the police everything and that the villain was surely "behind bars where he belongs." But the little voice inside of Tamiko was right after all; it was the voice of the closet girl … begging her to come and put an end to all her suffering. Tamiko had to go! She had to go now!

"Excuse me!" said Tamiko to the homeless man. "I … I got to go!"

"But I didn't finish my … did I say something wrong?" said the man.

So Tamiko ran home with Butterscotch and gathered a few things. Just before she left the house, something very important occurred to her. Tamiko knew what to do, but … where was she supposed to go? She had forgotten the exact location of the house! What was she going to do now?

So Tamiko put on her thinking cap and came up with a

solution. Maybe she had taken pictures of the place; if so, she could possibly get an address or something from looking at them. Remembering that she had a camera, Tamiko searched her room but without luck. Where could it be? She must have taken it with her on the plane trip, so it was long gone now.

Tamiko turned on her computer, hoping that she had at least downloaded the pictures. Sure enough, there they were. Looking at the pictures of the house, Tamiko could almost see the man beating the little girl and hear him yelling at her. Tamiko zoomed in on the pictures as she tried to see the house number; she also looked for street names. Tamiko looked and looked but couldn't find a single picture with a readable house number. However, she found at least one picture that showed a sign bearing the name of the street; that was all she really needed! Knowing the street name and what the house looked like, Tamiko would be able to find it. She opened Google Maps, entered the name of the street, and printed the resulting map; she printed a picture of the house, too. Tamiko raced toward the door, passing by Sakura, who was sitting on the living room couch.

"Tamiko! Is everything okay?"

"Oh yes, I'm fine! I just have to go somewhere. I … forgot something!"

"Are you sure? You seem rather … pumped up about something. Don't get into any trouble now," said Sakura.

"Don't worry. I'll be back soon. Bye!"

Tamiko jumped on her bicycle and sped off in search of the house. As she peddled, there seemed to be something in the air—something significant, something big. As for Tamiko, in her mind, she was already there … in the house with the girl.

When she arrived at the street, Tamiko stopped and

pulled out the picture of the house. As she continued down the street, examining both sides for the matching house, Tamiko appeared to be watching a tennis game, with her head pivoting from left to right and from right to left as she whizzed by. And then, there it was!

"This is it," Tamiko said to herself.

Finally, the moment had come—the moment where Tamiko's main mission would be fulfilled. Tamiko jumped off her bike, and studied the house and its surroundings a little. There was no car in the driveway, there was no noise, and there seemed to be at least one light on inside. Would it be easy enough to just knock down the door, get the girl, and take off? No ... it couldn't be quite that easy!

Tamiko went to the backyard and climbed up the fence; she saw nothing inside but an old barbecue and some bushes. As she made her way back to the front, she heard a car approach the house. Dodging behind a hedge, she watched as it passed by. Tamiko then crept up to the side window and peered inside. With the curtains shut most of the way, she didn't see much. What she did see, though, was a rather messy living room where several lights had been left on; she could also see part of the kitchen and the door to the basement. Once again, Tamiko heard a vehicle approaching. It slowed down in front of the house. Was the monster returning home? No, it turned out to be another car pulling into the driveway of a nearby house on the other side of the street. Immediately afterward, another car came rolling down the street; it looked just like the one in the picture. Sure enough, it turned into the driveway of the house. This was the car! Tamiko stayed on the side of the house as she watched the car. Quickly, the driver hopped out and slammed the door behind him. He was ... the monster!

Looking at him, Tamiko had a couple of flashbacks—of

the moment when the bad guy last defeated her, and of the little girl's basic location. Tamiko waited for the man to enter the house, and, after seeing him go downstairs from the side window, she scurried over to the unlocked door and slipped inside. She quietly raced to the girl's bedroom, opened the door, and saw ... an almost empty room! Then, she heard some muffled moans and groans along with some thumping sounds coming from within some other room. Where was she?

Tamiko had another flashback. Of course! She was locked inside some kind of a small walk-in closet within the room! But where was the door to the closet? Tamiko went back and forth along the wall from which the noise was coming. Was she in the bedroom on the other side? Was she in the wall? Just as Tamiko was about to leave the room and check the other bedroom, she had a flashback of the poster on the wall. Of course! There was that small, recessed door behind it—the one that led to the closet! Tamiko tore down the poster, and, sure enough, there was the door! Suddenly, Tamiko heard footsteps marching up the basement stairs. She unlocked the door and opened it.

Chapter 52~
Liberation (Part 2)

There she was, gagged and tied to a chair. She was also shaking with fear and gasping through her nose. The mystery girl was about five or six years of age, and had scrapes and bruises all over her face. She looked sick. She smelled awful. Her black hair was a mess, and her clothes looked like they hadn't been changed in weeks. Her feet were bare and badly bruised. It suddenly became apparent that the thumping noises came from the girl's feet knocking against the door.

The girl glared at Tamiko as though she was seeing an alien from outer space.

"Mmmm ... mmmm," went the girl.

Immediately, Tamiko removed the gag and untied the girl. The girl moaned and groaned and continued to tremble.

"It's okay. I won't hurt you," said Tamiko. "What's your name?"

The little one hesitated a bit, shaking and breathing fearfully. Then, she finally opened her mouth.

"K ... Kaylie."

"Kaylie—that's a beautiful name. My name is Tamiko. It's all over; I'm going to—"

Suddenly, the girls heard the man approach them.

"No! Please! Please!" said the girl, shaking with fear.

"You stay here, Kaylie," said Tamiko, as the noise of the nearing monster suddenly stopped. "He won't hurt you, I promise. I'll be right back. I'm getting you out of this place. You hear? It's okay. Like I said, I'll be back shortly!"

The little girl nodded her head, and Tamiko set out to confront the monster. First, she checked the kitchen and then the living room—no sign of him. Then, Tamiko heard movement from one of the other bedrooms; it sounded like the man was looking for something there. Tamiko made some noise, and the man fell silent.

Tamiko went into the living room and made some more noise as she peered around the corner. The bad guy exited the room and paced toward her to investigate the disturbance. He walked past the kitchen and into the living room but didn't see Tamiko, for she had moved into the hallway beside the living room a bit. The man marched all over the place as he tried to find the source of the noise. Then, Tamiko turned on the light in the hall. The bad guy took three more steps and then turned around. He was now face-to-face with Tamiko!

"What in the … who are you?" he said, looking at Tamiko as if she had three heads.

"I'm Tamiko … and I'm going to see to it that you never lay another finger on little Kaylie … ever again!"

"What? You think you're gonna take *me*?" said the man, chuckling. "Is this some kind of a joke? You're really serious. Well hey, I'll be so nice, I'll let you throw the first punch. Hit me right here with your best shot, Barbie Doll!"

With that, Tamiko jabbed him square in the face, and the man nearly fell. As he got up, he brushed his face and looked at his hand to discover that Tamiko had just given him a nosebleed; he now realized that Tamiko meant business.

"Why, you little …" said the man.

The monster took his right arm and attempted to slap Tamiko across the face, but Tamiko quickly avoided the swing and threw the man to the floor.

"Think you know how to fight, do you?" said the man. "You don't know who you're messing with, doll."

Then, the man threw some punches, and Tamiko blocked each one. Tamiko delivered a knee strike followed by a side kick; the man went down as though he were just a little boy.

"Come on!" said Tamiko. "Aren't you going to show me how you beat up little girls?"

Humiliated, the man pulled himself up.

"Okay … now I'm starting to get real angry," he said. "You don't want to see me when I get angry."

"Likewise!"

The man tried some karate-like moves against Tamiko, but the latter dodged each and every move and sent the man flying over the coffee table. By now, the little girl was watching the fight from just outside the bedroom door; she mimicked Tamiko's kicks and punches as she followed the fight.

The monster got up once more and turned into a kickboxer. Tamiko deftly avoided each strike and then spun around in a tight circle like a figure skater and kicked the man to the floor once more. By now, the monster was enraged, for he was being beaten by a young girl! He charged at Tamiko as he growled like a grizzly bear. Tamiko moved out of the way and sent the monster flying into the wall. The monster, almost conked out, made a final attack, grabbing a bat of some kind and swinging it at Tamiko. Almost effortlessly, she dodged the swings and knocked the bat out of the enemy's hands.

"This one's for Kaylie," said Tamiko as she delivered a

solid roundhouse kick to the face of the monster.

The impact of the kick sent the man flying into the wine cabinet behind him, filling the air with the sound of shattering glasses. The man dropped to the floor and lay there knocked out.

Tamiko ran over to Kaylie and wrapped her arms around her.

"It's okay. It's all over now, Kaylie," said Tamiko as the girl cried in her arms.

"I've come to take you away, Kaylie," said Tamiko while the little girl continued to shed tears. "Don't worry, I won't leave you, dear. You're safe with me. Let's go!"

As the two left the house, the man squirmed a bit, beginning to recover from Tamiko's roundhouse kick.

"Ever ridden a bike before?" asked Tamiko.

The girl shook her head no.

"Well, get on the seat here like this, and hold on to me. Can you do that? I'll do the peddling."

And the two were off. By the time the man got up, Tamiko and Kaylie were gone and out of sight. The monster grabbed a gun, flew through the door, and searched frantically throughout the neighborhood for the two girls. He couldn't find them anywhere.

"Oh, I'm going to get you … and when I do …" he said to himself.

CHAPTER 53~
TROUBLE'S COMING

When Tamiko arrived back home with the little girl, they scurried inside, and Tamiko examined Kaylie's scars and bruises in the living room.

"Oh, what did he do to you?" said Tamiko. "What kind of … person does this? Who is that man? Is he your dad or—"

"Uncle," said Kaylie.

"Are you hurting anywhere?" asked Tamiko.

"Here," said the little girl as she pointed to her nose and face.

Just then, Sakura came into the room.

"Tamiko, you're back," she said. "Where were you? I started to … who have we here?"

"It's kind of a long story," started Tamiko. "Her name is Kaylie. She's been—"

"Oh my! Look at her! She's got bruises all over! What on earth happened to her?" said Sakura, shocked.

"Her uncle … beat her. I think she needs a doctor."

"Where did she come from? Where did you find her?"

"Like I said, it's a long story."

"Oh, poor child! How could anyone do this to you?"

"That's just the half of it!" said Tamiko.

While Sakura's mouth was still wide open, Tamiko told her the "other half"—that Kaylie had been locked up in a closet and gagged and tied to a chair.

"My! How do you know all this? You still didn't tell me where you found her! Beaten and locked in some closet … I'm calling the police!"

"I hungry!" said Kaylie. "Very hungry! And a bit sick."

"I'll feed you, dear. Come over here!"

Tamiko gave Kaylie some vegetable sushi, fruit, and a tall glass of water while Sakura reported the situation to the local police. Afterward, Sakura and Tamiko patched up Kaylie's open cuts. Then, Sakura removed Kaylie's clothing, examined her for any severe wounds, and gave her a shower. Though not a doctor, Sakura had some good medical experience—she considered herself a "crackerjack quack." From her observations, she concluded that there were no immediate injuries to tend to. With Kaylie's numerous bruises, scrapes, and scars, however, she obviously had to see a doctor.

The man had pretty much given up his search when he got a call on his cell phone.

"Hi, Barnes," said the caller. "We just got an anonymous call about a little girl who, allegedly, has been beaten and locked in a closet. Go check it out. Here's the address …"

"Got it! I'm on my way!"

Like the monster had said before, he really was the police! Just when the man thought that he had lost and that this was the end of him, the call gets dispatched to *him*. "How sweet!" he mumbled. Now, he could just go out and get her … but it wouldn't be so easy. "How do I do it?" he asked himself. He thought and thought and finally came up with a plan. First, he called his rookie partner.

"Hi there, buddy," said the monster man. "It's Barnes. Look, I just got an emergency call from the big boss. He asked me to go check out some beaten girl on the west side of town, but my car's out of order. So how about you pick me up in ten minutes, say, at the front entrance of the mall? You know … the one where they have the annual fair?"

"Sure, boss! See you in a bit!"

So the rookie partner showed up with his police car in just under ten minutes, giving Barnes barely enough time to change into his police uniform. The two then sped off to Tamiko's house.

"You look kind of beat up there, boss. Did you get in some kind of a fight?" asked the rookie cop.

"Yeah … something like that. Uhummm," said Barnes, pretending to have a mild case of laryngitis.

"What's wrong with your voice? You sound a little …"

"I think I have … uhummm … a bit of laryngitis."

"What about the police conference? It's only forty-five minutes from now."

"Don't worry. After … uhummm … we get the girl, I can drop you off, and you can get a ride back from one of the boys."

Shortly, they arrived. Barnes's next move was to get his partner to go to the door and get the girl as well as Tamiko. Barnes would make up some excuse about having to stay in the car to check his BlackBerry. He couldn't go to the door, of course, for if he did, the girls would instantly recognize him. While his partner, Peters, was busy making his report, Barnes would take the driver's seat and drop off his partner at the upcoming police conference. Then, he would have Kaylie and Tamiko all to himself!

Barnes and Peters were among the very few English police officers—most were Japanese. Therefore, when Peters joined the force just weeks ago, it was only natural for him to have Barnes as a partner and mentor.

"Say, Peters, how about you ... you go pick up the girl. I'll stay here. Gotta check my ... uhummm ... can't really talk too much and I gotta ... check my BlackBerry."

"Sure thing. I'll be right back."

So Peters marched to the front door of Tamiko's house and rang the doorbell. Sakura answered the door.

"Good evening, ma'am. I'm Officer Peters. You called to report a little girl who's been—"

"Yes, of course. She's just around the corner here. As you can see, she's been pretty badly beaten ... and she had been locked up in a closet!"

"Oh boy! Poor little ... hi there. I'm Officer Peters. I'm a police officer. What's your name?"

The girl stood there, shaking somewhat. As she was just about to say her name, Tamiko spoke.

"Her name is Kaylie. I found her in some stranger's house not too far from here. She says her uncle's responsible for all of this. I'll tell you the full story with all the details later ... but now I think it's time that she be taken to a hospital. I'll go with you."

Peters agreed. Before they left, Peters asked some basic questions about Kaylie and took notes in order to make a report. Tamiko grabbed her little carry bag and cell phone before Peters led Kaylie and Tamiko to the car. Peters sat in front next to Barnes; the young ones took the back seat.

Chapter 54~
To the Hospital!

"We're going to the hospital now," said Peters to Barnes. "Like you said, she's been badly beaten. The conference is right on the way ... so you can just drop me off."

Barnes just nodded.

"How far is the hospital from here?" asked Tamiko, having forgotten where the hospital was.

"Oh, about another twenty minutes or so. You'll be there soon," said Peters.

"Nice car," said Tamiko.

"Yeah ... I bet it's the first time you're ever been in one of these," said Peters. "You've got a computer up here, and there's a radar system. There's even a ..."

After some more chitchat between Tamiko and Peters, there was a silence. Then, Tamiko asked the obvious question.

"And how about you ... driver up there ... you seem pretty quiet. What's your name?"

Barnes moved his head and looked at Peters as he "tried" to say something. As Barnes had anticipated, Peters explained his partner's silence.

"Oh, my partner here ... he has laryngitis. That means he can't really speak right now," said Peters. "He's Officer

Barnes."

The fact that Peters said the name "Barnes" didn't bother Kaylie's uncle, since this was really his middle name. Even though he signed up with the force under his full name, most everyone called him by his middle name, Barnes, and rarely by his first name Richard or by his last name Powell. Pretty much nobody else knew him as Barnes—not even his niece. Not only was the driver speechless, but the girls couldn't really see him either, as there was a mesh-like barrier separating the front and back seats.

"My partner here will be dropping me off soon; I gotta go to a conference. He will take over from there."

Then, there was another silence. Even though Peters explained his partner's inability to speak, Tamiko and Kaylie sensed that something just wasn't right. Was it the silence? Was it some kind of smell? Or was it something else?

"So … tell me more about this uncle of yours," said Tamiko to the little girl.

Kaylie trembled. She was about to say something but stopped; she still seemed rather scared, even though she had just been rescued. Then, she said something.

"Cop."

"You're telling me he's a cop?" asked Tamiko.

Kaylie nodded the affirmative. As for the men up front, they couldn't hear a thing the girls were saying.

"And his name …?" said Tamiko. "Can you tell me his name?"

Kaylie hesitated a bit and then started to pronounce his name when, suddenly, the car slowed down and Peters broke in.

"Well, this is it for me, so I'll say so long, Kaylie. Take good care, sweetie. And good-bye, Tamiko."

Peters gave Barnes his notepad and was gone. Now, it

was just Tamiko, little Kaylie, and some mysterious driving cop.

"So how are you feeling now, dear?" asked Tamiko.

"Better ... but scared," said Kaylie.

"I understand," said Tamiko. "Actually, I'm a little scared myself."

Just then, Tamiko looked out the window and saw the word "Maya" on a large sign; almost immediately, Tamiko remembered the hospital and, moments later, its approximate location. As she continued to gaze through the window, Tamiko grew more and more confused. What was going on? This wasn't the way to the hospital. Where were they going? Did the driver not know where the hospital was? How could he not? He was a cop.

"Excuse me, sir, this isn't the way to the hospital," said Tamiko. "You should have turned onto the parkway. We're already past it."

At a red light, the driver wrote something down on a small piece of paper and passed it back to Tamiko through the mesh barrier. Tamiko snatched it. "Missed turn—taking long route." Tamiko talked to the girl a bit more and looked out the window again. For someone taking the "long route" to the hospital, this was far too long—they were now driving through the countryside! Where on earth was the cop taking them? Suddenly, the car started to shake, as if the gas tank had gone empty.

"What's going on?" asked Tamiko.

Moments later, another note came through the barrier. This time, it read "Car trouble—must get out!" Still shaking, the car slowed down and came to a stop beside an old sawmill.

The driver jumped out of the car and opened the door on Kaylie's side; Tamiko's door couldn't open, as it was blocked by a pile of wood. With his face turned away from the girls, the driver pulled Kaylie from the car. As Tamiko got out, Kaylie screamed! Standing there was the monster—this time, in uniform.

"Aaaaaaah!" screamed Kaylie again. "It's Ricky!"

"So you are a cop!"

"And you're just a little girl who tried to be a big hero," said Barnes as he pulled a gun on Tamiko. "You and all those fancy karate moves. You thought you won, didn't you? Well, you're going down. So much for being the glorious hero that saves the day ... Tamiko!"

"You're a coward," said Tamiko. "And you're not very smart, either. Do you really think you were going to get away with all this?"

Tamiko was frightened somewhat, but nowhere near as frightened as any ordinary girl would be in her shoes. The monster sensed this; he was rather amazed at just how calm Tamiko was, for he had expected her to scream for help.

"Let's see," began Kaylie's uncle. "I have some car trouble. We get out of the car, and suddenly, to my surprise, I see my niece. Then, just like that, you pull a gun on me. I shoot back in self-defense, the girl freaks out, and we take off. Yeah, that's believable. What do you think?"

"Ugh! That's absurd! You really think they're going to believe all that?"

"Any last words ... hero?"

As the man was about to pull the trigger, Kaylie bit his arm, and the monster let out a little scream and pushed the girl away.

"Run, Kaylie, run! Don't worry about me! I'll be ... I'll be all right!" cried Tamiko.

"Hmmm ... strange that you seem so confident. You really think you're going to be 'all right'? Sorry, but now it's game over. Bye, Tamiko!"

The man fired two shots at Tamiko's chest, but nothing happened. Tamiko quickly jumped to the side just after the shots were fired. Astonished, the monster fired another shot and then another, but Tamiko just kept moving around. For Tamiko, the bullets felt like little love taps as they bounced off her body. She really was indestructible! The man tried to shoot some more, but he was out of bullets.

"What the …? But I shot you!" said the man, dumbfounded, as he looked at his gun.

Tamiko delivered a quick roundhouse kick to the enemy, knocking him out temporarily.

"Wimp!" she said.

Then, she raced over to Kaylie.

"I'm okay," said Tamiko while Kaylie trembled and looked at her with big eyes.

"You not die?" said Kaylie.

"Oh … he must have missed," said Tamiko. "He's really not much of a shooter."

After Tamiko hugged Kaylie, she took a curious little peek at her new skin … just to see if, maybe, the bullets had left any kind of mark or nick. Nothing—not even a scratch! Just as Tamiko was about to comfort Kaylie some more, Barnes got up, dragged himself to his car, and sped away. Tamiko ran after him and was just able to get the license plate number before he was out of sight. Then, Tamiko made her way back to Kaylie. On her way, she came across a notepad that had apparently fallen from Barnes's pocket or something as Tamiko knocked him down. She picked it up. On the front cover, it read "Gary P."

"Don't worry," said Tamiko. "I'm going to get you to a hospital and make you a nice, big meal, and then you'll feel a whole lot better."

"But … Zack … I want see Zack," said Kaylie.

"Zack? Who's he?" asked Tamiko.

"Brother," said Kaylie.

"You have a brother?" said Tamiko. "Tell me more about Zack. Do you know where he is?"

"He's … my twin … but … but …" Kaylie began to cry.

"But what?" asked Tamiko. "What's wrong?"

"He was living with me. Now, he's gone. They … took Zack away!"

"They? Who's 'they'?"

"The men …"

"Do you have any idea who they were? How many men were there?"

"Two."

"Do you know why they did this?"

"I don't know," said the girl, sobbing.

TO BE CONTINUED